SHOTS NOT TAKEN

NICOLE FALLS

ACKNOWLEDGMENTS

My alpha and beta readers: thank you for your valuable input

Cam: for giving me a reason to go this hard. Love you, kid.

Love Belvin: thank you for graciously allowing me to use your brainchild "Spilling That Hot Tea"

My alphabet gang (CJ, SL, AB, and ST): for being some of the greatest friends a girl can have. Y'all listen to me whine, make me cry laughing, and gas me up when I need it. Think I'll keep y'all forever.

And finally, to my co-collaborator, **THEE Alexandra "International Al" Warren**: We made it, friend! As founder & president of the Warrenistas you already know how hard I stan for you, girl. I don't even think there are adequate enough words to express how thrilled I was/am to take this journey with you. This experience has honestly been *the best*—a seamless creation of a new universe with oh so many possibilities. I look forward to writing about these ballers 'til we can't no mo'. Making sure I kept up with your pen pushed mine to places it'd never been before & I'm very grateful for the experience. I hope you know you're stuck with me noooooooow.

cheesy grin

ONE

I FELT the loud roar of the crowd coursing through my body more than I actually heard them. All thanks to my uncanny ability to tune anything that wasn't the twenty-two ounce, twenty-nine-and-a-half-inch spherical object currently nestled between my hands. I'd been at this stripe a few thousand times before, none of them as monumental as this one.

Dribble. Dribble. Bend the knee. Bounce twice. Release.

I knew that as soon as the ball passed through my fingertips it was going in. It had become a sort of mechanical action, one that seemed as automatic as waving hello or scratching an itch. The satisfying sound of the ball swishing through the net never got old for me. I accepted the easy high fives of my teammates before lining up at the stripe once again.

Dribble. Dribble. Bend the knee. Bounce twice. Release.

Like butta, baby I thought as that shot kissed the

bottom of the net like its predecessor and I backpedaled on defense. We were playing in a must win game seven of the first round of Eastern Conference playoffs. A game no one saw us, the *Tennessee Trojans*, getting to since we'd just barely eked our way into a number eight seed this year. After five years of horrible regular season follies and missing the post-season, we'd managed to get our chance to once again make it to the big dance. I'd be damned if I let some free throws stand between our chances to advance and being sent home to the couches once again. We were playing the number one seed of the conference in this first round. I was certain that they had assumed they'd get rid of us handily and would be sitting at home now watching the rest of the first round unfold. Instead, everyone was waiting with bated breath for the conclusion of our series, each of the other teams sweeping their opponents or only losing a game or two.

It took some getting used to, being the "scrappy underdog" team, but we didn't see ourselves in that light by any means. We believed that we had just as much right as anyone else to be in the playoffs, having ended our season on a run that had us looking like the twenty twelve glory days squad who'd brought a ship to Nashville in the early days of the franchise.

"Aye stay with him, man," I barked at our point guard, an arrogant lil rookie who was overly concerned with attention.

Kage Steele was a very talented, *vital* piece of our team acquired very early in the draft last year, but he was also like an annoying kid brother that I felt like I'd constantly had to wrangle as he stayed tip toeing the fine line of being teachable...*coachable* and thinking his shit didn't stink. What should have been a one game possession had been extended to two with the forced foul that had put me at the free throw line. Making both of those shots put us up by one and we needed to be monsters on this defensive possession, getting a stop and then managing to hold onto the ball as the final seconds of the last quarter trickled by. The opposing team's power forward set a screen, which now had me guarding the point guard, a mismatch that would have had any other person shook as the kid was known for his ball handling skills, but I could keep up with him. I wasn't some wet behind the ears rookie, easily dazzled by a bit of dancing back and forth with the ball. I kept up with him as he drove toward the basket and I kept my hands up on defense ready to block any attempt he made at shooting.

I wasn't ready, however, for him to switch trajectory mid-air and pass the ball to an open man since Kage had come over on the double. That quick kick out led to a catch and shoot three, effectively putting them up by two with three point eight seconds left on the clock. Immediately after the shot, Coach Kirkwood called a timeout. Jogging over to the bench, Kage looked at me in askance trying to figure out which of us had dropped the ball on that play. I shook my head. Honestly, it wasn't either of us. We'd both played impeccable defense on the ball but didn't account for the nigga who'd been bricking all night to come through for them in the clutch. I was barely listening to whatever play coach was trying to draw up, instead I looked at Kage trying to telepathically communicate with him that I'd get open for the shot no matter what. He nodded back almost imperceptibly, letting me know that he was on the same thing I was. We were winning this game at all costs, fuck whatever Coach was on.

"Verette, you got it?" Coach Kirkwood barked.

I nodded once, knowing damn well I wasn't listening to a thing he'd said. The ref blew the whistle signaling the restart of game play and Kage whispered to me, "Aight, your old ass got this, right?"

I smirked, "I hear Boston is nice this time of year."

"Say less," Kage replied with a grin.

I needed to shake my defender, get over to the left wing—my favorite spot to shoot the trey ball—and just wait for the kid to get me the rock. As soon as the ball was inbounded, I took off, easily leaving my defender trailing in my wake. Less than half a second later the ball was in my hands and I was launching it toward the hoop. A late, half-ass attempt to get in my face and affect the shot came a millisecond too late as the ball sailed through the net without even touching the rim as the final buzzer for the game went off. My entire team swarmed me on the floor, too amped at the fact that we'd done it. We'd advanced to the second round and knocked out the team that had been positioned as the one that would go all the way to win the chip throughout the entirety of the season.

I wanted nothing more than to be able to run off this floor, get showered and head back to the hotel to begin reviewing game tape, but first I had to do my most hated duty as the veteran leadership face of the *Trojans*—the postgame presser. Luckily, they'd had one of my favorite journalists on the sidelines covering the team tonight and

I knew she wouldn't ask me any stupid ass questions and would have me on my way back to the locker room after ten minutes at the most. I untangled myself from the sea of people that had swarmed the team and made my way over to Heather Cannon.

"Niko, you once again proved why the *Trojans* took a chance on promoting you from the G league a few years ago, how does it feel to be the one to seal your team's fate, punching your ticket to the next round?" Heather gushed.

I shook my head immediately, "It wasn't just me, HC. This was a whole team effort. As usual, Kage handled the ball perfectly every possession, taking care of it, making plays, keeping us playing at our pace. Zeb was a beast on the boards tonight...what he had bout twenty-five rebounds? Ed, Nate, Jared, Randy...all of these guys showed up in a big way tonight. This was a group effort, not just me."

"Next up, you guys are headed to Boston. Y'all ready for that? In the regular season you guys split those games —two apiece..." Heather trailed off.

"Yeah, we'll...you know...study some film, prepare our defense things like that, but yeah after this performance tonight I'd definitely say we're ready for whatever they throw at us," I replied, confidently, resisting the urge to smile with that. God forbid I show a little excitement about a matchup; I'd be all over the morning sports shows and blogs being called every sort of cocky nigga.

"Alright, thanks Niko."

"You have a good night, HC."

I turned and ran through the tunnel, slapping the

outstretched hands of the spectators who were still in the building. Most of them were local fans, with a smattering of *Trojans* jerseys in the crowd. Briefly, I locked eyes with a kid who couldn't have been more than six or seven years old, being held aloft on his dad's shoulders. They were both pretty far up, but something about the look in that kid's eye made me motion toward one of the security guards that traveled with our team.

"Ricky? You see that kid and his dad?" I said, pointing toward the general area where they were, "Bring them back to the locker room for me."

I jogged off without waiting for Rick's answer, quickly showering and dressing so I wouldn't keep the kid and his dad waiting too long. It was still a weekday evening and though we were close to the end of the school year, I didn't want to keep them out too much later than they'd probably anticipated. I grabbed my gear and headed out toward the exit I'd take to get into the Sprinter that would take me back to the hotel. I'd barely gotten two steps out of the locker room when I was stopped by one of our media guys, Mark.

"Hey Nik, where do you think you going?" he said, gesturing over my shoulder, "Post-game presser is mandatory tonight."

"I already talked to HC, though..."

He shook his head, "The whole of sports media wants their crack at you tonight, man."

"Aight, Mark, give me a couple minutes and I'll be right there," I said, looking over his shoulder where the kid and his dad stood, waiting with Ricky.

I strolled over to where the kid and dad stood,

biting back a laugh when the kid's eyes grew comically large and he tried whispering, "Daddy, it's Niko Verette!"

"Sup lil man," I greeted, hunkering down a bit to get on his level and give him dap, "This some pretty sweet gear you got on, champ."

He was wearing one of my old jerseys from when I played in China, *years ago*. It damn near drowned him, so it clearly belonged to his pops who was now staring at me with the same sort of wide-eyed wonder his kid had been, when I straightened up to greet him as well.

"Saw y'all up there representing and I just wanted to say thank you for the support. I can tell you a real one who been following the come up," I laughed, gesturing towards the jersey again.

"Yeah man, you been my favorite basketball player since we were in high school, dawg. McDonalds All-American...the years you played at Armstrong University...I definitely kept up, man."

"'Preciate it, big dawg. Lemme get y'all in some Cardinal and Silver now though..." I said, digging into my bag and giving the kid my game worn jersey that I quickly signed as he clutched it between his hands. You got a business card or something, man? Next season I'd like to hook y'all up with some dope seats next time we back in town. I gotta run over to this presser but give Rick your info and he'll pass it along to me."

"Thanks, Niko. That's what's up, dawg. We'd love that," the father said.

"Aye, what's your name, man? And lil man, what's your name?"

"George," they both said, simultaneously—causing all of us to bust out laughing.

"Aight, nice to meet y'all, Georges. And I look forward to seeing y'all again next season," I said, jogging backwards toward the media room.

As I took my seat to answer some questions, I thought I heard a mumbled, "*nice of you to make our acquaintance, your highness,*" but when I looked up no one seemed to be paying any attention to me. Kage finished answering the question that had been posed to him and the next journalist was signaled to lob their question.

"Ned Jacobs, Journal-Sentinel...this question is for Niko Verette. You guys had this series in the clutches of your hands after the first three games that you'd managed to win handily...what happened between games four and six and how do you think it prepared you all to come in here and pull off this, quite frankly, surprising upset?"

I took a deep breath before answering. There was one in every city and this prick Ned was on my list. He always asked questions with backhanded compliments that he wanted to use to bait you into losing your cool. I wasn't falling for the banana in the tailpipe tonight, my mood was too good...adrenaline surging too high to let some schlub who probably got cut from his local rec center's intermural league to bring it down.

"Look, we can't front like the Bucks aren't a great team. Hell, they had the best overall record in the league for both conferences. What happened? The Bucks bucked. And you know as well as I know, Ned...when someone is dead set on a particular outcome, there is nothing anyone can do to deter them from making their goal."

"So, are you saying tonight they lost their fire and that's how you all were able to come in here and snatch this win?" Ned prodded further.

I turned to Kage and laughed at him miming at me, "Who's mans is this?"

Shaking my head, I answered Ned, "Nah, man. Don't put words in my mouth. Both of us were scrapping to the bitter end tonight. But in the end...the game is the game."

Ned opened his mouth again like he wanted to further badger me, but I quickly cut him off by calling out, "Next question."

Whole room went up in laughter as Ned sputtered, red faced and clearly flustered. Soon the presser's energy was redirected back to reflecting on this win tonight and what we had to look forward to in Boston. After twenty more minutes of questions, we finally wrapped and the last lil bit of guys who were still in the arena, piled into the Sprinter and headed over to the hotel. Kage tried convincing me to go out on the town to celebrate, but I was cool with going to my room and laying it down. The time for celebration hadn't yet come. We still had a lot more work to do.

When I got back to the room, I still had the Georges on my mind. Damn it had been a long time since I'd even thought about that period of time that I played with the Golden Bulls. That shit seemed like a lifetime ago, but when I thought about it, it was less than ten years ago. I'd been the shit in high school, a highly sought-after player with the skills to match. Did the whole *McDonald's All-*

American thing, but then in my sophomore year of college all of my dreams of one day playing in the league were snatched from me after a pretty gruesome leg fracture that sidelined me for the rest of that season into the next. When I was finally healthy enough to resume the rest of my college career, I was never quite at the same level that I was prior to the accident. That plus, newer fresher faces had taken my spot. So, I was relegated to taking whatever off the bench minutes I was given. I kept my head down and did what was asked of me.

It was no surprise that by the time I'd finished my college career and declared for the draft that I heard nothing, couldn't even get an agent here in the states. I knew that basketball was what I wanted to do for life though, so I had to leverage some connections in order to assist me in getting to my end goal. My pops had some homies who were middling NBA players that eventually went on to play overseas. One of them got me in contact with an agent that he knew—who was retired by the time I needed him—but was able to refer me to someone else and the rest, as they say, was history.

That led me overseas to a world that was so foreign from the ones in which I'd previously existed. Changed me in a number of ways...some good, some bad. Traveling around China and other Asian countries as a six foot six, two-hundred-sixty-five-pound young Black man definitely put me in some interesting—at times, *very compromising*—positions. I wouldn't have traded my time over there for anything else in the world. I never managed to retain more than ten Chinese words, but the bonds made over there and the memories would stay with me for the rest of my life. However, when I got an email from my old college coach informing me of a G league tryout for a team that would eventually lead me to the *Trojans*, it couldn't have come at a better time.

I'd only been playing in China for about two years then, had made a lil bit of money, but that wasn't enough. I was still thirsting to get into the league and make that dream I'd held since I was a shorty watching all of the greats dominate. I wanted my name in the lights, to be the one that kids looked up to and tried to emulate when they were playing on the courts in their school yards, local playgrounds, or whatever. I wanted my family to be able to come to games and see me in action. And now here I was...not only achieving the goal that little Niko V couldn't stop talking about incessantly from the time I first held a basketball to now quite possibly putting myself in the place to win the highest distinction of this league. The shit was pretty surreal...and I wanted to make sure I allowed myself to take it all in, and not take any of it for granted because this shit could be snatched from me in an instant.

TWO

HERE WE GO, I thought before ascending the couple few steps I needed to make my way up to walk over to the microphone situated at the middle of the stage. I'd been gigging at this bar for a few months now and it was always a mixed bag. I knew that the crowd didn't know what to expect when they saw a little Black girl climbing onto the stage at a honky tonk, but before the end of the night they would know what the fuck they were getting. A woman with a damn powerful voice who could sing circles around more than half of these girls who were topping the charts right now. A woman with a singular focus to be not only heard but respected in her chosen genre of performance. A woman who wasn't with the shits and unafraid to get in these white people's asses if they disrespected me in the ways that some of their sistren and brethren had done on previous nights.

It was honestly nothing but the grace of God that kept my standing gig at The Purple Shamrock. I'd had too many encounters to count where I'd confronted ignorant ass rednecks who had something to say about me singing their so-called classics, as if it wasn't *my people* who had founded this damn genre, but were forced out—just like every damn thing we'd created in this country. It shouldn't have been surprising, but every time I was shocked anew. Mostly, I paid those folks no mind and got on this stage and sang my soul out...but some days? I just could not let their ignorance fly.

Shaking off the thoughts of idiots past, I turned to the house band flashing them a brilliant smile. These guys were my rock—Jacoby on guitar, Mikey on drums, and Daryl on keys. They were session players, having left their instrumental imprint on some of music's greatest songs, but they still showed up here faithfully, every Friday evening and played the house band to my prima donna. They also possessed an encyclopedic knowledge of music, which made singing with them fun because I could throw monkey wrenches in the planned set at any moment and they rolled with me. I usually sang a mixture of country standards and more modern tunes, covering music from everyone from Patsy Cline to Kellsea Ballerini.

I looked over at Mikey and he flashed a thumbs up and blew me a kiss. I laughed, returning the gesture. A glance at Jacoby garnered his too cool to be affected head nod, and Daryl tossed a wink my direction once my gaze had settled onto him. We began each set the same way, no matter the song. I would begin singing, acapella for the first few bars and each of the guys would fill in the pocket as the song progressed, building to an all-out jam session once everyone settled in. Just before coming onstage we put together a set list, comprised of eight songs. I'd perform four, we'd take an intermission of sorts and then come to close out our set before the next band took the stage. I'd been in my old school country divas bag tonight when I composed tonight's set, so it was Patsy Cline and Loretta Lynn heavy up top. I took a deep breath before closing my eyes and belting out the first lines of the first song in the set.

I go out walkin'/after midnight/ out in the moonlight/ just like we used to do...

And just like that I was in the zone, the guys filled in and we slow grooved our way through the rest of the Patsy Cline classic "Walkin' After Midnight" before I took a quick break to introduce myself and the rest of the guys onstage. The crowd was pretty impressive for it to still be fairly early in the night—the bars usually had an ebb and flow thanks to daytime tourists and nighttime partiers, but the Sham was packed out tonight. In between songs, I bantered with the audience a bit—trying to draw them in and hopefully convert some of them to fans of mine tonight. I'd recorded an EP a few years ago—a mix of original content and cover that I sold at the end of shows I did around town.

Before getting into the last song of the night I called out to the crowd, "All right we're about to get up outta here in a bit, but first I gotta ask. What y'all know about Tammy Wynette?"

I gauged the majority of the crowd to be made up of mostly twentysomethings with the occasional smattering of Boomers here and there.

"What do *you* know about Tammy Wynette?" an

older gentleman who was sitting near the front called back.

He'd been staring at me with a strange look the entire show and I couldn't get a read on him.

"Quite a bit, sir," I sassed, with a smile.

He scoffed, "I'd think a nice colored gal like you wouldn't..."

I'd barely heard a thing after the word colored left his mouth and before I knew it I was lighting into him calling him all sorts of ignorant motherfuckers and backwoods bastards as I cussed his entire family's lineage as well as gave a rundown of exactly who I was, where I came from and why I deserved to be there. I had to be dragged off stage and into the back room by Daryl because I was damn close to descending the stage and getting right up in that old man's face. This old guy wasn't the first and most likely wouldn't be the last, but I was tired of these bastards trying me.

"Jet...cool out. You can't keep doing this shit, girl," Daryl laughed as he placed me back down on my feet after literally carrying me off the stage and into our little "greenroom".

"Fuck that, D! Did you hear that? What he called me?" I screeched, not caring if my voice carried beyond the room in which we were currently situated.

"I did. But how many times have we had this talk about you needing to not let their ignorance knock you off your square, JT? We gotta do this every time a honky tonk bro comes in and challenges you being on this stage?"

"Why is it even an option for my presence on this

stage singing what I have grown up listening to and adore to be challenged? And what qualifies them to be the ones who are doing the challenging? You ain't no different from the rest of them, D. You might as well cut the shit," I huffed.

Daryl held up his hands, "Whoa, don't go lumping me with Bigoted Billy Bob out there, Jet. You know better than that. You know *me* better than that!"

"Do I? Because as far as I'm concerned, you're in here lecturing me when you should be out there talking to your skin folk. *He* is the one who needs the lessons, not me. They don't say shit when Casey prances her off-key ass up here and does a damned Taylor Swift revue," I gritted out, "There's no questioning of her presence even when she throws in an old Britney Spears tune."

"Probably not the best time for me to bring up you putting "Daddy Lessons" into sets every now and again, huh?"

"That is a *country* song, D! See...you're just as narrow minded as that motherfucker out there," I shot back, flailing my hands back toward the front of the bar.

"I was just joking, Jayde. Trying to bring you down a bit, but I see you're really committed to staying upset about something that really doesn't matter," Daryl argued back.

"Or that you don't understand where I'm coming from at all, no matter how many Black Lives Matter shirts you wear, rallies you attend, or times I tell you how I am feeling, and you try to minimize it. It isn't about the content that I sing, because you know I sing it *all* from country to r&b to pop to rock. It's about how I am only questioned when I get deep into my banjo swag. And if you don't see why that is problematic? Then, we honestly have nothing further to discuss about this, man."

I didn't even wait for a response from Daryl as I gathered my bag and stormed out of the bar. I was barely thinking as I flopped into my car, put the key into the ignition, but made no moves to actually turn it or start the car up. I blinked rapidly, willing myself not to let the tears that had been cresting ever since that man began his heckling fall. I wasn't going to cry over this stupid shit and waste tears on people whose opinions weren't worth them. There were far more bleak circumstances in my life for which these tears could be spilled, but this here? Not worth more than a blow up and then, moving forward. My body, however, was not in concert with my mind tonight because before I could control it, I was slumped over the steering wheel, heaving sobs as I cried about experiencing the stupidest form of...hell, I didn't even know what to call it? Was it merely racism? Bigotry? Ignorance? Whatever it was, I knew that it was something that I was tired of having to contend with...on all levels.

I should have been used to the ignorance honestly, coming from the teeny tiny town of Belt Buckle, Tennessee where me and my family were the outliers, but every time this mess was in my face it still stung. I honestly had no idea what the hell my ancestors were thinking when they settled there all those years ago and why my mother was okay with following my dad back there when they got married. That still boggled my mind, all these years later. But warts and all, Belt Buckle was home. And home should have prepared me for the bullshit I'd face in The Big City, but...I still hoped it would be less...*overt*? I pulled in a deep breath, willing myself to calm down enough to stop this flow of tears and drive home. I could continue this pity parade once I got there, with wine to accompany me. I didn't drink at the bars when I gigged, despite having an open tab most often, because of a bad experience years ago. I only drank publicly if I had a trusted companion by my side.

I'd finally gotten my mind right and turned the key in the ignition. I was about to back out of my parking space when my phone rang. I glanced over to my passenger seat where I'd flung it when I got into the car to see whose name would be flashing across the display. Fortunately, it was one of my favorite people on Earth who always had a knack for reaching out to me just when I needed her.

"Nasty Nyyyyyy," I squealed, "What's good, play girl?"

"Hey, Jay! You got a minute?" Nyema asked.

"For you, boo? Always!"

"You...aight, sis? You sound a little stuffed up?" Nyema asked, concerned lacing her tone.

"I'm good, girl. You know these damned allergies be acting up this time of year," I rushed out, "But what's going on with you, chica? I ain't heard from you in a month of Sundays!"

"I *know*. I've been a little...wrapped up in something," Nyema giggled.

"Something or some*one*?" I asked, teasing, "I know that 'I'm getting my back blown out on the regular' tone in your voice!"

"Jay!" Nyema giggled.

"Mmmmhmm...I see you haven't refuted it though!"

"Anyway...that's not why I was calling you—" Nyema started, but I quickly interrupted, "But it's why we're talking now, sis. So, who is he?"

She sighed into the phone, "So do you remember me talking about the junior associate my dad was always inviting over for dinner?"

"The stuffed shirt you called Khaki Randall Pearson? Mmmhmmm, I can say it now, right?"

"Say what?" Nyema asked, feigning innocence.

"You know what, heffa! I. Told. You. So! I told you so! Homeboy riled you up a bit too much for you to not be feeling him in any way. So, what's up, y'all fucking now? It was only a matter of time."

"Jayde Elaine!" Nyema scolded.

"Nyema *I can't think of your middle name right now*!"

A beat passed and we both collapsed into giggles.

"It's Jolene, fool!" Nyema giggled.

"Oh yeah that's right. How could I forget you're named after my favorite Dolly song?" I asked before launching into the chorus of the famed hit.

Nyema giggled, then sighed, "Whew, Negro Natalie Maines takes my breath away once again. When you gonna stop playin' and record that album, sis? The streets need some real nigga country tracks!"

I sighed, "Soon, hopefully. I think I've finally got a solid round of hits to get my next EP completed."

"It would have been completed if you stopped selling your best stuff," Nyema playfully chastised.

"Oh...so I'm not supposed to eat now? Besides...I've got some heat in the chamber that I'm not letting anyone have. I gotta send you the rough demo for the song I just wrote a few days ago. I'm sure if I sold it to one of these country girls it would take off immediately, but I'm saving it for myself. It's too good to let just anyone record, you know?"

Nyema murmured a sound of agreement into the phone, "Send that to me ASAP, friend. I got a couple things I wanna send to you, too. Get your input on any tweaks I need to make."

"Absolutely, boo. Anytime. You know I got you. Hey...speaking of...how are things going with Rich?"

Rich was a producer I'd become friendly with who was always looking for new talent to work with. When Nyema told me that she was trying to move beyond her steady DJing gig into songwriting too, it was a no-brainer for me to link the two of them. I'd hoped that linking would have led to some placements with some of Rich's artists by now. Nyema's pen was fledgling, but with the right amount of discipline and consistently, my girl could go down in history as a prolific writer. She just needed a little more experience and she'd be on her way. Rich had been good to me so far, giving my songs to more than a few of his artists—he'd tried getting me in at his homeboy's label, but the heads were not trying to let me do my own thing. They saw me and instantly formed an idea of the artist they wanted me to be, which wasn't exactly in line with where I saw myself going.

"Rich is cool. I've sent him a couple demos that I worked on with Trey and he provided some good feedback. I know I've got to pay some dues, but I definitely thought I'dve had something placed by now."

"Girl...this shit is a numbers game, honestly. And a lot about who you know, but you got *it*, Ny. And by it, I mean talent. And Rich knows that shit, too. So, keep on plugging away and your time will come."

Nyema and I chatted a bit more about music and planned to get together sometime in the near future. Either I'd travel to see her, or she'd come see me, but it had been entirely too long since we'd physically been in each other's presence. I met Ny through a friend who had a club at which she was the resident DJ. We clicked immediately, forming a bond that seemed rare for most trying to make friends in their adult years. We just vibed though. We were the same type of girl—a little too audacious, outspoken, and promiscuous for most to handle. But we welcomed each other without judgement or reservation, which is why our friendship worked so well. It was rare to have a synergistic bond with someone almost instantly like that, but when Trell introduced me to Nyema it felt like coming home. Meeting a kindred spirit that I knew would end up being a lifelong friend.

By the time I had pulled up to my place, I had about six text messages from the guys in the band checking on me. Daryl had sent the most, apologizing for our argument and wanting me to call him when I cooled off. I replied to Jacoby and Mikey as soon as I walked in the house, but D could wait. I was still smarting from his reaction and despite my display earlier, I did know how to give myself time to come down off a highly emotional situation before I responded in a way that would permanently alter relationships. I'd hit him back tomorrow when I was, hopefully, in a better headspace and we could squash this temporary beef. For now, the claw foot tub, a *LUSH* bomb, and a quarter of a bottle of Grenache rosé was calling my name.

THREE

"SAY MAN, *these niggas is barbecue chicken! Trojans in four*," is what Kage boasted in a post-game presser after we'd come into the second round of this series with the same fire that we'd held in the first. It also helped that the team we were playing had swept their previous series and were trying to get their legs beneath them once again. It didn't take them long as they ran through us effortlessly for the next three games. Now we were down, having won two games to their three and tonight's win was *critical*. The locker room before the game was pin drop quiet. Everyone keeping to themselves, trying to get into that "crush these niggas and avoid the L" zone. This damn near silence was disquieting though. I finally had to speak up and say something.

"Aye, y'all..." I said, my voice raised loud enough to carry over whatever was blaring through the various sets of wireless headphones and earbuds that decorated the ears of my teammates, "this what we on? This how we get down? Where's that same energy we had coming into this? Ok these niggas got three games on us....and? That mean we tuck our tails and hide? That mean we just roll over and let them get this dub? *Shit*, I thought y'all niggas —*all inclusive, Jared, Randy, and Pete*—was better than that."

"Aw nigga you been walking around here like somebody took your puppy, too," Kage crowed as he walked back into the room, "I'm the only one of us who still got faith in the team."

I shook my head, laughing at his ass. He was right though, even as we were fighting to stay in this shit, Kage still maintained his breezy air of confidence. Not one bead of sweat gathered on his brow when we were asked what the difference was between how the team was playing in this series and the last. The rest of us, however? Straight up pathetic. We needed to borrow some of Kage's unwavering and unyielding arrogance. There was no reason why we shouldn't be bustin' these niggas asses, but we went from playing with extreme confidence to playing scared now. Granted there were a couple of huff calls from the refs in a few games that really changed the direction of those games...and eventually the series. But we could either continue to cry about unfair officiating or we could dig our heels in and win this damn game...and hopefully the series.

Kage returned to the locker room from his pre-game PT session in the nick of time because his energy was infectious. Before I knew it the locker room was completely transformed, someone had pulled out one of those Bluetooth speakers and instead of everyone staying morose and turned inward, they were all up and about now, rapping along to Meek Mill's "Championships", loud as hell and rowdy...looking more and more like the group of guys I'd been playing with for the past few years. We kept that shift in energy through the pre-game shoot around and into three quarters of the game. By the time the third quarter ended, we had a commanding lead of fifteen points and needed to keep our heels dug in to pull out the win. The opposing team's point guard, however, had different plans for us. For those first three quarters he couldn't get a shot to fall in his favor at all.

Now, however, as we were midway through the fourth, the nigga suddenly had the *NBA Jam he's on fire* hot hand. No matter how good our defense was, it was no match for him. Homie was straight up in his bag, hitting shots from anywhere on the damn court. He even pulled up from the logo a few times and the shit swished through the rack, all net. That fifteen point lead we'd had had dwindled to a one-point lead with one minute left in the quarter. A timely TV timeout gave us a much-needed break to catch our breaths and regroup. I took a sip from my water and tried listening to whatever Coach was yelling about, but I couldn't focus. All I knew was that we needed this win. And I was willing to do whatever I had to do to ensure that. I tried catching Kage's eye as we headed back to the floor, but he was too busy talking some trash to the dude that was inbounding the ball for the opposing team. That timeout also gave them the time they needed to draw up and execute a perfect inbounds play, with the pass in actually being a lob to their center who slammed that shit right over the head of our guy, effectively turning him into a meme that would make the rounds for the next few months. Jared's ass cowered in the face of the monster hammer being levied upon him instead of playing defense and at least trying to prevent the ball from going in.

Granted there wasn't much he could do with dude, but damn at least try. *It's just a one-point lead,* I said to myself, *We are down but not out, stay focused, nigga.* I shook my head as I backpedaled up the court, waiting for Kage to set up a play. Two of their defenders were all over him, but his handles and speed shook them almost instantly as he crossed half court and headed straight to the rack, laying up a beautiful shot with his left hand. As they were inbounding again, we stayed tight in the half court press, not wanting to give them a chance to advance the ball. Kage stuck with the point, but right before half court when dude zigged, pump faked then zagged in the opposite direction, he got past Kage and was coming toward where I was guarding a man on the wing. I had to make the choice to either double buddy with the hot hand or stay on my man because he was known as a sharpshooter as well. I chose the double, the guaranteed shot and as soon as I moved to help on defense, he slung the rock out to the wing, and I was late on getting a hand in the shooter's face before the balls left his fingertips. The ball rattled through the rim; that made three-pointer putting us down by two now. Coach quickly called a timeout, our last one of the game. There were less seconds left in the game than the time normally loaded on the shot clock, so it was off, and we were down to the nitty gritty. Coach drew up a quick pick and roll, with Jared inbounding the ball to Kage, me setting a screen and then Kage passing the ball off to whomever had the best shot. Or...taking it himself if he had the space or opportunity.

It was a play we'd run countless times before and usually resulted in a victory if the defender who was guarding ball dropped to me when I set the screen instead of following Kage. Kage possessed superior ball handling skills and for a rookie played with impressive confidence and poise, even when we were in these do or die type situations. I had the utmost confidence in the rock being in his hand for the final shot. He was a guaranteed playmaker. Which was why I wasn't shocked when the defender skated around my screen to keep pace with Kage and avoid him getting that shot off. Kage anticipated that and passed the ball off to the right wing where our center Zeb was wide open since they were doubling both me and Kage. The big man was known to knock down a perimeter shot every now and again, so Zeb heaved a shot that rolled around the rim for a couple milliseconds before sliding through the net. The opposing team quickly called a time out, with less than three seconds left on the clock.

That usage of the timeout allowed them to advance the ball to half court. I walked over to Kage to assess what we thought they were about to try and do. Coach was rambling on about how our defense needed to be locked down tight, but I was more concerned with not only pressing, but getting a stop and maintaining our lead to carry us into game seven. Soon, the timeout was over, and I locked eyes with Kage. He was on the same thing I was —get a stop by any means necessary. I quickly found my man, as the ref blew the whistle to signal that game play was back on, playing defense that would have made my very first coach in the community basketball league I got started in proud. But all it took was a split second for a guy to get open outside the arc and heave up a shot. That motherfucker sailed through the hoop, only kissing the net, effectively ending our season.

The opposing team swarmed ol' dude who made the game winning shot and I quickly walked off of the court, *pissed*, ignoring everything and everyone that was vying for my attention as I moved through the arena to our locker room. I needed a moment of decompression before I was certain that both Kage and I would be trotted out to the media to do a post-loss press conference during which I needed to make sure I kept a level head. I hate doing these damn pressers already and that hate was exacerbated after a loss, especially one that was as monumental as this one. As I sat at my locker with a towel over my face, I could hear the rest of the guys coming into the locker room—a loud, rambunctious bunch fired up over what they thought was a missed call and should have had the basket made at the end of the game waived off. My teammates went on and on about how dude stepped out of bounds before heaving up his shot, but my eyes were trained on him almost immediately and he was definitely in bounds. We just fell down on the job. Coach came in soon after, demanding everyone's attention and giving a speech that would have made *Coach Carter* or whatever Rhea Pearlman's name was when she led the disadvantaged youth in *Sunset Park* to victory proud.

I wasn't in the mood to hear platitudes and late ass

praise. Damn all that. I kept that towel over my head, the last fifteen seconds of that quarter playing over and over in my mind, wondering what I or anyone on our team that was on the floor could have done differently. I finally took the towel off my face as I gathered my shit to shower before I would be dragged to the media room for the presser. On my way to the shower, I passed by Mark, the media guy.

"Say bruh, can you get Zeb to go out there with Kage? I ain't really—" he cut me off, "Now you know you're the face of the franchise, Nik, so you might as well not even waste your breath. Remember though, you don't owe them shit. Be on your Beast Mode swag if you need too, man."

I chuckled at his reference to Marshawn Lynch's infamous "I'm only here so I don't get fined" presser. I already had a reputation of being reticent and sort of difficult whenever we did press conferences, so I knew that wasn't even an option for me. Plus, my boy Langston and his new girl Nyema were in town for this game tonight. We were supposed to be meeting for dinner at my loft tonight—with one of his girl's friends. I wasn't really in the mood for entertaining tonight, but I knew that if I cancelled on them, I would just be sitting around watching all of the coverage of our loss on ESPN and obsessing. I had plenty of time to do that shit, but not as much time to hang out with one of my best friends from childhood since I didn't get back home that often.

Plus, I'd gotten to meet Nyema's home girl briefly before the game and shorty was bad. Couldnta been no more than about five one, five two—brown skinned, thick as hell, hair in long silky waves down to her ass. And that ass...I hadn't gotten to properly check it out in its entirety, but from the glimpse I'd been given pre-game. Shit, I could definitely use the distraction of a pretty ass woman and catching up with my guy after this shit show of a game. I showered and made my way to the press room, catching up with Kage as he was walking in as well. We were both pretty shocked to walk into a room that greeted us with an ovation, thunderous applause that we gladly welcomed—voicing our thanks before we both sat at the podium. That was exactly the energy we needed, our hometown press embracing us and the ones there for national coverage were asking questions that were thoughtful, respectful, and most importantly didn't seek to goad us into any negative reactions. Kage kept them in stitches with his signature quips and I filled in the gaps when questions were asked of me directly, but I didn't have too much energy for the shit overall and was extra excited when Mark indicated to a reporter to ask the last question of the night.

"Niko, we know that you're a free agent this summer. Any plans of moving beyond the *Trojans* and ring chasing next year?" the last reporter, Brian Lawrence, asked.

I took a deep breath before responding. I *hated* this dude. He always came out of nowhere with some left field shit and tried to play the innocent when someone called him on it.

Before I could get a word out, Kage piped up, "That's really how you choosing to serve the Lord right now, bruh?"

The entire room, including me, burst out into laughter. Brian's idiotic attempt at baiting me into giving a stupid soundbite completely forgotten as Kage went on and on about how he needed to be a better person and looking within for whatever made him such a lame ass. I was too damned weak to even think about formulating a reply, thankful for Kage's humor and quick wit deflecting from what could have been a terrible moment. Mark thanked everyone for their time, dismissed us and we headed out of the room.

"Kage!" I called out.

He was a bit ahead of me and turned around with his signature smirk, "It was nothin', fam. But uh...I got somewhere I'm tryna be right now, so we'll have to save this *Sister Sister* bonding moment you tryna have for another time."

I just laughed and waved him off, letting him get to whatever was so important. I needed to be getting home anyway to make sure everything was in order for tonight's festivities. When I invited Langston and his girl down, I definitely thought we'd be getting together under very different circumstances, not a season ending loss. I thought about calling my assistant and having him nix the champagne that was set to be served with dinner but forget it. This season was still one worth celebrating, even if the outcome wasn't what I'd hoped or expected.

By the time I got home, my assistant Pharris was on his way out of my place.

"Sup Nik," he greeted as we passed each other in the hall.

"You got it, bruh," I said in reply, "You sure you don't wanna stick around?"

Pharris was more than my assistant after working together all of these years. After Langston, I'd probably consider him to be one of my closest friends. He was the nephew of my high school coach, a sort of fuck up that Coach was helping guide through life. Luckily, he ended up being the perfect fit as my assistant. The flexibility of the job worked well with his temperament and his organizational skills were out of this world. He kept my life running smoothly as hell; a well-oiled machine.

Even though I was cool with Langston inviting his girl's friend, I didn't want this shit to seem like an awkward double date. I'd been in one of these setups too many times before and the mess always ended up wack as hell. Pharris sticking around would kill that vibe, in a good way though.

Pharris shook his head, "Nope, got a hot date tonight, boss man. Ain't no fifth wheeling and playing interference for you tonight."

As usual, Pharris saw right through me.

"Besides, I saw ol' girl earlier, she looks like a perfect distraction, g."

"She was bad as hell, wasn't she?" I mused.

"Yessir. Enjoy that," Pharris laughed, touching his hand to his forehead in a two fingered salute before turning and walking toward the elevator.

I stepped into my condo and it smelled damn amazing in here. I gave no instruction for tonight's meal, so I headed straight into the kitchen to see what we'd be dining on tonight. The chef grilled some steaks, shrimp, scallops, and lobster tails. To accompany that was grilled asparagus, mushrooms with garlic in a butter sauce, baked sweet potatoes, and a spring mix salad with a raspberry vinaigrette.

Against my better judgement I sat down and turned on the TV while I waited for my guests to arrive. Of course, I ended up on ESPN where they were rehashing the game I'd played in, the commentators examining all of my team's mistakes and insisting that our first-round win was just a streak of luck. I quickly changed the channel, landing on BET showing *Baby Boy* once again. I fell into that, trying to get my mind off of the bullshit of the ESPN commentary so I wouldn't be in a messed up mood when everyone pulled up. I laughed at Jody and Yvette's antics...and thanked my lucky stars that I'd dodged my own version of an Yvette way back in the day. The concierge called up to let me know that my guests had arrived, and I went to open the door to let them in since he'd already directed them onto the elevator.

When I opened the door, however, there was only *one* guest there, Nyema's fine ass home girl.

"Jayde, right?" I said in greeting.

"That's me. Nikolas, right?" she parroted back, stepping past me into my place, "Your boy and my girl are running behind. I got a text from Ny while I was in my Lyft. I'm almost certain that when they show up, DJ Nyla will have that freshly fucked glow that she greeted me with earlier at lunch."

I laughed at her candor, following her deeper into my place where she settled onto the couch.

"I hope you don't mind me making myself at home, immediately," she said, her eyes darting around the space, appraising everything she saw, "I tend to do that."

"You're good, sweetheart," I replied.

"This is a nice place. I love this building so much. My friend stays down on the third floor and every time I come over to his place I want to stay forever. Your floor plan looks a bit different than his though. Definitely bigger."

"What's your friend's name? I might know him," I said.

"You probably don't. He's a weird ass reclusive songwriter dude. Doesn't even make eye contact with strangers...even ones as well-known as you," Jayde smiled, "But his name is Edward Kane."

"Can't nobody sang like Eddie Kang," I said, without thinking. Her friend's name was too close to a character in one of my favorite films, *The Five Heartbeats.*

Jayde erupted into giggles, shaking her head, "The first time he introduced himself to me, I quoted that line and he looked at me like I had two heads."

"How did he not know that classic? Nights like this, I wish..." I sang, trailing off when she joined in, "that raindrops would fall."

"You sound good," I complimented.

"Well I should hope so. Singing for my supper pays the bills," Jayde quipped, "You got a lil tone on you too, though. I heard you, Nikolas."

"I can do a lil somethin'. So, you're a singer, huh?"

"*And songwriter.*"

"That's what's up. I love music," I replied, sounding stupid as hell to my own ears.

Before I could say anything else, my phone rang again with the concierge letting me know that the rest of the group was here. A quick exchange of greetings and then we were all sitting around the table as I moved everything from where chef had it waiting onto the table in my dining area.

"Y'all drinkin'?" I asked Langston.

"Hell yes, we are drinking. You are too," Jayde piped up before he could respond and I laughed, "What you got for us in here mister fancy basketball player man?"

"Water, juice, pop, wine, beer, champagne...whatever you want, basically?" I said.

"Whatever I want, huh?" Jayde queried, biting her lower lip.

"Jay!" Nyema giggled.

"The man said whatever, friend. I'm just asking for clarity," Jayde replied laughing, turning to grin at Nyema.

I smiled to myself, shaking my head as I headed back into the kitchen to grab red and white wine, along with glasses. This girl was a lot...but I *liked that. A lot.* After dinner, Langston and I stepped onto my balcony to enjoy a couple cigars while the ladies holed up inside sipping their beverages and watching something on TV.

"Love looks good on you, brother," I quipped.

Langston didn't reply verbally, shaking his head and throwing a hand in my direction that said cut it out. He and Nyema were a fairly new development, but I knew him. This wasn't some fly by night shit for him, he was *into* this girl. And she was a good match for him. Langston could be a bit uptight at times...a little too rigid, but Nyema brought out his less serious side. He couldn't keep a grin off his face, keenly attuned to her in ways that I didn't even think either of them were even aware. It was the little things—from the way they unconsciously touched one another as they spoke—tripping over each other's words to finish sentences. It was wild witnessing this, especially knowing that Langston had held a little crush on Nyema from the first time they met. Watching the two of them together now, almost had me thinking about revising my unofficial official lifetime bachelor status.

"Could look good on you too, bruh..." Langston shot back with an easy grin.

I shook my head, "Gotta knock a few things of my bucket list first, man. Too many irons in the fire and I ain't got the time or proper energy to give to a woman right now. I'm in grind mode."

"Man...*okay*, right. Grind mode, that's what we'll go with," Langston laughed.

"Damn nigga you really have been hit by the love bug if you tryna talk me into settling down with someone," I replied, chuckling at the starry-eyed look in his eyes.

"I'm just saying bro; life is improved when you have someone to share all of your highs and lows with. Like... tonight for example...you good?"

I nodded once, tightly, before shrugging, "Yep. Par for the course."

"You don't have to play it cool with me, Nik," Langston said.

"I ain't playin' it cool, man. I just...it hasn't really sunk in yet, you know? Still pretty fresh, but also doesn't seem real. I keep getting flashes of those last couple of minutes, thinking about things I should have or could have done differently. Still processing that..."

"Look, I won't even front on you and say that I know any of what you're feeling right now, but you know if you need to talk it through once you're done processing I got you."

I took a puff of my cigar before replying, "Preciate it, bro. For real...but say...how much do you know about shorty in there?"

"Enough to know that I am telling you to tread lightly. She's Nyema's bestie and I don't need you fucking her over and making our eventual wedding awkward. Abort whatever mission you think you're about to be on."

"But..."

Langston shook his head, "Nah, bro. Jayde's cool peoples. I don't need you messing that vibe up."

"Damn, you act like I won't let her know what's up from jump. And I know you know she's ready to go the moment I give the signal."

"Nik."

"Langston."

We stared at one another in silence before breaking into laughter.

"Damn, bro...you really feeling Nyema like that?" I asked, "Enough to cockblock this tough?"

"She is it for me, man. You call it cockblocking, but I call it protecting my interests. If you still feel as strongly about getting at Jayde after I make Nyema my wife, then you can have at it."

I narrowed my eyes at Langston, "Are you serious?"

"Hell nah, bro. Leave that girl alone at all costs."

'Nah fool, about Nyema? She's the one?" I asked, shocked honestly.

Don't get me wrong, Langston had always struck me as the type who wanted to settle down with the right little woman, have two point five children, the picket fence, the dog—all of that. But the read I'd gotten on how he felt about Nyema in our conversations wasn't quite what I was picking up currently. I definitely had discounted it more as a purely physical thing and not anything much deeper.

"Man, she's the one...two...three through ten, my guy. If I didn't think she would cut and run, I'd be down on one knee this weekend."

"It's like that?" I asked, brows raised so high they damn near blended into my lining.

Langston nodded strongly, "I'm slow rolling it for now, but mark my words, man. That one there? She's my inevitability. You can take that to the bank."

"Aw shit, boy!" I crowed, "But wait...who's gonna break the news to your other *other half*?"

Langston quirked an eyebrow in askance.

"PL! You know he gon have a fit when you and Nyema make it official,' I laughed.

I'd grown up with both Langston and his cousin Paul Lawrence. We were all fairly close growing up, but Langston and I had a stronger bond than I ever forged with PL, which led to a lot of misplaced anger and undue strife. Langston was my boy whereas I merely tolerated PL. Though as of late I barely did that since he'd cut his ass with me years ago when I came back to the states and I'd pretty much terminated our association. It wasn't a thing that Langston and I discussed in depth because I didn't want to put him in the awkward position of having to choose friends over family, but dude was unnaturally possessive of Langston at times, which was just strange. I know that the two of them grew up more like siblings than cousins and maybe that was why. As an only child, I had no frame of reference for that, really. I just knew that a far as I was concerned, PL was someone I preferred to keep at a distance.

Langston howled with laughter, "You know that man got mad that I brought my girl on this trip instead of him?"

I joined in Langston's laughter, "That's unsurprising, man. Dude can't accept the fact that y'all lead and live separate lives."

"Man, he's gonna have to get used to it. Nyema's here to stay...unless she decides she's ready to vamp."

I shook my head, "Nah bruh, I don't see that happening. She's just as sprung out on you as you are on her. So, I guess I gotta respect your wishes and not push up on her home girl."

"Please. Do it for the children," Langston joked.

"Aye, I'll try to do my best. But if shorty gives me any sign that she's going..."

Langston shook his head, "You're hopeless."

I glanced inside briefly, my eyes locking with Jayde's as she happened to be staring out toward the balcony at us in this moment, "Naw man...I'm hope*ful*."

FOUR

"YOU KNOW I wanna climb that big motherfucker like a tree and ride him off into the sunset right?" I sighed, looking out to the balcony where Langston and Nikolas sat looking like they were engaged in a pretty serious conversation.

"So, what's stopping you?" Nyema laughed.

"*You*," I said, turning back to face her.

"Me?" she asked, reaching for her water glass to take a sip, "How am I stopping you from doing what you like?"

"Because," I whined, "He's your man's friend. So that means he finna be around for the indeterminate future. And I can't just hit and quit him like I'd normally do, because it'll probably be hella awkward to be walking down the aisle at your wedding as maid of honor with a one-night stand. Though, *if it was good enough,* we could recreate that one night on the night of your wedding and you wouldn't be the only one having a great time that night."

"Jay!" Nyema screeched, laughing, "How have you created an entire scenario for an event that is nowhere near coming to fruition?"

"Oh girl, you and Beige Urkel are a foregone conclusion. That man is *smitten* with you. And your nose is just as wide open for him even though you're trying to be on your cool girl shit. And that's cute...for y'all. As for me and my house?" I sighed again, grabbing my own glass to take a prolonged sip of my wine, "I should get out of here before I do something stupid."

Nyema laughed loudly once again, "Dang, Jay. It's like that?"

"Look...it's been a minute and I'm *vulnerable.* And you didn't make matters any better, limping in here like Langston knocked the bottom out of your pussy. You know nobody likes a braggart," I groaned, rolling my eyes.

"Something is seriously wrong with you," Nyema giggled, "But...what's stopping you from pursuing something with Niko? Seriously. He seems to be kinda taken with you too."

I shook my head, "Nah, he wants to *fuck me*. Which, who can blame him, honestly? Have you seen me tonight? I look good."

I stood up, showing off the cute mustard yellow jumpsuit I'd paired with flat, gladiator style sandals. I hit a few poses while Nyema pretended to take pictures of me.

"You are a damn fool, Jay, I swear," Nyema cackled before sobering and saying, "But seriously though...you know you could actually like...get to know and possibly date, Nikolas. There's nothing wrong with a non-hit and quit situation. No laws against it or nothing..."

"Woooooow, Khaki Randall Pearson really got you caught up out here, huh?" I asked, pretending to wipe away a tear, "Lemme pour out a little liquor for my partner in hoe shit's jersey being raised to the rafters."

Nyema rolled her eyes and shook her head, "We're not talking about me, we're talking about you."

I ignored her attempt at trying to start a conversation that I did not want to have right now. This wasn't the time nor place. Instead I began singing Boyz II Men's "*It's So Hard to Say Goodbye to Yesterday*" while pantomiming raising a jersey to the rafters.

"*And I'll take...with me the memory...*"

"Fine!" Nyema pouted, rolling her eyes, "I'll let it go. For now."

"Whew, your girl gets booed up and immediately tries to make everyone else see the monogamy light. You hate to see it," I jeered.

"I'm just saying. You never know what life will bring. Y'all could be each other's meant to be," Nyema rebutted before launching into one of my favorite songs, "*Meant to Be*" by an indie singer/songwriter named Melissa Polinar.

I couldn't help but join in, harmonizing with Nyema and grinning right along with her when we got to the end of the chorus and she said, "Damn, we sound good. We should cover that at you and Niko's wedding."

"I can't stand you," I groaned.

"The lies! I'ma leave you alone though, even though you should give him a chance," she mumbled.

"But...we...I...*can't*. Besides we don't even know that he's into me beyond what he sees."

"Oh, so that's why he is more focused on you right now than he is on whatever Langston is talking to him about?"

I pulled my lower lip between my teeth wisely staying silent, but also feeling slightly validated that I hadn't been imagining it. All night as we ate and sat around talking about a bevy of subjects, I'd felt Nikolas' gaze on me, but I brushed it off as paranoia that he had noticed how much I'd been trying to check him out on the low. He was a gorgeous mountain of a man—standing at six foot six, weighing nearly two hundred eighty pounds if the Wikipedia article I'd read about him was accurate. Stretched across all of that man was blemish free pecan brown colored skin, decorated with tattoos on both biceps and a lush beard that framed a grin that was guileless and inviting whenever he graced any of us with it. Not only was he big and fine as hell—*my general type*, he also had the kindest, almond shaped deep brown eyes that crinkled at the corners slightly whenever he smiled. Nyema wasn't wrong about him being the type of guy who could possibly be someone worth building with, but I wasn't exactly the girl a man wanted to build with. Not yet, anyway. I was hyper focused on ascending in my career on my own terms, without the distraction of falling in like or love or anything adjacent. Having my needs satiated on demand was more of my speed for now, anyway.

So, I had to get up outta here, now. Before my mind

got too carried away with the seeds of what if that Ny was trying to plant in it.

I pulled out my phone and opened up *Lyft*, but Nyema reached out a hand to stop me.

"We can drop you off," she smiled.

"We've been drinking, sis," I replied, taking another pointed sip of wine.

"*Y'all* have been drinking. Not me. I'm fine to drive and you don't need to be getting into a *Lyft* by yourself, possibly inebriated, at this time of night. Too many cautionary tales on social media of a rideshare gone wrong. Babe," Nyema called out, before I stopped her.

"Y'all shouldn't have to cut your night short because I don't have self-control."

"It's *fine*," Nyema insisted as the guys came back into the condo.

"What's up, baby?" Langston asked, plopping down onto the couch next to Nyema and immediately burying his face in her neck.

She giggled before informing him that we should be calling it a night. I couldn't hear his response, but whatever it was made Nyema flush bright red before she thanked Nikolas for his hospitality, then scurried off in the direction of the bathroom. I started to apologize for cutting the night short, but Langston piped up quickly, interrupting my little speech.

"You're all good, Jayde. This man been needed to put us out of his crib. I know that high from all of the adrenaline of today's events has worn off but he's too polite to say anything. Besides, we ain't got nothing but time to catch up now."

"Damn bro," Nikolas laughed, "*Really*? Nothing but time?"

"Oh..." Langston quipped, "Too soon?"

Nikolas just shook his head laughing, before moving closer to me and saying, "Jayde, I hope tonight won't be the last time we see each other, since we're practically neighbors and all. I've been here a few years, but most of my friends aren't locals. Since I spend the majority of my year here, it'd be nice to have a friendly face around."

"I...um...yeah," I croaked out, nodding, "I'm sure we'll see each other."

"Let me get your number," he said, smoothly, "So, we can keep in touch."

"Sure," I replied, rattling off the digits as Nyema reemerged.

"Okay," she said, "Y'all ready?"

"Let's roll," Langston said, raising up from where he was seated to give Nikolas that little man hug dap thing that men did, "Say, bro. Why don't you bring your ass home this summer?"

"Moms been pestering me to come visit, so I might pop up there on y'all sometime this summer."

"Nikolas," Nyema said, extending her arms for a hug, "A pleasure to finally meet you."

"No need to stand on formalities, DJ Nyla...Niko is fine," he said, returning her gesture with a warm smile, "I'm glad you got this negro to finally take me up on an offer to come down and check out Nashville. It took him trying to impress a girl to get the nigga down here despite the years I've been tryna get him to come visit."

"You talk too much, man," Langston grumbled, and Nikolas chuckled in response.

The deep rumble of his laughter reverberated through my body as he turned to me.

"Jayde," he said.

"Nikolas," I replied.

He laughed and shook his head. I held out a hand for a shake, which he promptly ignored, pulling me in for a hug as well. As we embraced, he rumbled into my ear, "I'll be in touch."

All I had in return for him was weak nod and smile as I was way too preoccupied with the strong bands of his arms sweeping me into him, and the frisson of attraction it sent through my body despite the embrace lasting no more than five seconds. My accelerated heart rate and the way my pussy throbbed like a pulsing bass drum after that brief moment further cemented the fact that I needed to carry my ass far and away from Nikolas Verette.

I'd deftly avoided all contact initiated by Nikolas in the ensuing weeks after I'd hung out at his place with Nyema and Langston. He'd texted a few times and called, but I used my phone's settings to put him on a restricted list so that I wouldn't be notified of the notifications when he did reach out. I guess he eventually took the hint as the messages had petered off this week. But imagine my surprise walking onto the stage at the Purple Shamrock on a random Tuesday evening and seeing his massive person trying to be incognito while seated at a back-corner table. I hadn't seen him when I arrived, so he must've come in after I'd made my way to the back room to relax before I had to be *on*.

Tonight wasn't a scheduled night for me and the guys to play, but it was actually an open mic night. In addition to my regular gigs with the band, I was the backup hostess for the Sham's weekly open mic session. The normal host, Randi, was touring as a background vocalist for the next two months, so I'd be filling in until she returned. Nikolas' appearance tonight made the bar seem stiflingly small, his presence filling the room in a way that made me a bit more keyed up than I preferred. That combined with the people who vacillated between trying to ignore him while blatantly staring in his direction or going up and asking for autographs and pictures and I was completely unnerved. I took a second to close my eyes and take a deep breath, before speaking directly into the mic.

"How y'all doing tonight?' I purred into the mic, "Welcome to No Shame at the Sham, an open mic extravaganza. For those of you who aren't regulars—*I know, Terrie, I'll try to keep it short*—let me give you the rundown of how this evening will progress. We got Keith on the ones and twos, if karaoke is your thing. He's got the hits that span genres from Aaliyah to ZZ Top. If you prefer to do your good singing acapella? That ain't no problem. Ain't no problem at all."

The crowd chuckled a bit at my Shannon Sharpe impression as I continued, "Sign up is at the bar with Terrie. T, throw a hand up and shout hey, for the unfamiliar ones among us."

Terrie, a statuesque, bleached blonde beauty did

exactly as directed as I stared down at my clip board. I looked over to where Nikolas was sitting and our eyes met, his revealing a sort of pleased surprise at seeing me on the stage. I quickly racked my brain wondering if I'd mentioned the Purple Shamrock was my spot during the conversations we'd had at his place when Nyema and Langston were in town. I couldn't recall, honestly, and had a much more pressing issue at hand currently—being an engaging and witty hostess tonight.

"Now, we've got a few sign ups already and honestly, there is zero surprise at this first name on the list it's... me!" I laughed. Terrie had jokes and signed me up as the first person whether I was here or not every week. More often than not I *was* here and the folks who were at the Sham regularly just got used to me kicking off the night. If I wasn't there, my social media feeds would blow up with people tagging me in pics of the stage at the Sham saying they were missing a little something *something* that I always brought to the table. Unlike the last time I was in here, there didn't appear to be any jerkoffs who'd have a running commentary on my performance, but for some reason tonight I was in a different sort of mood.

Instead of singing a hit, I'd decided to do something new. It was a tune that I'd just finished writing that morning. The idea was sparked a few weeks ago when on my morning run, I'd inadvertently stopped at a familiar intersection that brought memories of a liaison in the past flooding into my mind. The chorus of the song came to me immediately as I recognized my surroundings and I sat on the curb with my Notes app in hand, writing the words down. The rest of the song was slow coming, but eventually it all came together in a beautifully, forlorn melodic expression of longing. This was one of those songs that I know could go on to make me a bucket load of money if I pitched it to any of the popular singers to whom I had ties, but I'd continue to hoard it for myself.

"Y'all mind if I go off book a lil bit tonight? Now, normally I'd keep this close to the chest but y'all I finished writing a really good song this morning. And it was one of those things that just sort of happened organically. Any writers in the house will tell you that you can be triggered to create from the smallest thing. For me? It was a few weeks ago that during a jog in my neighborhood...I ended up on 12th and Halcyon...right in front of the bike shop, y'all know? Now...I'm probably telling too much of my personal business, but stalkers please try to keep your creepiness to a minimum and respect my privacy at this time, please and thank you."

The crowd chuckled; Nikolas' low rumble of a laugh slithered to the forefront of the cacophony of sound. I shivered imperceptibly and continued on with my tale about how ending up at that corner taking a breath turned into writing a song about a past lover.

"Aight y'all, so without further ado...here is "The Corner of Me and You"...ooh that rhymed!" I giggled before stepping back briefly to clear my throat to sing, "Well I should say I'm gonna give you the first verse and chorus of the song. Can't give it all away for free, right?'

More laughter from the crowd.

"Oh," I said, popping forward to speak into the mic again, "And I'ma do it *acapulco*, since I'm still working out the melodies. Shout out to you if you get that reference! Alright, here we go."

Took a walk down memory's lane
Traveled far enough to pass the pain
Visions of your face played in my brain
Thought we'd last through the end of time
But fate had other plans in mind
You crushed my heart
Left me broken, cryin'
But time healed my wounds
My mind you no longer consumed
I was past the notion
Devoid of emotion
When it came to losing you

HINDSIGHT IS twenty twenty
Lessons from you I learned plenty
And I'm thankful for them every day
Now I can finally say...
These memories are bittersweet
Yet I wouldn't change a single scene
Painted on the edges of my mind
Wandering blind, didn't know what I'd find
Took a moment to stop and take in the view
And ended up on the corner of me and you...

THE UNEXPECTED EMOTION of performing this song for the first time in front of an audience caught me off guard as the crowd applauded. I swallowed the lump that had formed in my throat before moving forward with the next person in the lineup—a regular named Marge. Marge was a sturdy sort of woman...I could never quite tell how old she was because some days she looked old enough to be my mom and others old enough to be my grandmother. But Marge's low contralto was a thing of beauty and we lived when she got on stage to bless us with a few tunes. She always brought her acoustic guitar and blessed us with a minimum of three songs, most often her unique spin on popular tunes from the radio.

Listen, you have not lived until you've heard a velvety voiced middle-aged white woman sing the hell out of her remix of "*Hotline Bling*". I wasn't a fan of the Poutine Prince from the Six, but Marge flipped his repetitive, robotic sounding song into a plaintive lamentation of a former lover's presence being so seared into your brain that their absence leaves you bereft in the deepest of ways. I kept trying to make her start a YouTube channel, but Marge wasn't too much for technology. After Marge's performances, a couple of tone-deaf Taylor Swift wannabes graced us with their presence and God-awful warbling through Kelsea Ballerini's "*I Hate Love Songs*". I loved Kelsea—*and that song*—but boy did they screw it up.

I should have been consumed with hosting, but I found myself keeping one eye on my duties and the other on Nikolas. He seemed to be enjoying himself, joining in and singing the songs he'd recognized, bobbing his head to the ones that were unfamiliar. The novelty of a celebrity being in the house wore off about halfway through the night and he was sitting by himself, nursing a beer when I finally decided to go over and speak.

"Nikolas, funny running into you here," I greeted, jovially.

He cut his eyes at me briefly acknowledging my presence, and dryly responded, "Jayde."

"I...um...just wanted to come and say hi."

Nikolas again, didn't respond verbally, just picked up his beer and sipped again.

"All right I...won't bother you. I'll let you get back to it. Have a good night," I said, turning away to head back to the front of the bar to the stool I'd abandoned to come over here and apparently make a fool of myself.

I got it, honestly. I had played the hell out of him and it was stupid of me to do so knowing that this town was way smaller than I liked to pretend it was and our degrees of separation were even smaller than that so it was inevitable that our paths would cross again.

"You know, if you weren't interested in the opportunity I had for you, saying so directly would have been a better approach instead of behaving like an unemployed person dodging bill collectors and completely ignoring me," Nikolas spoke up after I'd taken a few steps away from his table.

"Opportunity?" I said, turning back in his direction, "So you weren't trying to..."

He shook his head once, "And now, you've screwed yourself out of a potential well-paying job because your ego thought I was trying to stick my dick in you. Sucks to be you."

I narrowed my eyes at him, "Oh please don't act like

you didn't hit me with the velvet teddy bear voice and your best mack moves when you asked for my number. How was I supposed to know that you wanted it for professional reasons?"

"I don't shit where I eat, sweetheart," Nikolas replied smoothly.

"Excuse me?" I shot back, irate.

"I don't mix business with pleasure. Nyema shared with me some of the songs you'd written, and I came across others when I googled you. I wanted...to collaborate with you, see what kinda vibe popped off. Nothing more. Yet you and your *ass*umptions..."

"Okay, so now that I know that...we can..." I started, but Nikolas raised a hand to cut me off.

"Nah. We can't do anything but try not to make it too awkward when we run into each other in the future at any events thrown by our mutual friends. I'm good on anything else involving you, Jayde."

"Oh, you're so good on it that you just happened to show up in a place that you knew for a fact was a place that I was more likely to be than not since I have a regular gig here. Sure," I rolled my eyes.

"Don't flatter yourself, sweetheart. This place came up in a google search for the best open mic nights in Nashville. Wasn't nobody coming to see you, Jayde!" Nikolas grumbled, raising up from his seat and getting nose to nose with me.

I took a couple steps back, putting some space between us, "I'm not doing this with you right here with you...or at all actually. You don't get to come to my job, act an ass, and expect me to sit here and take it. Just forget that I even came over here. Or that I even exist, honestly."

"Your wish is my command," Nikolas replied, reaching into his back pocket, throwing a few bills on the table and sauntering out of the bar.

I shook off the unpleasantness of that interaction and headed back up to the front to finish my hosting duties before turning the night over to Keith to get his deejay on. My mind was reeling at this Nikolas I'd seen tonight, a seemingly completely different man than the affable, charismatic guy I'd met a few short weeks ago. *Tuh! And to think Nyema was tryna get me to date his wack ass* I thought to myself. I'd definitely be giving her a call tomorrow to tell her about this Dr. Jekyll/Mr. Hyde act that buddy pulled tonight.

"SO...YOU know the both of you were completely wrong here, right?" Nyema said, calmly.

I could tell she was working at keeping her voice placid in order to not rile me up, but her efforts were futile as I instantly fired back, "The hell you mean the both of us? Did I insult him? Noooooo. Was I rude to him in his workplace? Noooooo."

"Did you dodge his calls like he was Navient? Did you try to act like everything was all good when you walked over there, knowing that he would likely feel a way? You could've just left well enough alone, Jay. Especially once you realized that he didn't come there to see you specifically. Because I know that was something that ran through your brain before you went over to him embarrassing yourself. Now was he right to react in the way that he did? Nah, there's never an excuse for anyone to get that bent out of shape at someone's job. He coulda caused harm and perhaps termination if anyone had noticed you all going back and forth. So, I'm not taking his side over yours, but sis you know I'm gonna call you on your shit too. You're culpable here as well and you have to own that."

"I don't have to own shit, Ny! He was out of line, full stop!" I screeched.

"And I agreed with you on that," Nyema replied, soothingly, "You probably just need some space from it to let the rest of what I'm saying really sink in."

"Sink these balls, sis," I fired back, laughing.

Nyema blew out a breath, which I knew was also accompanied with an eye roll. Her go tos when she was exasperated.

"Okay...okay, *for real*...I probably could have handled things a whole lot better regarding Nikolas. Do you... know anything about this opportunity he was talking about that he had for me? Because if this rich negro is tryna loop me into a damn MLM scheme..."

"Jay, please," Nyema giggled, "I don't know about any opportunity. Langston didn't either and he is refusing to pry because he says he told me to stay out of grown folks' business. But I mean...technically...if you bring me into it, who are me not to pipe up with my little two cents worth?"

"Two cents? Oh, girl more like five dollars. You've never met a problem that you don't have an extensive solution to. And I love you for that, but let's not act like you don't sometimes go overboard."

"See...that mouth of yours is why that man went off on you in the middle of the Sham, Jay, damn!" Nyema grumbled, trying to keep the laugh that was brewing in her belly tamped down.

"Kick me while I'm down!" I replied.

"Oh, girl bye. You ain't that down with your haughty ass. Oh hey...are you coming up for Ma and Daddy's 4th of July bash? Lena has been stressing me about her daughter from another mother being in attendance. Did you get her punchbowl invite?"

"I did and yes, I will be up there, barring any unforeseen occurrence. I'm overdue some of Mama Lena's peach cobbler."

"Girl you know as soon as I mention you want some, she's gonna make one the size of Wyoming so you have more than enough to take back with you to Nashville. Just keep me abreast of your plans so I can make sure to pick you up at the airport and all of that. Since I'm spending most nights at Langston's you'll have free reign of my place and I can even leave you my ride if you wanna make some moves on your own once you hit the city."

"Sounds like a plan, sis."

FIVE

"YOU KNOW you done messed up now A-a-ron!" Langston laughed, doubled over as if his Key and Peele imitation was just that damn funny.

I failed to see the humor in the situation at hand and was now questioning why in the hell I even reached out to him.

"Fuck you, man!"

"Naw, you finna get this roasting. Because how you go from ready to smash and dash to now wanting to work with the girl on some for real shit and *not* think she'd think something was strange?" Langston asked, "Stevie Wonder could see that you wanted to take her down, man."

He wasn't lying, but I still wasn't trying to hear shit that Langston had to say. Besides, he'd been the one trying to warn me off of her, so he should have been satisfied at my one-eighty. Did I still think Jayde was bad as fuck? Absolutely, but when the opportunity to fulfill my second most coveted dream was thrown in my lap and I knew that I had access to someone who would help take that to the highest level it could go? I put my dick to the side and tried to be about business. Shortly after Langston and Nyema had left town, I heard back from a label I'd sent a rough ass demo that I recorded in my closet. It was a cover of Donny Hathaway's "*A Song for You*", set to a cheesy karaoke track that I'd found on YouTube.

I'd sent the demo in on a whim, in response to a contest they were running on their social media pages. Pharris had seen the *#forthegram* contest advertised and sent me a link. They were looking for fresh new talent to cultivate and encouraged folks to submit a song that was the bedrock of their musical identity. It had taken Pharris' constant nagging and reminders before I finally sat down, sang and sent it off. I had no designs on actually being chosen, since singing was just a hobby that I happened to be a little above average at doing. I could have easily just booked some studio session time and cut my own shit, but something about the structure of the contest and getting the validation of someone who wasn't being paid by or wasn't related to me was...*appealing*. The entirety of the result would be determined by public opinion, essentially. So, I sent that shit in under an alias and hoped for the best.

I'd heard back from the A&R at the label, a real down to Earth cat named Roosevelt who let me know that I'd progressed to the final round of the contest. Ro and I set up a face to face meeting soon after he notified me, and of course I then had to disclose my real name since my face was very recognizable due to the past few years in the league. Ro's reaction was priceless when I rolled into the private room of the restaurant where he'd requested that we meet, but that shock was quickly replaced with glee as he went on and on about the endless possibilities of where this could take me if I won the contest. And that was where Jayde came in...or where she would have come in if she hadn't played the hell out of me over the past few weeks. I wanted her to be my...coach of sorts. Since singing had always been sort of a hobby of mine, a natural talent. But I still had a lot to learn about the technicality of the entire process, which is where I'd hoped she would have been able to help. I'd planned to compensate her handsomely as I wasn't certain if there would be any travel involved for the duration of the contest, but I'd wanted her to be there with me at all times if that was the case.

"Fam, I really can't believe you about to be on some *American Idol* of the 'gram type of joint. Being a superstar in the NBA ain't enough, this nigga gotta be Ruben Studdard too," Langston joked.

"Chill, bruh," I laughed.

"My bad, man. This is my sorry for two thousand nineteen."

I shook my head, laughing, "Gon head and keep getting your jokes off."

"Oh, that's one thing you do not have to worry about Justin Guarini. Better hope you don't get upset by a down home Kelly Clarkson type, man."

"Ha. Ha. Aye, can you ask Nyema if she knows anyone else who would be up for this gig? I know she's on the other side of the music, but I know she did do some time down here, so she might know someone..." I trailed off.

"I'll ask when she gets back home," Langston replied.

"Back home?" I asked, brows raised, "Damn, you done already moved her in, man? Aight, I ain't mad at it, playa. Stake your claim early and often."

"For your information, I am currently laid up in her house while she's out at brunch with her home girls. I've been tasked with staying ready, so I don't have to get ready when she's gone off the 'mosas. Her words not mine, but I damn sure ain't a fool, so..."

"You stayed your ass there."

"Already."

We both laughed again, knowing how sex with your girl was a little different after she'd had a few glasses of champagne or wine. I didn't know what chemical reaction those two things incited in women particularly, but I did recall reaping the benefits of it a time or two myself. Langston and I talked for a few more minutes, with him trying to convince me to come home for Nyema's parents' big Fourth of July party, and I told him I'd play it by ear. I still didn't know how much of a commitment this vocal contest would entail, so I was trying to stay local as much as possible for the next few weeks. Ro had been very vague with how everything would unfold, but he dropped hints of some sort of...seclusion being eventually involved.

I really hoped Nyema did know someone, so I didn't have to go through the effort of trying to find someone to help me. Well...so Pharris wouldn't have to go through that effort of doing the initial groundwork and then passing the ultimate hiring decision off to me. The person would have to sign a nondisclosure immediately, as I did not want any of this getting out. I needed something in my life that allowed me to show off my creativity, but still keep a modicum of anonymity. Ro insisted that they would do everything they needed to in order to keep my privacy intact, and I hoped that wasn't just him blowing smoke.

"YOU KNOW this wouldn't be so hard if you just got over your pride and hit up old girl again, right Boss Man?" Pharris sighed as he walked back into my living room after seeing our latest potential vocal coach out.

I shook my head, "Ain't no pride to get over, fam. And where did you even get these people from?"

"Man, you can thank Nyema for this one who just left. He was one of her referrals. The rest have come via a variety of ads placed."

"Wherever you placed that ad, yank it down immediately," I sighed, running a hand over the top of my head before flopping backwards onto the couch.

"I honestly think you should go with Bernadette," Pharris said, referring to a woman we'd spoken with earlier in the week.

"Man, you're only saying that because she was giving you the *I'll do anything including suck your dick for this opportunity* eyes during our entire conversation."

"And who am I to deny her the chance to show how seriously she'd take her role here?" Pharris shrugged, laughing, "But fine. You want to be a hater. Now what was wrong with buddy who just left here?"

I threw him an annoyed look, "Man, you didn't hear that noise? Whenever he said a word that had the letter s in it, it sounded like the wind whistling through the trees. I'd rather not have to listen to Hurricane Harold every time I needed to practice, man."

"You are bugging, Nik. I didn't hear anything out of the ordinary beyond his slight lisp," Pharris reasoned, "Just admit that you're going to find something wrong with everyone who comes through these doors to interview because they aren't *Jayde*."

"There's nothing for me to admit, P."

"Aight, bro. Well look, we outta options and a little birdie told me that your girl was gonna be hosting that open mic night tonight, so I suggest you put together your best hat in hand, baby baby please, apologetic tune and get your big ass up on that stage tonight. You know women love those big gestures like that."

"That might be the worst idea you've ever had, man. What I look like hopping on stage in public, using this voice that we've been trying to keep anonymous in this contest, and effectively ending my shit before it even gets a chance to pop off. Hard pass, man. I dunno, I gotta figure something out."

"And fast...you seen Melina's upload? Sheesh..."

Melina was one of the other contestants that I was competing against. *Double R Records* had begun the rollout of the contest by posting teasers of our audition submissions on their social channels. Right out the gate, both Melina and I were crowd favorites and the frontrunners to win it all. I'd had to create a burner Instagram account to use for the purposes of the contest, but I'd been slacking on uploading consistent content. Melina, on the other hand, practically lived on the damned app—inviting the people of the internet into her life beyond the singing thing, going live and showing off the most innocuous parts of her life. I'd yet to come up with a way to be able to be as accessible while still maintaining a modicum of privacy so she had me beat on that front.

"What upload?" I asked and Pharris pulled out his phone, presumable scrolling on Instagram to show me.

"Take a look for yourself," Pharris said, extending his phone in my direction.

Sure as shit, here was Melina on her newly created contest specific Instagram, @mel4dagram. She was dressed...well more like undressed in a crop top and the tiniest pair of shorts as she moved through a series of yoga poses while singing an acoustic rendition of Janelle Monae's "Yoga". Whoever was playing the guitar was just off screen, but it was clear that the music wasn't the focus of this upload underscored by the fact that she'd chosen to face away from the camera with her ass being the focus of the video more than anything that came out of her mouth.

"Oh, you gotta be kidding me," I groaned.

"You know you gotta put some shit up to compete with this, right bro?"

"Or I can just upload a regular video?" I reasoned.

"Bro, how many likes shorty got now?" Pharris asked me.

I glanced back at the phone to look, "It doesn't show

likes but...nigga she got almost a quarter million views on this shit?"

"I'm responsible for at least ten percent of those. I mean...take off your competitor hat for a second, bruh. You see that ass?"

I shook my head laughing, Pharris was right...that thang was poking, but damn all of that. She was the competition, so my lust was short-lived as I sat watching the video as it replayed. I had to top this shit in some way. Pharris grabbed his phone back and navigated to something else before handing it back to me.

"This is your only resort, man. You gotta fight fire with fire," he said, laughing, "But uh...you gon have to use the self-timer and take as many takes as you need because I'm not gonna be the one to record this one, big homie."

I laughed, looking at the song he'd brought up on YouTube, "This would be a good choice if I was interested in gimmicks to get me by in this contest, but I'm tryna win off talent, man. I am not stooping to Melina's level, no matter how tempting it may be."

Pharris grabbed his phone back again, shaking his head, "Aight man, you might wanna think about it a little bit more, but I'm telling you this could be your ace in the hole. Until then...you going to see ol girl to convince her to come on board or you gonna just go the rest of the way by yourself?"

I flicked my wrist up, looking down at my watch. I still had about thirty minutes before the open mic night started at the *Purple Shamrock*.

"Aye, what you got going on tonight?"

"Not a damn thing, what you tryna get into?"

"Come run a lil errand with me. I'll let you drive the Tesla," I said standing up and tossing Pharris the keys.

"Aye man, you make too much money to need a getaway driver..." Pharris teased.

"Just bring your ass on before we're late. Last thing I need is to be making spectacle."

Pharris shot me a look of disbelief, "Oh...your big ass ain't a spectacle just walking into a room? Yeah, okay fam."

I ignored him, shaking my head and walking to get my wallet before we left the condo. Minutes later we were pulling up to the *Purple Shamrock*. I tried walking into the bar as inconspicuous as possible, but mere seconds after we crossed the threshold; I heard my name being called from the direction of the stage. I turned around to see some brotha with a fucked up lining getting up from a table and coming in my direction. He spoke my name with such familiarity that I was scrutinizing his face trying to see if he looked familiar, but nothing sparked.

"Aye, Phar, do I know this cat?" I asked under my breath, indicating with an almost imperceptible head motion toward the guy.

Pharris quickly shook his head no as the guy approached, hand out, awaiting a shake.

"It's good to meet you, man," the guy gushed as we shook hands, "I'm a season ticket holder with the *Trojans*. End of the season was a bit of a bummer, but what can you do, am I right?"

"Oh...ok, nice meeting you brotha. If you don't mind,

I'm meeting someone here and I'm a little late," I lied, not really here for the fan meet and greet shit.

I'd come here with a specific purpose in mind, convincing Jayde to get over whatever perceived issue she had with me and signing on to help shepherd me through *#forthegram*.

"You mind taking a picture with me really quickly? The guys on the farm won't believe me when I tell them about this later."

Instead of waiting for me to give him an answer, buddy crowded my space while trying to throw an arm around my shoulders and snapping a selfie. Before I had a chance to think about it, I was stiff arming him, softening it with a sly grin.

"How bout we let my guy Pharris take it, man?" I said, affably.

Considering that I was damn near seven feet tall and dude looked to be a strong five three at best, any angle he got wouldn't be flattering toward either of us. And since I knew the shit would end up on social media in some fashion, I preferred to not take awkwardly positioned selfies with folks. Pharris was used to having to step in to be Gordon Parks every now and again since he was with me most often when folks asked for a flick. Luckily he took it in stride, a lot of that having to do with the very handsome salary I paid him, I was sure. After taking the pic with the guy and scrawling an autograph on a cocktail napkin, Pharris and I finally headed back toward the table that I'd occupied the last time I was in this spot, way in the back in a sort of inconspicuous spot.

Moments after we'd settled and a waitress brought us

a couple brews—a guy bounded on stage welcoming everyone to *No Shame at the Sham Open Mic Night.* According to his little speech, he was the back up for the backup—Jayde which drew a series of groans from folks in the crowd.

"Well, there goes that brilliant little plan," Pharris said, taking a long sip from his beer.

I shook my head, "Nah, it ain't the end of the road, G. Did you forget I had an in?"

Moments later we were in the car, Nyema on FaceTime with a dubious look on her face. I'd called Langston trying to get him to give me her number, but to no great surprise, they were together, and she had him initiate a video call instead so she could grill me about what I was asking her to give to me.

"Please?" I insisted, flashing a grin that had talked women out of far more than the little bit of information that I was trying to extract from her.

"I don't know, Nikolas. Jay is for real crazy. My sis might cut me for giving you this info. And honestly? This face is too fine to have a massive scar running from temple to sternum because I know for sure that she'd go for the money maker over anywhere else."

"Baby, you could have a Frankenstein stitched scar running the entirety of your face and nobody would be touching you out here, still," Langston piped up.

I rolled my eyes. The man was *whipped.*

"Man, you can save all of that for y'all own time. Nyema—I wouldn't ask if this wasn't on the up and up, I swear. I mean I kinda already know she lives in the 12 South neighborhood and drives a custom pink Fiat 500,"

I started—one of those little tidbits she'd shared before she sang the last time I was at the open mic; the other had come up during dinner at my place that night we first met, "So I can use the rest of my context clues and have Pharris driving around all willy nilly until I find her or..."

"Ok fam, you realize that makes you sound like a stalker, right?" Pharris piped up.

"Phar...whose side are you on here?" I groused.

"Yours always, man. But...come on...you gotta admit..." he trailed off.

Nyema and Langston were cracking up, finding this little back and forth between us funny.

"For real though, I *need* her for this project, Nyema. No one else will do. You can ask Pharris, we've definitely tried to find someone else."

"Have we ever!" Pharris yelled and I cut my eyes at him.

"Why Jay? Why do you *need* her?" Nyema asked, eyes narrowed peering at me like she was trying to look into the depths of my soul.

"Something just tells me that she will bring that passion and fire I need to come out on top for this," I said.

I hadn't given them the details of the contest, not wanting to get too many people looped into the biggest secret that I'd have to keep in quite some time. I just told them that I was working on a music-based project and wanted to collaborate with Jayde. It wasn't that I didn't trust them to keep the information to themselves, but it was just that I knew that the more people who were in on the details of this particular endeavor; the more likely it was that someone would spill the beans inadvertently.

Nyema stared at me for a few moments more, the silence from her a bit unnerving before she rattled off an address.

"And if she asks where you got it from, just know that I will claim plausible deniability...or that you sent some goons to beat it out of me," she cackled.

"Baby? Goons? Really?" Langston chuckled.

"Aye, I can't let my girl know I rolled over so damned easily. But I'm a sucker for a good story and these two working together? Will definitely be a good one," Nyema said, cryptically.

"What's that supposed to mean?" I asked as Pharris plugged the address Jayde had given us into the GPS.

Nyema ignored my question and bid us good night before she disconnected the call.

"Oh she in Green Hills man, not 12 South," he mused as he pulled away from the curb, "We should still be there in no time though. Baby girl must be racking in some bread though if she lives in Green Hills. It's nice as hell over there."

I'd only been in the area to go to the mall that was there but had noticed that there were a lot of nice houses in the immediate area. About ten minutes later we were turning onto a semi-dark street with small homes lining either side into a cul de sac.

"Man, did that sign back there say *plantation*? Where the hell are we going?" Pharris grumbled.

"Hey...you were the one who was so insistent upon me making amends with Jayde. You get what you get," I said as we pulled up to the last house on the cul de sac, angling the Tesla into a narrow driveway behind that damned pink Fiat. I shook my head, it was obnoxiously pink too. Looked like a damned Barbie car.

"You want me to come for backup or you good?" Pharris joked.

"Ha. Ha. Bring your ass on, man."

I didn't need him for backup, but I definitely wasn't just going to leave him in a very nice car in this unfamiliar neighborhood by himself. Who knows what would happen if a trigger happy cop on patrol just happened to breeze through? An extreme thought, but I preferred to be safe rather than sorry when I had the opportunity to control the narrative. I walked up and saw an ornately carved lion head knocker decorating the door. I used it, knocking three times before I stepped back with hands in my pockets as we waited for her to answer the door. A few moments passed with no indication that she was coming to answer the door. I stepped off the small porch that was in front of her house to peer into the front window. There were slivers of light coming through her blinds, so I assumed she was home and walked back over to the door. This time I noticed a doorbell that I'd missed the first time and pressed that instead of using the knocker again.

"Say, maybe we shoulda called first?" Pharris mused.

"Perhaps, but we were already in rotation, so I mean..." I trailed off, when the door finally opened and Jayde peered from behind the massive teal door.

Her eyes were narrowed in confusion that quickly turned to recognition as she looked me directly in the eyes and stepped from behind the shelter of the door. Despite being completely sleep rumpled, she was still bad as hell in a tank top and itty bitty shorts that showed off her dope ass frame.

"Can I help you?" she asked, leaning against the door, annoyance clear on her face.

"Hey...I was...*we* were wondering if you had a few spare minutes. To discuss some business?" I said, gesturing to Pharris who'd backed a little off the porch once Jayde appeared.

"How did you even know where...I am going to kill Ny," she gritted out before addressing me again, "I thought you said that whatever business you had with me before was dead now. What was it you said...my overinflated ego had you fucked up? Or something to that measure? Nah, I'm good Nikolas. Y'all have a good night," Jayde said before stepping back and closing the door to her home.

"Jayde, please. Give me five minutes, that's all I ask. I think this could end up being mutually beneficial if you'll just hear me out. I...admit that I didn't exactly handle my approach in the right way when I first thought of you for this opportunity, I'll own that. But...if you think I'm about to get on bended knee and ask you to work for...no...with me, then you've got another thing coming. I think your talent is rare—top notch, bar none—but I'm not exactly the type of man who will grovel over a simple misunderstanding. Now, with that being said, can we bug you for no more than five minutes or nah?"

"I'm not exactly dressed for company," she said.

I chuckled, "We'll give you a few minutes to make yourself presentable, so long as it doesn't cut into my promised time. C'mon...I can see it in your eyes that you're intrigued by what would bring me all the way over here to bother you tonight? I actually went to the *Shamrock* first...but clearly you weren't there, so I had to use other means. By the way, you all right?"

Looking at Jayde a bit more closely, her eyes were reddened and a little puffy, not completely due to being asleep before we arrived unannounced. Her nose was also pretty red as well and she'd rubbed it a couple times while I was giving my little speech.

"Allergies," she groaned, "been kicking my ass all week and today I finally let them win. Thanks...for asking."

"You're welcome. So...you gonna let us in or nah? It's a little breezy out here," I joked, giving Jayde the same smile I'd laid on her home girl earlier.

Only this time I received the desired response, even if only for a split second. Jayde quickly schooled her features into a mask of nonchalance, but for a moment a faint blush of red covered her cheeks as she bit down on her lower lip. Wordlessly, she stepped aside, and then backed into her townhome waving us through the entrance.

"Well I'll be damned. That shit really worked," Pharris muttered under his breath, following me into Jayde's place.

"Did you doubt me, fool?" I whispered back as Jayde told us not to make our way anywhere past the front room where an abnormally large television was mounted onto the wall. The place was very cozy looking, the little bit of it that we could see anyway. The front room was outfitted with a medium sized heather grey sofa stuffed to the gills with decorative pillows and two very comfortable looking teal side chairs. I opted for a chair while Pharris shuffled some of the pillows on the sofa aside to take a seat there. I observed the crap ton of concert posters she had on the walls, some advertising shows that I knew took place way before her birth. They gave the room character and definitely advertised that Jayde was a music head—if not a musician in her own right. The posters were cool as hell, multi-colored with that vintage letterpress style advertising acts from Willie Nelson to Janet Jackson.

"Alright, so what was so damned important that you pulled up to my house at eight seventeen pm in the evening?" Jayde teased as she walked back into the room and flopped down onto the chair across from me. She looked over at Pharris and rolled her eyes, "And I see you've made yourself right at home, Mister Man Whose Name I Still Don't Know?"

I chuckled, "My bad, Jayde. This is Pharris, my assistant. And actually, Phar, why don't you give Jayde the four one one on the details of what we're proposing exactly?"

"Me?" Pharris said, sitting up, "Nah, player, this is *your* show. I'm just here for moral support."

"Time is ticking, boys," Jayde replied, yawning, "You're down to three minutes now."

"Fine," I said, throwing Pharris an exasperated look, "You've heard of *Double R Records*, right?"

"Ryan Rucker's label? Of course I have," Jayde replied, "But what's that got to do with you?"

"Well, I'm a finalist in their *#forthegram* contest and... I need your help," I said.

"No fucking way! That's dope, Nikolas! Congratulations!" Jayde screeched excitedly, "Wait...wait...though, I've been following that contest because my mortal enemy is also a finalist and I don't remember seeing you at...oh my God...you're the *faceless* nigga!"

Pharris busted out laughing at the journey Jayde's thoughts took in such a short period of time and I couldn't help but join him.

"Does Ny know you're the faceless nigga? She and I have been trying to figure out if we knew him since *Double R* was being cagey with details and you obviously weren't showing your face. Are you on your 'I'm an artist and want to be respected for perfecting my craft' steelo? What's with the cloak and dagger of it all?"

"I...which question do you want me to answer first?" I asked, to which Jayde responded with an eye roll, "No, your girl doesn't know. The only people who do know are in this room right now, with the exception of Ryan Rucker and Ro Ashe from *Double R Records*."

I also explained the lead up to me entering the contest in the first place and a little bit about my passion for singing which had been cast aside in favor of basketball since it seemed the surer bet. As I talked, Jayde's eyes stayed engaged with mine, locked in with a laser-like focus as she listened intently.

"Awwww, Ro Ashe is involved with this? He's a dope dude. Heard he finally settled down with someone, damn I missed out with that one," Jayde said, shaking her head, "Anyway...anyway...if you're a finalist already then why, pray tell, would you need my help?"

"Because I mean, I can sing. But if I wanna beat

Melina, I gotta be able to *sang*, you know what I mean?"

"Ugh, that yamp," Jayde replied, rolling her eyes once again, "Lord knows how her and that thin ass voice even got to the finals in the competition. She probably blew *Double R* or something to claw her way in."

"Damn, hold back a little, Jayde," I laughed.

"Sorry, but not really. I'll never pull any punches when it comes to talking about that trash bucket. You'll learn that I...can be a little loose with my mouth as we work together," she replied, grimacing slightly.

Even with a mean mug, she was still spectacularly gorgeous. I shook my head to rid my mind of that thought. *Keep it professional, nigga,* I said to myself before her words registered.

"Wait, did you say 'as we work together'?" I asked.

She nodded once, giggling, "I was waiting for you to pick up on that."

"Why?" I asked, not knowing why it was important for me to know, but also knowing that I couldn't begin this working relationship without knowing her reasons.

"One because even before I knew the faceless nigga was you, I was rooting for him to win as he sang my draws off with that acapella cover of "Love's In Need of Love Today". And secondly...*and I cannot stress this enough*...if I can be a part of the team that is the reason why Melina is relegated to second place? That's a team I will always be a part of."

"Whoa, if you signing on to help me is about whatever bad blood you and ol' girl have...I..." I started before Jayde held up a hand cutting me off.

"I promise you, it's more about seeing you win than it

is about her. Scout's honor," she said, putting three fingers over her heart.

"Oh, she is *legit*, bro. That's the real-life girl scout symbol of promise," Pharris, who'd been uncharacteristically quiet this entire time, piped up.

"Man, how you know?" I laughed.

"Aye...I had three older sisters and three younger ones. We had 'em all in the crib from daisies to brownies to full-fledged scouts. I know things," Pharris said with a shudder as if the Girl Scouts was a dangerous gang.

Both Jayde and I laughed at his ridiculousness, with Jayde sobering before I did as she impressed upon me that she really did want to be a part of helping me achieve a dream of mine. She was earnest, eyes shining with genuine positivity, so I believed her and welcomed her to the team.

"Great, now that you're on board," Pharris started, a mischievous twinkle in his eye, "Can you help me convince this man that this needs to be his next video?"

He handed Nyema his phone and she grinned broadly.

"You, my new friend, are a genius!" she clapped gleefully, "Do you trust me, Nikolas?"

"As much as I can anyone at this point," I smirked.

"Great! Now take your shirt off," Jayde smiled.

My head jerked back, and my eyes narrowed, knowing that I did not hear her say what I thought I heard her say.

"Excuse me?"

"You heard me," Jayde replied, speaking slower than previously, "Take. Off. Your. Shirt."

SIX

THIS WAS either the smartest or dumbest idea I've ever had I thought to myself as I watched a half-naked, fully greased up Nikolas Verette in my back parlor. Gone was the black tee that he'd paired with jeans and casual loafers when he showed up on my doorstep unannounced. And those jeans rode dangerously low on his hips now, giving me a delicious view of the v-cuts on either side of his waist and a bird's eye view of that light dusting of hair that began right below his belly button and led down into...

Nikolas cleared his throat and I re-centered my focus upon his face.

"I can't believe y'all talked me into this shit," he grumbled, the pout on his face just making him look *impossibly* sexy.

Definitely the dumbest idea I surmised, considering that he was like cake when you're on a low carb diet —*completely* off limits. That still didn't take me from taking him in most of his glory all in. I didn't know what actually propelled me to say yes to his little proposition, knowing good and well the distraction of his fine self around me was not something that I needed in my life. But it was summer...and I was known to be a little reckless during this time of the year so here we were. When his homie proposed this song to be the next one that Nikolas tackled during this competition, I readily agreed. And then urged him to take it off so we could get it on film. He balked at the idea, but I told him that if Melina wanted to use sex to sell, then Nikolas—*who had sexiness emanating from him in spades*—needed to match her same energy if it would keep him from being left behind. He was still a bit dubious, so I pressed onward, getting to the part that would ultimately count. I knew that this contest would largely be led by the impressions and views on social, but also having dealt with the guys at *Double R* before, I knew a gimmick wouldn't get him too far with them.

The visual wouldn't be enough, he needed out of this world vocals; so I'd asked him to sing a couple lines of the song acapella before we set up to record. I wanted to really hear him sing in an uncontrolled environment. I'd heard him a little bit that night we first met, when we bonded over *The Five Heartbeats*, and on the couple of videos that I'd watched obsessively since I started keeping up with *#forthegram*, but those were carefully curated.

I wanted to hear his raw tone, without time to prepare for execution, just instinctual singing. And he delivered...*boy did he deliver,* crooning the opening lines to the song in a smooth tenor that just about melted my panties clean off.

Girl it's only you

Have it your way

And if you want you can decide...

At that moment, I should have reneged on this whole thing. Begged off, and provided Nikolas with a robust list of others who could assist him in achieving his goal, but instead I sat there with a moony grin on my face. When he finished and asked me what I thought, I gave him a couple quick breathing tips and urged him to run through it a couple more times before we actually filmed it for upload.

And now? He was in my spare room that I used as a recording studio slash soundstage, situated in front of the camera behind which I was currently perched. Nikolas' deep brown skin looked flecked with minute speckles of gold, as his coconut oil covered chest glistened under the amateur ring light set up that I had rigged.

"You ready?" I asked.

Nikolas threw me a skeptical glance, before shrugging, "I guess. This shit feels mad awkward. I can't front."

"Well, if it makes you feel a little better, most of your face isn't in frame at all," I laughed, "We're taking the inspiration to heart all the way here."

Unlike in the D'Angelo video where he bared way more than Nikolas was currently, we were going to keep a tight shot on Nikolas' body. The camera would pan from his lips down that beautiful terrain that was his pectoral and abdominal regions periodically, but not giving too much away because of his quest for anonymity.

"Alright, let's do this," he said, a begrudging tone lacing his words.

"If you don't feel comfortable with this, we can...find you something else?" I said, already scrolling through the mental rolodex of music in my brain to find something different.

Nikolas shook his head, shooting me an impish grin, "Nah, y'all said I gotta show off the goods in order to stay in the hunt, so we'll do what needs to be done. I'll get used to it."

"Oh please, let's not act like you haven't shot a thirst trap before, I've seen your Instagram," I said, laughing.

"I don't even run that thing," Nikolas said, joining me in my laughter, "Pharris and my photographer put in a joint effort in keeping that up to date with relevant content. I couldn't even tell you the password to the account."

I shook my head, "Alright superstar, well for this contest here, you're gonna have to switch up your approach. I know you're on your secret squirrel vibe, but the people feeling like you're accessible is going to go a long way in helping you succeed here too. Anyway, I digress...let's get going. So y'all aren't in my house all night."

"Is this fine?" Nikolas asked, "Where I'm standing?"

"*You sure are fine*," I mumbled before I could catch it, "I mean...move a little to the right, so I have you centered in frame."

The slight grin on Nikolas face let me know that he'd heard what I said initially but chose to sidestep it. *Interesting*, I thought, I guess he really was on his strictly professional thang. Which, was honestly, the best approach for us both. I adjusted a few settings on the camera before finally reconnecting my gaze with his as I set the camera onto the tripod.

"Okay, take it from the top," I said, using my remote to start recording and looking at the screen instead of Nikolas directly.

That seemed to be the safer choice. The fact of the matter that closing my eyes completely and just hoping that the camera stayed in focus would have been the safest choice, as I made the mistake of looking up right before Nikolas got to the chorus. He looked me directly in the eyes as he sang the last few lines before the chorus.

Won't you come closer to me baby,

You've already got me right where you want me baby

I just want to be your man

And for a minute I almost forgot what the task at hand truly was, as I let myself get lost in his voice, the moment, and those damned abs. He was really unfair. Made no damned sense for someone to be this fine and be able to sing like this. Nikolas was like a big ol pile of catnip and my kitty was ready to go, raring for the signal to indulge. I got lost in my thoughts, trying to shake the incredible urge to let him know *exactly* how *it* felt...how *I* felt...and how I hoped *he'd* feel deeply embedded inside of my body.

It took a minute for me to realize that he'd stopped singing right after he got to the first chorus, trying to keep the video within the time limit needed for *Instagram.*

"That...okay?" he asked, his voice a little raspier than usual.

I licked my lips, clearing my throat before responding, "Let's check it out."

I walked over to where he stood in front of my backdrop and angled the camera so that we both could watch the playback. The video wasn't but a minute long, so it was a quick watch and he sounded good, but it seemed like something was missing. I vocalized my thoughts and Nikolas felt the same way, but neither of us could articulate exactly what was missing. For me, the look and vibe was definitely right, but there was still a distinct lack of...*something*.

"Ay yo, Phar, bring ya ass, G," Nikolas called out, crossing the room to open the door, "Come check this out."

"You got your shirt on? Ain't nobody tryna be looking at you all twankling and glistening," Pharris joked as he walked into the room, "What's good?"

I walked the camera over to Pharris, playing the video back and he agreed with the two of us that something was missing.

"Well, what is the something?" I asked.

Pharris' eyes wandered around my room before landing on the hot pink, custom Fender bass that sat propped against a wall.

"You play that or is that for show?" Pharris asked.

"Play it, of course!" I exclaimed, "For show. Tuh!"

"Well give my brother some accompaniment then. That's what missing. I know we'd been doing everything *acapulco*," Pharris grinned, "But you can't sing a Michael Eugene Archer tune without *any* instrumentation. It's almost like a damned direct display of disrespect to the musical architect that man truly is."

I grinned broadly, "Check you out, dropping Brother D's whole name like y'all went to elementary school together. You know your shit, huh?"

"I know *his* shit. I owe that man a massive debt of gratitude for the sheer amount of ass he and his music have gotten me," Pharris said, crossing his hands over himself and kissing his fingers up to the sky.

Nikolas groaned, "Stay on the task at hand, G. And take that camera from Jayde. Her hands are gonna be otherwise occupied and we need you to take over."

"Man, clause ninety-two g in my contract clearly states that at no time will I be obligated to take shirtless thirst trap pictures or videos of you for the gram. Don't be tryna switch it up on me in the name of ya lil music career or whatever," Pharris groused.

I let out a loud peal of giggles before I even thought to contain it as Nikolas rolled his eyes and huffed, "Man if you don't take that damn camera. We done already taken up too much of Jayde's time tonight. Hell, she might not even sign *her* contract if you keep on."

"Contract?" I asked, an eyebrow arched.

Nikolas nodded, "I know my approach was beyond casual, but I'm dead serious about this being a professional gig, with no end date in sight until I've been eliminated from the competition. Which...that ain't gonna happen, so I mean...we gotta get my lawyers to draw something up, but it'll be a standard contract with nondisclosure. You can have your folks look over it, but I'm certain the terms will be agreeable..."

"Oh..." I said, handing the camera into Pharris' outstretched grasp, "All...right."

I don't know why I thought this would be a handshake, much more informal agreement, but it was all good. My big brother Sidney was a lawyer—granted his specialization was like environmental something or other—but he usually was who I ran my contracts by before signing off. Legalese was a language in which he was fluent, and he'd saved my behind more than once when some producers had tried looping me into some shady songwriting deals.

Like Pharris, D'Angelo was also one of my favorite musicians, but I hadn't attempted to play this song in quite some time. I did a quick google search for the tabs, ran through it a couple of times and then we were ready to go. We ended recording three different takes, with Pharris sending the raw footage to their usual guy who handled their edits to upload to Nikolas' contest *Instagram* account. I'd decided before they left to go ahead and actually follow *Okin4thegram* instead of continuing to creep since we would be working together in the future. When the guys left, my energy was still pretty keyed up, so I channeled that into working on a tune that I'd been trying to get right for the past couple of weeks. Not long into trying to work that out, however, my earlier fatigue returned with a vengeance and I dragged my ass back into my bedroom collapsing onto my bed. I had an alarm set for an early morning run before a writing session I had with Eddie, but I made sure to shut that off quickly. There was no way in hell I'd be ready to hit the pavement that early without falling flat on my face.

I awakened the next morning to my phone consistently pinging with notifications from Instagram. The sound was so distinctive, I wondered why in the hell my account was blowing up as I rolled over and snatched my phone off of the charging pad to silence it. My Instagram notifications were at over a hundred and steadily climbing and I wracked my brain trying to remember what in the hell was the last thing I posted. I swore it was a repost of a stupid platitude that someone had carefully handwritten on a torn off piece of paper that was strategically held aloft in some natural setting. When I logged in, however, what greeted me was tag upon tag to a post on the *Spilling That Hot Tea,* a celebrity gossip and general negros on social media shenanigans page. *Now, what in the hell about me would be of interest to STHT* I thought as I clicked one of the comments to navigate to the page.

When the post finally loaded, it was the video I'd shot with Nikolas and Pharris last night, which...apparently all of us were a little too tired to notice that there were a few of my knick knacks in the background that would have been recognizable to anyone who followed me on YouTube and watched my videos since we were in the room I regularly used as back drop, but more importantly—none of us noticed that there was a mirror situated just over Nikolas' shoulder and in that mirror, clear as day was the reflection of me playing the bass and mouthing along, clearly feeling myself and the music as Nikolas effortless crooned and sang the e-panties off of everyone who'd viewed it. All—*holy shit*—two million and counting folks that had just viewed on the *Spilling That...*page. That didn't even include those who were following his contest page and had seen the video as well.

I watched the video, noting the barely detectable cuts that whoever edited this had done. I'd clearly been able to tell that he'd spliced together several takes, only because I was there and recognized the slight adjustments that both Pharris and I had Nikolas making as we worked to get the best angles, lighting, and made sure his voice was in peak shape. Despite Pharris keeping the camera pretty stationary, the video editor employed some tricks to give the appearance of extreme close-ups of Nikolas' body and during one of those sweeping pans he lingered on my reflection in the mirror. I let it loop a couple times, taking advantage of my freedom to ogle Nikolas freely and let his warm baritone wash over me in waves. After the third time, I pulled myself away to see just how bad the comments were. The shady caption by whoever was the intern on duty today for *Spilling That Hot Tea* didn't go unnoticed by me, but I was more concerned with if this little slip would endanger Nikolas' anonymity that had been kept air tight so far.

Most of the comments, however, were asking who's the girl—which is what garnered me so many tags. There were a few shady hoes with something so say about my two second appearance and others were speculating about what was going on between the two of us with my appearance in this video. And then you had the folks who spilled over from the gossip page onto my personal page, leaving wild comments and following me just on general principle of my association to the faceless dude in the singing competition, likely hoping that I'd slip up and give them more clues. I quickly navigated out of Instagram and was about to shoot Nikolas a text when my phone began vibrating and sounding off in my hands with an incoming FaceTime. I pressed the green button quickly accepting it with a smile.

"Man, what the hell have you gotten me into?" I asked while Nikolas barely let me get those words out of my mouth before offering up an apology.

"Hey, I had no idea that you were even in that footage let alone that Ant would make it that noticeable, I can have him scrub it again and reupload if you want me to," Nikolas said, his tone filled with contriteness, "I don't want us getting back on the wrong foot when we just got off."

After that he flashed that grin that I knew *he knew* had the ability to get him out of any jams with those of us of the farer sex who were not immune to it. And I was certainly within that number because he could have asked me for my mother's maiden name and entire social security number when he hit me with that smize and grin combo and I'd've gladly given both without hesitance.

"It—it's fine," I stammered, shaking my head a little to regain my sense, "Comes along with the territory and besides? It's doing exactly what we needed it to do. Did Melina's little stunt get her on *Spilling That Hot Tea*? Sure didn't! Because no one knows or cares about her wack ass."

"I..." Nikolas started before dissolving into chuckles, "don't hold back, Jayde, tell me how you really feel."

"I just...ugh, this isn't the first time she's tried her hand at getting a foot in the door at *Double R* and I'm honestly surprised that Ryan is even letting her be a part of this contest after the stunt she pulled. These new folks must have no clue about her diabolical ass," I grumbled.

Nikolas' jaw dropped, "Diabolical, damn...so y'all beef wasn't over some dude?"

I scoffed before rolling my eyes, "Oh please, no wack ass dude is enough to get me declare someone my mortal enemy. The only way one can earn that lovely title is by messing with the things I hold most dear—my family, my music, and my money, in that order. No, what Melina did was way beyond the realm of messing with some dude I might've bagged back in the day. How about she wormed her skanky behind into the A&R at *Double R*'s life and started sleeping with Ryan's *female* personal assistant simultaneously so she could have access to submissions that different singers and songwriters were sending to *Double R* and claiming them to be her own. I never got the dirty details of how far reaching her treachery was, but I did know that Ryan completely cleaned house and made sure anyone associated with all of that mess was gone. Somehow—*and I don't even know how*—Melina convinced Ryan that she wasn't the mastermind behind the mess and that it was the machinations of the people who got let go, but...nah, I never bought that shit. And because there were at least three songs of mine she tried to steal? Oh, that skank can take a long walk off a short pier. Expeditiously."

"So, I should be watching my back?" Nikolas asked, warily.

"I mean, so long as you got some distance between you all, you should be okay. But...being associated with me might've just put a target on your back, for the record."

"Well your association with me has not only made me the clear favorite in the competition, it's also widened my audience reach with that *Spilling That Hot Tea* post so... I'm good with continuing our thing if you are?" Nikolas asked, eyebrows raised as if he were bracing himself for me to rescind my acceptance of his job offer.

I nodded my head grinning, "Oh I am definitely still on board to mop the floor with Melina's ass. If she thinks today is something, she's just seeing the tip of the iceberg."

"...I don't know whether to be glad about that or scared about that," Nikolas joked.

"Oh dear, sweet Nikolas...you should be both," I giggled.

"Have you received the contract?" Nikolas asked, sobering up a bit, "I want to make sure everything is in order before I get my hopes up."

"Honestly, I hadn't looked at much this morning, literally just woke up right before you called."

"Damn," Nikolas murmured, before asking, "You... know Beyoncé?"

"As the queen of the industry? Absolutely. Personally? No...why?"

"Because she clearly wrote that song about you," he replied before briefly singing, teasingly, "I woke up like this..."

"Oh stop, I look crazy as ever," I replied, feeling my face growing warm and seeing that warmth manifest into reddened cheeks onscreen.

Nikolas bit down on his lip, "Nah...crazy is the furthest thing from what you look right now, sweetheart."

I blushed even harder over him calling me sweetheart, taking a deep breath before speaking, "I thought we weren't gonna..."

"Gonna?" he prompted.

"Do...this..." I trailed off.

"What? I can't state facts? You *clearly* know how fine you are already. I'm...merely...making an observation."

"All right, Mr. Making An Observation," I started, just as my phone buzzed with another incoming FaceTime request...that I should have known to expect, "I'm getting another call so we're gonna have to table your observations for now. I'll be talking with you later though."

"That a promise?" Nikolas asked, teasingly.

"Bye, Nikolas," I giggled.

"Bye, Jay," he replied.

Hm, that was different I thought as I disconnected that call slipping right into the next. Hearing him calling me by that nickname was a fairy new adjustment that I tried not to read too much into. Maybe he was just one of those people who bestowed nicknames on everyone he met. Nikolas calling me by a shortened version of my name was just that...right? I was shaking my head, trying to redirect my thoughts from Nikolas as the next call connected, then Nyema's skeptical face appeared on my screen.

"So...what happened to not being able to stand that —*and I quote*—overgrown nigga who thought he was God's gift to women and the world?"

I rolled my eyes, "Good morning to you too, sunshine!"

Nyema laughed, waving a hand, "Yeah yeah, good morning...whatever. Wait a minute...pan left then right. I wanna make sure I'm not speaking out of turn if you still have company."

I sucked my teeth, "Good damn day, Nyema. That man is at his house *not* mine."

"Huh, well he was certainly there last night..."

"And do we wanna talk about how he got here or..." I asked, brow arched ready to lay into her for giving him my address in the first place.

I knew it was no one else he couldn't have gotten my info from despite him mentioning that he was at the Sham before he and Pharris popped up on me last night. No way in hell anyone there gave him this information. Besides, none of them had hearts and sparkles in their eyes from a new relationship thusly trying to set up everyone else in their lives. That designation belonged to Nyema alone. Loved that girl like a sister, but whew child, Langston had her behind *sprung*. And she was loving every minute of it, so she thought we needed to possess twin feelings or something, which is why she kept trying to force me into something with Nikolas.

"So...I take it you took him up on his offer?" Nyema replied, deftly sidestepping my lingering question.

"Nikolas and I will be working together over the next few weeks...yes...wait...how did you know that I let him in after you sent him to my place last night?" I asked, narrowing my eyes in suspicion.

"I...didn't?" Nyema replied, her voice taking on a

decidedly higher pitch as she squirmed a little as I remained silent, "Okay, fine. I saw the video on *Spilling That Hot Tea*!"

"Wait..." I started, finally piecing some things together in my head, "did you know he was the faceless guy from the contest when you sent me that video? Oh my God, Nyema Jolene! Whew, child you are really in it to win it tryna push us together huh?"

"Okay...well...see..." she hedged, stammering all over herself.

"Spit it out, chick!"

"Fine! I didn't know it was him, when we first found out about the contest. Not at first...until one day I was watching one of the videos and Langston was at my place and asked where I'd gotten a hold of Niko's singing. And then I showed him the video and taking a little too close of a look at the background of some of the videos we pieced it together."

"And that's why you suddenly became so obsessed with this contest and started sending me every available thing about it, huh? Including that yamp Melina's videos. So clearly Nikolas hasn't the slightest idea that y'all know his secret, huh?"

Nyema shook her head, "And we're gonna keep it that way until he feels comfortable sharing it, right?"

"I don't have a dog in the fight either way. Not my secret. I'm just worried about the terms of this contract looking right because the money he was talking for this short bit of time is worth me pushing back recording this second EP, honey!"

"Oh, he is spending bread *bread*?" Nyema asked.

"Call him Wonder, baby girl, because my mans is coming through with the bread, okay?" I laughed, "But nah seriously...the money isn't the only thing that's got me committed to seeing this thing through. He really seems like he could use this win, especially after how the season ended for the *Trojans* and all. I just...I'd like to help him get there, however I can."

"Awwww, Jaydeyyyyyyy," Nyema gushed, pantomiming wiping tears.

I rolled my eyes at her antics, "Here you go. Don't read too much into it, Landry."

"Yeah yeah, whatever you say, girl."

"There's no whatever, I'm serious. I'm here with a single focus–help Nikolas traverse this competition and come out the victor. That's it."

"Okay with the wild formal victory speech," Nyema giggled, "Girl...just...don't forget to have some fun along the way, okay?"

"Have you met me? I always manage to have a bit of that, no matter the circumstance," I said, with a toss of my hair over my shoulder.

"Mmmmhmm, I know you do," Nyema murmured.

"Oh, here you go!"

"What? I ain't said nothing."

"Yet saying nothing is saying more than enough. As much as I'd love to sit around saying nothing with you a little longer, I gotta let you go, girlie. I got a writing session with Eddie in a few hours and since *your boy* had me up late last night recording his little video, I didn't get up for my run. So, I'm gonna do some HIIT before I have to head out to Ed's."

"All right...hey, you still coming up for the fourth, right?"

"Yep...I'll send you my flight details after I book it. I still have free rein of your place, right?"

Nyema nodded quickly, "Yep, it's all yours boo!"

"Aight chica, we'll rap about it more later. Tell Lang...ston I said whassup."

"I'ma tell him you playin around with his name," Nyema giggled.

"*I'ma tell him you playin around with his name*," I mimicked, "Boy, I never woulda thought I'd see the day that DJ Nyla got slayed, but whew child you are definitely no longer a wild cat, but a kept kitten. You hate to see it."

"Goodbye, Jayde," Nyema said with an eye roll, but the twitching of her lips trying to hide a smile belied the annoyed state she was trying to give off.

"Bye, boo!"

SEVEN

THROWING *my hat into the ring for #forthegram might either be the smartest or dumbest idea I've ever had* I thought as Jayde crossed the threshold of my place wearing the tiniest shorts and a cropped shirt that showed off what seemed to be miles of smooth, tawny skin. Despite being knee high to June bug, as my grandfather would say, Jayde's legs were deceptively long and the heeled sandals that she wore with her outfit made them look even longer. Her popping up at my door was unexpected and I told her as much.

"I was in the neighborhood," she giggled, "Writing with Ed this morning and decided to come up and see what you boys were up to."

Jayde had made herself very...comfortable in my life, with us seeing each other and touching base at least every third day. She'd taken to sending me songs on the days that we didn't have any official time set aside to go through vocal techniques or weren't recording something for the contest. She called it trying to expand my musical palette, but I wasn't quite sure about some of this shit she sent me. Like the song I'd been just about to listen to when the knock sounded on my door.

"Didja listen to what I sent you today yet?" she grinned, eyebrows raised, eyes full of mischief.

I knew this face. It was one I'd come to very well over these past couple of weeks. This was her *I'm about to get you into some bullshit but you'll enjoy every minute of it* face. I shook my head as I walked back to what had now become the music room in my place. Jayde followed closely behind me, talking mess about me not having listened to the song she'd sent me just over an hour ago. I sat down at my desk, hand poised over the mouse about to click on the link she'd sent.'

"Eddie and I think that you should do this one next. Show some range. Sing more than the panty dropping tunes you've been singing since that lil D'Angelo cover went off like it did."

"Hey...that was you and Phar saying that I needed to keep striking while the iron was hot," I reasoned, laughing.

Since the "How Does It Feel" cover, I'd also sang "That's What It's Made For" by Usher, "Mission" by Robin Thicke, "Make Love to Me" by Luke James, "Earned It" by The Weeknd, and "So Anxious" by Ginuwine in addition to some old school 70s and 80s r&b from the likes of Stevie, Luther, and that ilk. We were expected to upload a new video thrice weekly, but I'd been uploading every week day, applying hella pressure to the rest of my competitors. We'd finally reached the elimination portion of the contest. At the outset of the competition, we had been fifteen strong and now we were down to seven. By next week's end we were supposed to be down to four and I'd been warned that there would be a switch up in the competition, but that details about it would be forthcoming if I made the cut. Considering that I'd been the front runner in the competition since the D'Angelo cover and showed zero signs of losing any steam, I figured I'd be a shoe-in to make it to whatever these final rounds would look like.

Along with being in the lead, however, also came more and more speculation about who exactly I was. Even some of my fellow competitors were getting in on the action, comment creeping with suggestions when the general public began their fishing expeditions. Some of the guesses were hilarious—with folks suggesting random washed up r&b superstars and Nashville local singers and songwriters due to their proximity to Jayde. She was taking it all in stride though, I'd expected some of the residual spotlight being shone in her direction helped catapult her reputation a little bit higher. She was already pretty known behind the scenes within the industry for being a pretty prolific songwriter, but it was good to see her getting well-deserved recognition from folks on the other side of the curtain.

I'd learned that she was a pretty huge country music fan, to the point of that actually being the genre in which she wanted to make her first full-length record, which surprised the shit out of me when she shared that. We'd been sitting around listening to tracks from her first EP which was a mix of the yeehaw agenda and early 2000s r&b—a combination that shouldn't have worked, but she managed to make a seamless, cohesive vibe. I asked if she'd recorded the first half of the EP to get in good in the Nashville scene and she damn near cussed me out for coming for her passion before explaining that she'd grown up on country music almost more so than r&b. Her mother was a huge music fan—not musically inclined in any way but passed her love of music down to Jayde who managed to pick up some sort of family musicality gene from back in their familial lineage, according to her. She'd moved to Nashville with a single-minded focus, to record an album in the genre that soothed her spirit and nurtured her soul—*her words, not mine.* Unfortunately, when she got a foothold in the industry, she allowed the folks that surrounded her to influence her a bit too much and she put her dream on hold a bit while she wrote massive hits for others. She was on her way back to achieving her initial goal, though, and after she was done being my coach for this competition, she was slated to get in the studio to record some of the original country tunes she'd been storing away for herself.

"Hello...Nikolas...are you listening to me?"

I shook my head, returning my focus back to Jayde as she stared at me with an annoyed grimace on her face.

"Nah, man. You gotta stop pushing your yeehaw agenda on me. I told you I'm good on the banjos for the next decade or so," I joked.

"You know you get on my nerves right," she replied, rolling her eyes with a smile.

"You know you like it," I replied back with a grin of my own.

I received no verbal reply, just another eye roll as she

stood from the couch on which she'd been lounging when she followed me into the office, maneuvering in front of me to manipulate the mouse and pull up the video in the link she'd sent me. Her movements placed her ass squarely in my face, something I'm certain of which she was blissfully unaware, but I took the time to unabashedly enjoy the view. Seconds later she was turned around and perched on the edge of the desk, bopping her shoulders as an upbeat, clearly honky tonk ass song played.

"Jayde...what in the hell is...*this*?"

"You...don't know Charley Pride?" she asked, aghast as if she was naming someone painfully obvious that I should recognize like Jesus or Barack Obama.

I shook my head slowly, "But you're gonna tell me, right?"

"You're damned right I'm gonna tell you," Jayde said, pivoting to stop the song from playing and then turning back to me, "I can't believe you don't know who Charley Pride is. He's a very important part of Black music history as one of the first Black men to achieve great success in country music. Hell Charley Pride and DeFord Bailey walked so Darius Rucker and Kane Brown could fly!"

The only name I partly recognized in the men she named was homie from Hootie and the Blowfish, but I let her go off.

"It's amazing how a genre that our people played a huge part in pioneering and perfecting is one that is often rejected by so many folks who look like us. Hell, country music ain't shit but r&b with a banjo and twang. They're both rooted in the same thing—love or pain. Sometimes both simultaneously. I'ma put Charley back on. Push past your initial reservations and judgements and just listen to the words. Tell me that if it wasn't slowed down and put to a beat driven by a bass guitar instead of a banjo that it wouldn't sound like something that your parents woulda listened to back in the day."

She clicked the play button for the video to begin again and I could feel my face pulling into a slight frown as I wasn't really here for buddy's tone as he began singing and Jayde shook her head.

"Close your eyes and concentrate on the words... forget everything else and just listen to what he's *saying*," she urged.

And it took a minute for me to get past my biases, but when I did finally just let the words wash over me, Jayde was...right. And she knew the moment it hit me when I opened my eyes, she stared at me with a self-satisfied grin.

"You get it now, don't you?"

I shrugged, "Yeah, but...I'm not...singing this, Jay. You gotta find something else...actually...why don't you find something we both can sing?"

The grin that played around her lips dropped into an open mouth, "Why would I do that?"

"Because...I wanna see if I can hold my own with you. See if I got what it takes to go the distance with Jaydeofalltrades," I said, teasingly employing the usage of her Instagram username.

"Tuh, I don't know if you can keep up, baby boy," she replied.

"Sounds like you're afraid to be out sung," I shot back.

"Oh negro, please...you? Out sing me? *Whew*, the man learns proper breath control and thinks the student can surpass the master. Lemme find something easy for ya," Jayde said, sitting back on the desk, crossing her legs and tapping her index finger on her chin, "Oh I got it!"

She hopped up from her perch, once again giving me the unobstructed view of her perfect ass as she hurriedly typed a song into the search bar on *YouTube* and hit the play button. The voices that began singing sounded vaguely familiar, but I didn't know why until Jayde shifted slightly and I was able to see the artists' names who were singing and then they got to the chorus.

"Oh wait...I know this one," I laughed, "Well...I know the "Ghetto Superstar" version. But I get the gist. Aight bet...let's go. Find a karaoke version and I'll figure out the melody and lyrics quick. Lemme school your ass on what the real yeehaw agenda is."

"Can you *please* stop saying yeehaw agenda?" Jayde groaned.

I shook my head, "No can't do, sweetheart. Now queue that shit up!"

It took her a little bit of searching, but she finally found a karaoke version of "Islands in the Stream" by Dolly Parton and Kenny Rogers that didn't sound like it was being played on a MIDI keyboard and we ran through it a couple times.

"Yo...we sound kinda good together why don't we up..." I started but Jayde quickly cut me off.

"Absolutely not."

"But you didn't even let me finish," I said.

"You were going to suggest we upload this to the 'gram on ya lil channel, but no way Jose! This contest is about *you*, not me. I got enough residual attention since the D'Angelo debacle. I'm good."

"...you haven't enjoyed the attention...even a little?" I asked, light teasing in my tone.

"I didn't say all that mister basketball man, but...we're getting down to the nitty gritty. We need to make sure the major focus in all of your content is that golden throat of yours," Jayde smiled, "No distractions or gimmicks. Just straight up, flat-footed, God given vocals from you here on out. We got a contract to win."

"Yeah..." I said, softly, "A contract..."

"You...don't sound so sure about that," Jayde said, "What's up with that? Winning is still our goal, right?"

"Absolutely," I shot back quickly.

"So...what was that...just a moment ago?"

Truth was...I was having second thoughts about how far I wanted all of this to go. I had different intentions at the outset of this competition than I did now. I was motivated by recognition not based on who people already knew me to be...but of my own merit and talent. And now...having gotten that...I was a bit...confused on my intentions going forward. The ultimate prize of this competition was closely working with *Double R Records* to record an album. That sounded like another job in and of itself, when I had an already demanding one. I was still working through my feelings, so I wasn't quite at the point where I could adequately articulate them to anyone else without it sounding like I was throwing in the towel on this whole thing after all of the hard work we'd already put in to get this far. So instead of answering Jayde, I lobbed a grin her way and shook my head.

"Just nerves. And you know what would help me get over them?"

"What?" Jayde asked, skeptically.

"Seeing how a pro gets things done. Don't you have a gig tonight?" I asked.

And that was how we ended up at the Purple Shamrock a few hours later. Me sitting at what had become my "usual" table, sipping on a beer, waiting for Jayde and the guys she played with in the band to make an appearance. The regulars at the bar were used to me being there on nights that Jayde was, so no one bothered me too much, which was a far cry from the first few times I'd set foot in the joint. Soon Jayde and the band took the stage and I got to lose myself in her performance. Despite this bar being the size of my condo, Jayde performed with enough energy and vigor that would make you believe that she was headlining at the Bridgestone Arena. She commanded that scant stage, drawing the audience in from the first note, keeping them ensnared until she decided she wanted to let them go.

Jayde possessed a special blend of charisma, talent, and chutzpah that demanded that she be a star. Too bad folks were too narrow minded to let her fully fly in the genre in which she wanted. She'd been offered contracts by a few record labels—*Double R included*—but they all wanted to turn her into someone she wasn't. So instead of succumbing to their demands, she stood her ground firmly, pressing forward determined to do her own thing on her own terms. It was admirable—enviable, honestly. Jayde was that self-assured, that confident in her gift, in her lane, in her capacity for success that she refused to be boxed in. I took a quick video of her singing and uploaded it to my *Instagram*, praising her talent and drive. I'd hoped that it would get her the right sort of attention and not spur on the rumor mill even further, but social media was a fickle machine.

I woke up the morning after our night at the *Shamrock* to more speculating about whether or not Jayde and I were more than coach and mentee instead of folks focusing on what was important, much to my chagrin. I had hella direct messages on *Instagram* that were all about Jayde. I ignored them all, in favor of posting a meme about folks minding the business that minds them, which I was sure would go over well. I was waiting for a call from Ro Ashe regarding a new development with the competition. He wouldn't give me too many details and I racked my brain trying to figure out what curveball they could be throwing at me next. My curiosity was sated almost immediately after the call between Ro and I connected.

"I'm sorry...you want me to do what now?" I asked, voice raising in octave by the time I reached the last word in the question I asked.

As far as I knew this competition was all viral sensation, virtual reality until we reached the end and the winner was crowned. Then they'd go on to work closely with the development team at *Double R Records* and possibly become the next big thing. There wasn't supposed to be any...reality TV-esque vibe associated with this, but since the contest had blown up a bit larger than initially anticipated thanks to a couple of appearance by contestants on *Spilling That Hot Tea*—some in a positive light like me and others being clowned on their way to elimination. Seeing how we were picking up steam, Ro and—to a larger part, Ryan Rucker thought that bringing the remaining three contestants together in a *Making the Band* type of set up would be an interesting curveball. They called it an artist's boot camp, in which we would be placed in a house with some of their in-house writers and producers who would help us curate our own sound. We were past the point of covers of other folks' songs keeping the general public interested and *Double R* wanted to see if we could keep an audience with original content.

As Ro patiently and repeatedly explained the setup, he tried to ensure me that since there wouldn't be any of the actual leaks *live* footage from the house—because they would have cameras filming our every move like *Big Brother*—nothing would be released without being carefully curated and scrubbed. We would still be able to preserve my anonymity. But this, agreeing to live in a house with the other finalists and these producers and shit? It ...seemed like a terrible idea. The worst idea, in fact. I didn't grow up in a house with a lot of people. It was just me, moms, and pop—no siblings, no other random family members living there. Just us three for all eighteen years that I lived at home to moving into undergrad and being able to have my own place as a perk of being a star athlete.

Despite being all in for teamwork when it came to

my occupation, I was a solitary sort of dude in my personal life. I liked being able to retreat to my own space and work through whatever was in my head without intrusion of others unless I invited them in. I would be giving all of that up if I agreed to do this part of the competition. But the heat of competition, the spark that came from head-to-head, looking my temporary enemy in the eye as I cruised past them to victory? That part fueled me like no other. I had to remember that there was nothing personal about this competition though and that I needed to ensure I came out on top by any means necessary.

Ro's voice broke in the journey of my thoughts, "Look, Ryan said he'd give you 'til the end of this week to decide since he wants everyone ready to move into the house he rented after the holiday. I know you said you were doing some traveling, so just let me know. I do have to inform you, if you choose not to do the boot camp, then you will forfeit your spot in the final three."

"Wait...so basically I need to say yes or completely give up on achieving a long-held dream? Y'all are..." I chuckled, humorlessly.

"If it's any consolation, the house you all are gonna be in is within spitting distance of where you live now. Some one-horse town called Shelbyville is where Ryan rented this mega mansion."

"Man, I stay where I stay and don't be traveling much further beyond the suburbs of Nashville's city limits," I laughed.

"Ask your coach, she's probably very familiar with the area. Look, I'll send you the specs on the house, the details of expectations written out, and the disclosures that you need to sign if you're in, aight?"

I signed, running a hand over the top of my head, "Yeah man, send it over. I'll look over it with my people and get you an answer by the end of the week."

"Alright, looking forward to hearing some good news from you, Niko. Talk to you later," Roosevelt signed off.

"Aight, talk to you then."

"You know you just need to gon head and say yes, right?" Pharris said, peeking his head through the door of my office.

"And you know you need to stop eavesdropping like a little old lady, right?" I shot back as he pantomimed clutching his pearls.

"I'll have you know, boss man, I actually had one up on you this time. Rucker called me a few days ago trying to get a beat on which way you'd lean when they would pitch this Real World Nashville shit to you," Pharris came all the way into the office, collapsing onto my couch.

"And you couldn't warn me? Just let me get put on the spot?"

"Well, one—I knew you wouldn't be put on the spot because you don't say yes to anything without running it by Jenkins. And two—man, that deposit Rucker made into my cashapp after our five minute conversation and the unspoken nondisclosure it signified had me keeping my mouth shut tight."

I shook my head, "Damn it's true. Everyone in your life does have a price."

"Hell, you go with the dramatic shit. Ain't nobody

done sold you up the river, man. I had a simple conversation. A heat check. That's all."

"Yeah, yeah...whatever...so you really think I should do that shit? Live in this house with these strangers? That Willie Gee cat look like I'd be ready to punch him in the face after five minutes of conversation, man."

"You really think that cat made it? According to Ruck, it's just the top three finalists that they're moving into this house. So it's you, Melina, and that white boy who sounds like the lovechild of Jon B. and Robin Thicke are it, playboy."

"How do you know more than I do, man?" I asked, chuckling.

"Because I ask the right questions. Now for the real reason I'm in here, I just emailed you the itinerary for your trip back to the crib for the holiday. Langston said he'd pick you up when you landed so you can surprise your folks when you touch down."

"...and you comin' too, right? Langston will pick *us* up?" I prodded.

Pharris had been avoiding going back home to visit ever since he began working for me when I accepted my slot on the *Trojans*. I didn't know all of the circumstances surrounding him leaving our hometown, but I knew that whatever the particulars were? He had no desire to be back there any time soon. Every time I traveled back up that way, he begged off claiming alternate plans or just flying his people down here to do their holiday gathering.

"Man, you know ain't shit good for me up there. Besides Cyn and her people invited me to their Fourth of July extravaganza blowout something or other."

"Wait...who is Cyn?" I asked, joking because it seemed like at any given time Pharris had about a smooth twenty women in his rotation. I honestly didn't know how he kept up with them.

"Don't play, fam, Cyn might be wifey one day!" Pharris replied, fake offended.

"Aye, didn't you say that about Marshall...and Teresa...and Brande...and Samona...and..." I trailed off.

"Okay, man. Tread lightly..." Pharris chuckled, "Back to business though...I've arranged for car service to get you to and from the airport here so we don't run into that issue that happened the last time you tried driving yourself there."

"I miss one lil flight and you try to act like I can't ever get myself anywhere on time," I laughed.

"Look, you weren't on the receiving end of your mother's wrath because you missed one *little* flight as you call it. I'm taking all precautions to not have to endure that again. You ain't been properly reprimanded until you've had your ass handed to you by a Black mama who doesn't use a solitary cussword when she's dressing you down and it still manages to cut to the quick," Pharrell shuddered, "I still get flashbacks every once in a while."

"And you call me dramatic," I droned, deadpan.

"Anyway...enjoy your time at home with your folks and the rest of the old hood. Really give this idea of turning your life into," Pharris paused, changing the inflection of his voice to sound like a television narration voiceover, "This is the true story, of seven strangers, picked to live in a house and have their lives taped. Find out what happens when people stop being polite and start being real."

I broke down laughing, "Man, how do you even remember that whole spiel?"

"My older sisters were obsessed with that damned show. And when you're outnumbered? You get dragged into marathons of stupid MTV reality shows. After about four episodes the shit is permanently seared into your brain. Anyway...focus, man! Take your time away, think about your decision and then get ready for whatever the fall out is—either way."

"So, you really think I should consider it, huh?" I asked again, honestly seeking Pharris point of view.

"I think you shouldn't not consider it is all. You didn't come this far to get punked by a little in-house comp, right?" Pharris shrugged, "Maybe it just me, but it sounds like easy money. Skate to victory and get a leg up on any external competition when you're putting your debut album together right before the next season of hoop starts when you and the *Trojans* make it all the way to the Finals. Just imagine a platinum plaque and winning the Larry OB within months of one another."

"Aight, Phar, chill. My whip can't take all this diesel you are fueling me up with," I laughed.

"I'm just saying man, think of the possibilities of what could be. It all starts with one little word though."

"Yeah, yeah...we'll see."

EIGHT

"I'M GONNA DO IT, Ny. I'm gonna fuck that man. And I'm gonna do it in your bed. And it'll be all your fault. Because you got me drinking this...what in the hell is this even?" I sighed, raising my glass for another sip.

I'd been with Nyema for the past few days and we were currently sitting on the patio of her parents' place as their party went up in full swing around us. I thought I was grabbing a simple glass of punch but imagine my surprise about three sips in to discover that I'd definitely filled my cup from the wrong container.

"Jay," Nyema giggled, "Just how much of that have you had?"

"This is my first glass. I thought you said the one with the red A was good to go!"

"I said the one with the damned scarlet A was the one to avoid unless you were trying to get tore up," Nyema giggled, "You should have just stuck to bottled water if you weren't listening. I told you mama's punch wasn't nothing to play with."

"I figured you were bullshitting since your light-weight self doesn't even drink like that!" I exclaimed, quickly throwing a hand over my mouth as my last word ended in a loud burp.

I shook my head at myself, amateur move. No way should I be this twisted this early in the day, but here we were. Well, here I was since little miss straight edge over there had been sipping on the same bottle of water since I'd arrived. She had been here since earlier in the day, helping her mom prepare for the sizeable amount of guests that were now spread across her parents' land. The party was comprised of a mix of family, friends, coworkers of Mr. Landry and Langston's and various neighbors who had wandered over lured in by the music being played by my favorite DJ's favorite DJ—DJ Trainwreck.

"So..." Nyema started with a sly grin on her face, "What happened to your whole thing about not mixing business with pleasure, hunh?"

"Who said that?" I replied, giggling, "Besides—*technically* I am no longer in his employ."

"And you're no longer concerned with things being awkward since you and he will likely be maid of honor and best man at the eventual nuptials between me and Langston?" Nyema asked, a brow raised in askance.

"Hold on, bitch. Are you holding out on me?" I asked, frantically grabbing both of her hands to check for a ring.

Nyema giggled, "No fool. I'm just saying what you said back to me a few short weeks ago."

"Ny, look at him," I said, dreamily, "You knew I was

lying when I said I was going to stay away from him to begin with."

"Mmmhmmm."

"You didn't have to agree so fast, damn!"

Nyema giggled again, "I'm just saying sis, it's almost like that man has a flashing neon sign above his head that says, 'take me down, Jayde!' He's one hundred percent your type of hype and I'm honestly disappointed that you've made me lose my bet with Langston because I was certain that the two of y'all would have bumped uglies by now!"

"Really, Ny? No faith in your girl?"

She shook her head slowly, "Absolutely not. You forgetting I know where all your hoe secrets are buried?"

"I...I can't cross the line with him, for real though. Not while we're working together," I said, resolute in my stance.

I'd wavered because ever since he had arrived, Nikolas was the central focus of my attention. We spoke briefly before he was dragged into a game of dominoes with some of the men on the other side of the yard. While Nyema and I sat talking, I'd discreetly been peering in his direction, taking advantage of being able to take him in uninterrupted or unnoticed. Over these past few weeks, while working together on the *#forthegram* content I'd come to find myself somewhat enamored with Nikolas—the man and the artist. He had a single-minded focus when it came to time to work, but he knew how to cut loose and have fun too. We just had an easy vibe, talking about any sundry of subjects as we worked on perfecting his craft and finding that we had more in common than either of us knew before this collaboration.

It would have been so much easier if...he was a jerk. Or we kept things strictly professional when we worked together, but nope. Those lines were blurred fairly quickly once I'd gotten over my initial annoyance with Nikolas. Not that he'd been anything but a perfect gentleman towards me, but I'd definitely felt his lingering glances when he thought I wasn't paying attention. I also noticed the way he would go out of his way to find some reason to touch me in some way while we were talking—a hand on my knee or shoulder or the small of my back. The way he peered into my eyes intently whenever I spoke, whether it was the simplest correction on a breathing technique or a rant about whatever current societal issue had me riled up.

And I fought valiantly not to read too far into any of that, since none of those actions had been backed up with any intent on Nikolas' behalf. Maybe he was just a super friendly and attentive guy is what I told myself time and time again when I was talking myself off the ledge of throwing caution to the wind and mounting him like a stallion. Tonight, though? Whatever was in this punch was making it damn near impossible for me to ignore the feeling deep down in my loins to just give in to temptation and have one good night with him. We were consenting adults, and I knew that attraction was mutual. So, perhaps we just needed one good fuck...to ease my mind...and my pussy.

Nyema sighed, "So you ain't bout to do shit and you just talkin' right now? Because girl from where I'm sitting y'all are two consenting adults and what does a working relationship have to do with a little...*recreation* on the side?"

"Look, if word gets out that I'm having...*recreation on the side* as you say...with clients, how long before it gets around the industry that I'm like that doorknob Melina."

"Wow, so you just jumping completely out the window tonight, huh?" Nyema said, reaching for the red solo cup I now was just clutching as a safety blanket, having not sipped from it again after my initial taste.

I snatched my hand out of her reach, taking a small sip, "Whatever, you keep pushing and I'll fuck him in your California King and not change the sheets."

Nyema shrugged, "Not like Langston and I haven't done worse."

"First—bitch I hope you changed the sheets before you allowed me to sleep at your place for this weekend. And secondly, I'm a considerate friend. *If* I were to take Nikolas home with me tonight, I'd smut him out in the guest room like a respectable houseguest."

Nyema giggled, shaking her head, "I swear you get on my nerves, Jayde!"

"You love it. You love me. Otherwise you wouldn't have begged me to come up here before I go on lockdown."

"Speaking of...have you shared that little detail with...?"

I shook my head quickly, "Not yet. Not sure how to...broach it."

"Head on...apply directly to the forehead," Nyema droned.

"Girl what?"

"You face it head on, girl. No beating around the bush. Besides...I mean if all goes well with your plans tonight, wouldn't the rest of this be kind of perfect. Proximity..."

"Ugh, no...it could have the potential to be very awkward. Which is why I need to keep my pocketbook to myself."

Just before I left Nashville to come out here, I got a call from Ryan Rucker. It wasn't unusual as I worked with *Double R* Records artists from time to time on songwriting collaborations, but he was reaching out to me on behalf of the *#forthegram* contest. He wanted to me to join the squad of songwriters and producers who would be shepherding the finalists through what would eventually become the recording of their debut album. I of course disclosed, to zero surprise, that I was actually working with one of the contestants already and it could be considered conflict of interest.

Ryan laughed me off, clearly in the loop with everything happened with this contest, its contestants and their lives as it concerned the contest. He was cool with my previous relationship with Nikolas but emphasized that I would be tasked with submitting work for all three finalists during this "artist boot camp". Ryan wasn't specific about who would be involved, but knowing he knew the history between Melina and me—I knew he made it a point to emphasize that my contributions needed to be universal to give hint to the fact that I would possibly have to work with that trick ass yamp.

It wouldn't be my first choice, for sure, but Ryan also

dangled another carrot in front of me that made me immediately sign on board to be one of the mentor artists. He mentioned possibly bankrolling some studio time for me to finally give myself a proper country debut album. A mutually beneficial association is what he referred to my involvement in this process. After hammering out the details through my brother, contracts were signed and I'd be reporting to Shelbyville, TN bright and early Monday morning. I hadn't had a chance to tell Nikolas about my shifting involvement in the contest yet since Nyema had me on the go since I landed. I'd hoped that this wouldn't bring any friction between the two of us—in case he wasn't cool with me working with his competition, essentially.

"You sounding like a real punk right now, Jay. I'm... disappointed in you," Nyema said in a very dejected tone of voice.

I swiveled my head around to see if she was serious and I'll be damned, but she was literally sitting there pouting.

"What about me getting involved with Nikolas seems like a good idea for anyone involved?" I asked.

"That's what I mean, sis! Old Jayde wouldn't have had a second thought. What's up with this pragmatism all of a sudden?"

"It's not sudden, it's just..." I trailed off not wanting to tell her what I'd already come to realize in my own mind.

I knew that I wouldn't be able to just hit and quit with Nikolas. I liked him a lot as a person and friend... and I knew, *knew* it would be dangerous for my heart and mind if I allowed myself to cross that line into anything else with him. Keeping things strictly professional was a defense tactic, a surefire guarantee to save me from myself. But that shit wavered every time he hit me with damn sly grin, like the one that was currently pasted on his face as he and Langston made their way over to where Nyema and I were sitting.

"Getchass up, babe, it's our song," Langston said, pulling Nyema up from her chair and leading her out to the makeshift dance floor where couples were stepping, moving in perfectly timed syncopation to the beat of K'Jon's "*On the Ocean*".

Nyema easily acquiesced grinning broadly as she and Langston grooved effortlessly, lost in their own little world as he sang the words to her as he pulled her closely into his body. I couldn't help the smile that spread across my face watching the two of them interact. No two people could have been more opposite, but their thing just worked for them. I was happy to see my girl happy. She definitely deserved it after some of the shit she'd been through with men.

"You gonna let my arm fall off?" Nikolas rumbled in a low tone that finally caused me to look his way.

I'd been so wrapped up in the cuteness that was Nyema and Langston that I hadn't noticed that he extended an arm toward me to lead me toward the dancefloor.

"Lemme see what you know about stepping, girl," Nikolas laughed.

I grabbed his hand and giggled, "I don't know much, but perhaps you can school me a lil bit?"

"I could teach you, but I'd have to charge. Just...

follow my lead," he replied, easily leading me in a series of steps, twists and turns that I easily fell into as the song faded out and into another one that had a decidedly slower tempo. I tried pulling away, but Nikolas' grip on my hands didn't ease up, instead he pulled me flush against him, settling his hands on my lower back, just above my ass as we swayed back and forth to the music. He was so damned tall that I had to thread my arms around his waist since I couldn't reach his neck.

"You knew a lil more than you led on," he murmured, leaning down so that the words caressed the shell of my ear.

I pulled back slightly so I could look him in the face, "I can do a lil bit out here..."

He bit down on his lower lip, eyes low as he gazed down at me. Just as he opened his mouth to reply to me a hand on my arm and a meek voice asking if she could cut in sounded and Nikolas immediately stiffened in my hold, speaking before I could.

"Nah...we're good," he replied, pulling me even closer into his body.

"Nik..." the woman tried again and he shook his head.

"I said we're good, man. Move around," Nikolas said.

I wisely stayed quiet, still kept dancing and this time when the song melded into another one Nikolas pulled away, gave me an apologetic smile and said, "I'm about to get up outta here. See you back in Tenn?"

"Ye-yeah...I'll see you then."

He squeezed my arm and then moved on to say his goodbyes to Langston and Nyema. Then all of three of them were heading over in my direction.

"Hey sis, I think we might be a little too twisted to give you a ride back to my place and Niko said he'd be able to give you a lift back if you didn't mind taking off now?" Nyema said.

I narrowed my eyes at her knowing good and damn well she was lying about being too twisted to do anything since her ass didn't drink. I saw right through her little ruse and replied, "I don't wanna inconvenience Nikolas, sis. I can just take a rideshare when I'm ready to boogie."

"Alright, I'll see y'all later then," Nikolas said, trying to walk off but Nyema grabbed his arm before he could stride off.

"No! There have been way too many stories about women getting into the car with these people and something going awry. I'd rather you be safe in the hands of someone I know won't do anything with you that you don't want him to," Nyema said.

"Babe!" Langston said at the same time I exclaimed, "Ny!"

"She does make a good point about the rideshare thing though," Langston piped up.

"It doesn't look like Jayde is ready to leave quite yet, y'all. And I...need to be up outta here ASAP," Nikolas said, casting a glance in the direction that the woman who tried cutting in our dance earlier was standing.

"No...they're right. I should get going. I've got an early flight back home tomorrow anyway. So if it's no trouble," I said.

Nikolas quickly shook his head, "It's no trouble at all. You'll just have to give me Nyema's address and I got you."

We said our goodbyes to Nyema and Langston, with me whispering threats to Nyema as I pulled her in for a hug and then got up outta there. We got in the car and rode in silence for a minute before Nikolas reached over and switched on the radio. It synched with his phone and picked up playing the song that must've been on when he got out of the car—PJ Morton and Yebba's cover of "How Deep Is Your Love". I immediately began singing along and Nikolas eventually joined in. The song switched to Jill Scott and Anthony Hamilton's duet and we kept right on singing.

We were stopped at a light when Nikolas turned my way and said, "Hey...I wanted to just let you know about why I needed to get out of there so quickly."

I said nothing, just inclined my head in a way that let him know I was listening.

"Ol girl who tried to cut in is...an ex. My...only true ex, who I had no idea would be at that party. I'm certain Langston didn't know either otherwise he would not have invited me to occupy the same breathing air as her."

"Bad breakup?" I queried.

"Only if you call trying to pin a baby on someone she thought was on his way to being a paid baller is bad," Nikolas laughed, humorlessly, "Not quite sure what she was doing there or why she thought shit was sweet, but nah. I was good on staying where she was."

"You coulda had her put out," I tried joking, but the grimace that covered Nikolas face told me that maybe I shoulda kept that one.

"Nah. You know I don't like making a scene like that. Figured it was just easiest for me to get up outta there and leave her to it. The last thing I need is for us to be going back and forth and have the shit end up on *Spilling That Hot Tea* minutes later."

I nodded, "Yeaaaaah, I get that. But your night shouldn't have to be derailed because of that. It's still pretty early."

Nikolas quirked an eyebrow, "So what you tryna get into?"

"Me? I'm tryna get into bed...I mean, I gotta be up early tomorrow to fly back. So, I'm tryna get...into bed, to sleep."

"Aw c'mon you just gon leave me hanging like that?" Nikolas asked, grinning that grin that I knew would get me in nothing but trouble.

We were making the turn that would lead us onto the road to Nyema's townhome, but there was also a little hole in the wall bar on the corner at which we were currently stalled.

"Fine...I'll bless you with my presence for a little bit longer. But I'm not staying outside, you good with coming into Ny's for a nightcap?" I asked, lower lip pulled between my teeth as Nikolas appeared to mull it over as he made the turn onto Nyema's street.

"Sounds like a plan to me," he said, after a few moments of silence.

As we slowed to a stop in front of Nyema's house I kinda wanted to rescind the invitation. The entire ride over I spent with my thighs clutched together tightly in direct response to being in such an enclosed space with Nikolas, smelling whatever deliciously overpowering scent he wore for the past ten minutes had me like fuck a nightcap, let me be your cap tonight. I shook my head briefly before opening the door and leading the way into Ny's place. I kicked off my sandals at the door, calling over my shoulder for Nikolas to discard his shoes as well since Nyema had a thing about folks wearing their shoes past her foyer. I headed straight to the kitchen, knowing I needed the distraction of fixing a drink in order to get over the idea of climbing Nikolas like a tree and yelling timber as I took him down.

Despite not being a drinker herself, Nyema had a nice selection of alcohol in her place—a little brown, a little white, and wine as well.

"What would you like?" I asked an approaching Nikolas, "Your choices are vodka, whiskey, or some random ass red wine that is probably nasty as hell if the label has anything to do with it.

"I'm drinking whatever you're drinking," Nikolas responded, smoothly before walking off into the living room to settle onto the couch.

Because of the open floor plan on the first floor of Nyema's townhome I had a bird's eye view of him making himself comfortable on the couch. He snagged the remote off of the coffee table, then sat on her large sofa with the built-in recliners at either end and surfed through the channels until he found ESPN. I shook my head, mumbling, "Typical," then set about making our drinks. Since I was drinking some sort of rum punch at Nyema's parents' party, I should stick with white liquor tonight. The very last thing I needed was mixing formats and possibly oversleeping, then missing my flight. I looked in the refrigerator and just as I expected Nyema had the flavored sparkling waters on deck, so I made us a coupla vodka sodas and took them into the living room. I handed Nikolas his drink and took a seat on the opposite end of the sofa that he sat on.

Nikolas took a sip from his drink, nodded then sniffed the air with a strange look on his face. Lifting both of those powerful arms, he pantomimed sniffing his pits before speaking, "I don't smell...so why you so far away? It is my breath?"

I giggled and shook my head, "Self-preservation."

He quirked an eyebrow in interest, nonverbally cueing me to continue that thought. But...I'd already said too much as it was. I did not care to elaborate at all.

"So...how's your time at home been?" I asked.

"Real smooth segue, Jay," Nikolas laughed, "I'll let you hoop though. It's been good. I hadn't been around my folks since Easter so it felt good to get some of that good old love from my ma. Pops, on the other hands, couldn't stop talking about the season so I'll be glad to not have to hear from him about what I need to change in or expand with my game. How about you? You having a good time up here visiting with the Landrys?"

"Absolutely," I gushed, "Lena and Neill are like my second parents. They were so welcoming from the first time I came up here to visit Ny. So it's always fun to come up here and get some of their brand of love. And of course, Mama Lena's peach cobbler...oh my gosh, now that? I would slap my biological mother over it."

"Say word? It's that good?"

"Better...there's only one thing on Earth that's better..."

"Oh yeah, what's that?" Nikolas asked, innocently.

"You...um...ever had any of Lena's cobbler before?" I asked, trying to dodge the answer to that question, but I could tell from the look in his eyes he knew exactly what I was alluding to.

Nikolas shook his head slowly, "I'll have to experience it for myself one day. Especially if you think it's better than everything except..."

"Well!" I said standing up quickly and moving toward the kitchen, "Lucky for you, I have some here. And even luckier—I'm willing to share. But...like, not a corner piece because that's my favorite part. But you can have a middle piece. Let me hook you up right fast."

And I carried my ass off to the kitchen before he could get another word in edgewise. I quickly retrieved my Tupperware container of cobbler that I'd been pinching off of since Lena presented me with it the first night I arrived. I grabbed two small plates from the cabinet, dishing out a couple of small portions for the both of us to enjoy. I popped the plates into the microwave for thirty seconds, returned my Tupperware to the fridge, gathered a couple forks, and then took the plates into the living room. As I sat his plate down in front of him, I told Nikolas to get ready for the best thing that would hit his taste buds tonight.

"It's that good, huh?" he chuckled, the low sound sending a shiver coursing through my body.

"Better," I replied, emphatically, picking up my plate and taking a nice healthy bite of my portion.

As usual, I moaned in delight, my eyes closed as I gave into the urge to hit a little shoulder shimmy. Something about Lena's peach cobbler always put a dance on my spirit. When I looked over to Nikolas to see how he was enjoying the dessert, I saw that he'd not taken a single bite, but was instead staring at me with a laser-like focus. I stared back, unable to break the gaze. I saw him coming closer and closer, should have tried avoiding his approach but instead girded myself for the inevitable. His lips were a scant distance from mine as he whispered in a throaty groan, "If you don't want this, you gotta say something, Jayde."

I didn't say a goddamned thing because I was done resisting. Done trying to convince myself that I didn't want him because I did. *And badly.* And the first press of his lips against mine—soft and questioning before becoming firm and insistent—solidified that I'd made the correct choice in staying silent. Nikolas ran his tongue over the seam of my lips, and I opened for him immediately, greedily lacing my hands behind his neck and pulling him deeper into the kiss that he'd initiated. That move spurred him to further action, pressing me backward into the couch to lay supine as he hovered over me on the couch. I opened my legs slightly, welcoming the mass of his body pressing into mine as my legs threaded around his waist. Nikolas ground into me insistently, hands traversing my body from my waist to my ass where they settled in a firm grip on my cheeks as he plied me with decadently sensual kisses in time to the languid movements of his hips. Trailing kisses from my mouth to my neck, Nikolas gave me a few moments to gather my breath, but that was short lived as he suckled a particularly sensitive area of my neck right below my ear.

"*Shiiiiit,*" I moaned, as he kissed his way up to my ear and whispered, "You gotta let me know how far I can take this, sweetheart."

Instead of answering, I pushed at his shoulders, separating us just enough so that I could sit up. Chest heaving, I maneuvered from beneath Nikolas and stood from the couch. He ran a hand down his face, before speaking.

"Jayde, I didn't..." he started before I quieted him with the press of my fingertips to his lips.

Biting down on my lower lip, I slowly removed my hand from his lips before inclining my head, "C'mon."

I walked off in the direction of the bedrooms upstairs and wordlessly Nikolas trailed me into the room I'd occupied during my stay. We were barely over the threshold of the door before he snatched me up, effortlessly hauling me into his body and reconnecting our mouths. Cradling my ass with his big ass hands, he palmed me like a basketball, keeping me suspended in the air so that my mouth was right where he wanted it. His tongue tangled with mine, darting and swooping with purpose—and that purpose was to drive me out of my mind with desire. When he had his fill, he slowly released me down his body, keeping us pressed closely together as he bent down and whispered into my ear, "Take this shit off," gesturing towards the cute romper I'd worn to the party.

I bit down on my lip, shaking my head, "you want it off, you gotta take it off yourself."

Nikolas chuckled before swooping me into his arms again turning us around and gently laying me on the bed, on my stomach. As he unzipped the back of the romper, he plied my shoulders and back with lingering, open mouthed kisses turning me into a writing mess of arousal. He trailed those kisses lower and lower as he removed the fabric from my body, nibbling his way down my sides and hips before nipping the cuff of my ass cheeks. Then he removed the romper from my body completely, leaving me clad in a tiny pair of red lace panties. He indulged himself with a squeeze of my ass, groaning as he palmed it roughly before turning me over. His gaze zeroed in on my titties, and my nipples immediately beaded into hard peaks like a damn beacon signaling for his mouth to come on home. Nikolas immediately caught the hint, lowering his mouth to my titties with fleeting, barely there kisses as I tried grabbing the back of his head and directing his mouth to exactly where I needed it to me. He deftly dodged my attempts, smirking up at me and giving me a slight shake of the head to let me know he was moving on his own accord. I groaned in frustration as he pressed kisses along the sides of my titties, nibbled the undersides and pressed long suckling kisses to my breast plate, but completely ignored my nipples which at this point were painfully hard, damn near screaming for his attention. He slowly brought his hands up from where they'd been resting on my hips to encase my titties, his thumbs strumming my diamond hard nipples once, twice, before I groaned once again, "quit playing with me."

He must've liked that shit, as he chuckled, and kept using his thumbs to flick at my nipples, each glide of the pads of them over me making me cry out for him. He played like that for a few moments more, watching the emotions of arousal and impatience battle on my face before finally lowering his mouth to take my left breast into his mouth, his tongue wrapping around the nipple as he suckled hard. My stomach contracted immediately at the contact as I sighed in relief. He went back and forth between my titties alternating between long, deep suckles of my nipple into his mouth and quick, flickering glances of his tongue against it, both making me shudder, shiver and shake, damn near on the verge of an orgasm and the man hadn't even taken my panties off.

And that wasn't a fact of which he wasn't aware as he slid his hands down my body once again, hooking his thumbs in the waistline of the aforementioned panties, removing them in one sweeping glance down my legs. As he spread my legs I looked down at Nikolas and he met my eyes with a lecherous gaze before he licked his lips and dove in. I pushed out a breath as he wasted no time having his way with me. With his forearms braced on my thighs to keep them apart, Nikolas face planted in my pussy tonguing me with a fierce determination. His tongue worked like a marauder, pillaging through my folds as if the most precious of treasures were housed within. He was rapacious with me, growling about how I was wrong about the peach cobbler being the most delicious thing he would have in his mouth tonight. If I were in my right mind I would have giggled at that revelation, but I was too far gone, reveling in the feelings that he was drawing out of me with every lick, lap, suckle, and kiss.

I cursed him for keeping a low fade, so I had nothing to hold onto while he drove me out of my mind instead leaving me grasping at the sheets to gain some semblance of control over my body which seemed to be hurting through the stratosphere as he did something with his tongue that almost made me black out. I let go, falling headfirst into the sensation of feeling that Nikolas and that dastardly mouth of his invoked. The sound and feeling of me cumming did nothing to deter Nikolas from getting his fill as he went even harder, tonguing me with abandon, adding a couple fingers to the mix for a penetration that intensified my orgasm. Momentarily it felt like I lost a few senses, oblivious to sight and sound as I became a quivering mess. By the time my sight had returned, Nikolas was kissing his way up my body with a smirk covering his face that let me know that he was more than aware of the skills he possessed. He swiped a hand down his beard, the sheen of my arousal clearly coating it before he tried reconnecting our mouths.

I swerved, shaking my head, "You. Naked. In me. Now!"

Nikolas' chuckle to my cavewoman-esque command sent residual shockwaves through my body as he followed my command, shedding his clothing quickly. I positioned myself up on my elbows to take in the show, frowning when he stopped briefly. He was clad in just a pair of boxer briefs that had me thanking every deity whose name I could readily recall in my head for bringing me this far in life to have *this* moment.

"Protection?" he asked.

"You...don't..." I trailed off.

He shook his head once.

I popped up off the bed, quickly shifting into action, "BRB."

I took off toward Nyema's room at a clip, praying that she had something, *anything* we could use. At this point I didn't even care if Nikolas had to don a damned rubber glove, I was getting that dick tonight, hook line and sinker. Luckily, I didn't have to look past the top drawer in Nyema's nightstand before striking gold. I grabbed a couple few—*just in case*—before running back toward the guest room just as quickly as I'd run out. I stopped just before I crossed the threshold into the room and tried walking in calmly like I had some sense as if I hadn't darted earlier. Nikolas' low rumble of laughter greeted me as I took him in, stretched across that bed looking better than every single wet dream I'd had about him over the past few weeks that we'd been working together.

In my absence in the room, he'd ditched the underwear and was now completely naked and ready to go. I tossed the condoms in his direction before slowly strolling toward the bed to join him on it. Nikolas smirked as he easily caught the little foil packages, instantly opening one with his mouth, sheathing himself quickly and pulling me onto the bed with him. Barely giving me a chance to settle atop him, Nikolas slowly plunged into me. I inhaled sharply as I sank further onto him, fully seated. I moaned at the feel of him inside of me, warm and heavy, stretching my walls to capacity. I looked down at him, lip tucked between my teeth as he laid back with his hands laced together behind his head. He raised a brow, as if to say, "This is your show". I took another half a second to adjust before moving my hips in slow, undulating movements as I braced my hands on his shoulders. I rode him very slowly at first, needing a chance to adjust to his size. Nikolas hands rhythmically squeezed my ass in time with my movements as he lowered his mouth to my titties once again to lick and suck.

We kept on like that until he was no longer able to hold back and began thrusting his hips upward to match the rolling of my hips. In next to no time I was shaking and sputtering, cumming all over his dick as I yelled out his name. Chasing his own nut, Nikolas gripped my hips as he continued to glide between my slick folds, pistoning his hips rapidly before finally thrusting one final time and grunting his way through an orgasm. He fell backwards onto the headboard and I slumped into him, content to stay this way forever. Despite cumming as hard as he did, Nikolas' dick remained rigidly encased in my walls, taking up space as if it had finally found home and I was in no rush to evict him from the space. I slumped onto his chest, feeling my eyes grow heavy and let the sandman carry me away.

NINE

THE SOUND of two voices that sounded faintly familiar, but not readily recognizable to my sleep addled mind filtered through my consciousness as I struggled to fully come awake. When I finally peeled my eyes open and realized my surroundings, I looked to my left expecting to see Jayde but instead there was a disheveled portion of the comforter. Groaning I sat up, noticing that the little items of hers I'd seen strewn about the room were all...*gone*? *Wow she pulled a Houdini in this mug* I thought, laughing a bit to myself as I got up and dressed in the clothes I'd had on last night. Or at least I attempted to dress in the clothes I'd had on last night. I found my underwear and shorts, but the shirt I wore was nowhere to be found. I could have sworn that I'd lost all items of my clothing in this room last night, but maybe my mind was playing tricks on me and it was downstairs.

Downstairs—from where Langston and Nyema's voices were still carrying as they went back forth in an argument. Faced with no choice, I had to walk down there and face the music as I embarked on my version of a walk of shame. Although, I thought, there was absolutely nothing shameful about last night to me. Getting indulge myself in Jayde's body, learning what made her moan, squeal, and turn into a gargled mess as she was cumming was the opposite of shameful. I shamelessly enjoyed myself as I explored her body over and over and over again until she begged off claiming to need at least a couple hours of sleep or she'd miss her flight. She was adamant about making it, despite me saying several times I'd pay for her to take the one back to Nashville with me later.

Her little Casper the Friendly Ghost act was cute though. Before heading downstairs, I stripped the bed of its sheets, throwing them into the washer that I peeped last night on our way up to the room. I started the load and then checked my phone for the time. A little after nine am so Jayde was still in the sky somewhere getting ready to land. That didn't stop me from sending her a text, teasing about her abrupt exit.

Couldn't even leave any money on the nightstand, huh?

Almost instantly three dots appeared, as if she was typing something in return but disappeared as quickly as they'd popped up. I shook my head, chuckling a bit under my breath before continuing downstairs in search of my damned shirt so that I could get back to my parents' place, shower and change before I needed to be heading to the airport myself. As I came down the stairs, I could still hear Langston and Nyema going back and forth.

"Well if they aren't yours then whose are they? Am I

to believe that some sort of shoe fairy left those damned boats in my foyer? Because I *know* you are not implying *anything* else," Nyema grumbled.

Langston immediately fired back, "I'm not implying anything, baby. I'm just saying...those don't belong to me. I don't know who they belong to. Won't presume to figure out who they belong to, but I know they ain't mine."

"Langston...I'm up under your ass far too much for there to be time for any other dudes to be in this house like that, so you need to stop."

"I...uh...good morning, y'all," I finally spoke up, coming around the small wall that separated the stairs from the kitchen area in which the two of them were standing.

"See...not my shoes?" Langston shrugged as Nyema stood there open mouthed.

She quickly recovered, clearing her throat, "H-hey, Niko. I um...*we*...didn't know you were here."

I rubbed a hand over the back of my head, "Yeah... Jayde and I...uh...had a little too much to drink so she let me crash in your guest room until I sobered up. She was supposed to wake me for her ride to the airport though."

"Mmmmhmmm, I'm sure she got that ride one way or another," Nyema murmured under her breath.

"Bro," Langston laughed, "where is your shirt?"

I grinned sheepishly, shaking my head, "I uh...it's probably in the living room. I don't remember much about last night."

Lying my ass off, I remembered last night in painstaking detail. Details I would never forget flooded through my mind as soon as I told that lie as if my brain wanted to taunt me for daring to test its capacity. I shook them off quickly, heading toward the living room hoping to find the black tee I'd worn last night. It was nowhere to be found though, *shit.* I went on, putting on my shoes like it was nothing and turning back to Langston and Nyema to say bye before opening the door.

"Say bruh, you really finna be out on your slut walk shit, huh?" Langston called out, laughing.

"Babe, it's actually called the *walk of shame.* Slut walk was Amber Rose's..." Nyema trailed off shaking her head, "Never mind, unimportant. Langston has a couple spare tees over here if you need one, Niko. Must've been a pretty wild night of...sleep if you lost your shirt huh?" She couldn't help snickering to herself as she delivered that last line which let me know she definitely wasn't buying my I'd drank too much excuse. And rightfully so because drinking wouldn't cause me the need to come out of all of my clothes unless that drinking led to *something else.*

"Yeah...actually that would be clutch. Last thing I need is to have to answer moms' questioning if I walked into their place without the shirt, I wore last night," I chuckled.

Laschelle Verette was like a dog with a bone when seeking answers. Relentless. I wasn't up for the Spanish inquisition when my time was so finite. At this point I had about three hours to shower, dress, and be through TSA to board my flight. Nyema reappeared holding out a shirt of Langston's that I gratefully accepted.

"Thanks, y'all...I'll see you...when I see you," I said,

quickly donning the shirt and making my way out the door.

"This is a safe space," Langston called out behind me, "We won't judge your slut walk too harshly."

Laughing, I threw up the middle finger over my shoulder and kept it pushing. I thought I heard him telling Nyema to pay up and I scratched my head in puzzlement over what that was about. I know their asses didn't have a bet about when or if Jayde and I would...get together. Either way, I was sure I'd be hearing more from him later once his girl pumped his head up to interrogate me for details. Right now, I needed to make sure I got my ass back to my parents' crib quickly so I could make my flight. The last thing I needed was to miss it and then delay my time getting back to Nashville. I was expected to report out to Shelbyville by midday tomorrow. The house that the finalists were living in *Real World* style for the next couple of weeks was about an hour outside of Nashville—in a "quaint, small town" as the email with all of the details had described it. The house looked dope though. The email had contained a link for us to get a lay of the land, so to speak, before we arrived. It was a rustic looking, sprawling ranch house that had twelve bedrooms and five bathrooms. I'd already peeped which of the bedrooms I wanted to take, a tiny out of the way one that was conveniently ensconced above the garage. I'd planned on arriving a little bit earlier than our designated meet time in order to be able to slide into that bedroom before anyone else.

When I got back to my parents' house neither of them were anywhere to be found, thankfully. As I looked at my phone again for the time I realized that my timing was perfect as they were in the midst of their morning stroll around the neighborhood and wouldn't be back for another twenty to thirty minutes. I took advantage of being able to dodge an interrogation and quickly jumped into the shower before packing my things up to head out to the airport. By the time I made it back downstairs, my mom and dad had returned.

"Good morning, my favorite son," my mother sang as she stood at the stove, flipping a pancake.

I ambled over to her leaning down to press a kiss onto her cheek in greeting, "I'm your only son, ma."

"Don't make you no less my favorite. And I know you don't think you were getting ready to leave out of here with nothing on your stomach this morning. Sit your tail down. I'm almost done with this and you'll have plenty of time to get out to the airport before your flight," she said in one breath.

I wasn't stupid so I didn't argue back, just took a seat at the table where my dad sat reading the paper.

"Morning, Pop," I said.

He put down the paper, staring at me with a sly grin on his face, "Oh hey there son, nice of you to finally join us today."

I smirked and shook my head, "Here you go. How was y'all walk this morning?"

"Man you already know it was the damn same. We traversed the same streets. Waved to the same ugly neighbors. Petted the same mangy dogs. All the same."

"The sameness is keeping your pressure down though ain't it? While you over there running your mouth," my mother called out, looking over her shoulder pinning Pops with a look that woulda singed him alive if the fire in her eyes was real.

The whole reason why they started their daily walks was because Pops had a little episode with his health that scared us a while back. In his retirement, he took the term "easy life" a bit too literally and was stagnant and lethargic. Gained a helluva heap of weight within the first six months of his retirement that put undue stress on his organs. Trying to compensate for the weight gain, his incessant eating, and lack of physical activity landed him in the hospital for nearly a week as doctors eventually diagnosed him with high blood pressure and pre-diabetes. The doctor put him on a strict diet and Mama ramped that up with the required daily walks around their subdivision. They covered a mile or two a day between mid-morning and evening walks. Pop complained about it, but I knew he looked forward to them too. Especially since he loved calling me and catching me up on the latest neighborhood gossip. I didn't know why he was fronting now.

"Forget all that," my dad said, waving his hands, "you heard anything from FO yet?"

I shook my head, "It's the holiday, Pops. Chill. They know I'm not looking to make any moves and I trust them to take care of me. The Lloyds won't hang me out to dry."

"Yeah okay, I'm certain Kawhi, DeRozan, and any number of these young bucks who got upended already this season—*like that Ball boy*—would beg to differ. Don't let misguided loyalty let you lose out on a bag," he tutted.

"Man, who taught you about a bag?" I laughed.

"I listen to them young boys in the shop, pick up

some of their slang every now and again. And stop trying to change the subject...maybe if you were a bit more focused on securing your bag and not singing into the camera for the twistagram you'd have already signed a new contract already."

"Gerald!" my mother called out.

"Nah, Ma. It's cool, Pops gon air his grievances whether I care to hear them or not," I said, "Like I said, old man, I'm good. *However* anything shakes out."

I deftly ignored that jab about my participation in the *#forthegram* contest because Pops was never too much for my singing. He hated that I was in the children's choir growing up, never came to any of the musicals I acted in during my high school years and wasn't trying to hear me when I minored in music during my stint in undergrad. To him, music wasn't worth my time because he felt my skills and natural talents were more developed in sports. For some reason he was on the one or the other train, which for a very large portion of my life I'd ridden on, but after being knocked down a bit too many times with regard to my sports career—I was open to exploring other avenues to bring me fulfillment.

Did that mean I was through with the league? Not by a long shot, but I was definitely open to the possibility of exploring the dual career life. Who knew what this contest would lead to? And I definitely wasn't the first dude in the league to step into the music arena—though most of my contemporaries fancied themselves rappers, my dude Victor Oladipo released a whole r&b album late last year that had some heaters on it. And hell, back in the day Wayman Tisdale became a whole jazz sensation after a storied NBA career. If that was an avenue I chose to pursue, Pops would have to build a bridge and get over it. And I had little doubt that he would do anything other than that because he hadn't been anything but overly supportive of me. Even when I was at my lowest, he was always in my corner giving me words of encouragement and telling me to keep fighting to reach my goals. So, while he gave off grumpiness and disapproval on the surface, I knew that deep down he was only thinking of all of the things I told him I wanted to achieve once I'd been drafted to the NBA. Goals, for some reason, that he seemed to think I'd forgotten in lieu of taking a bit of time off for a diversion this offseason.

He couldn't be further from the truth though. And I was in constant contact with my agent, breathlessly awaiting the final word from him about my final contract numbers. They were trying to get me at least one hundred fifty million over four seasons, fully guaranteed. It was a big ask, but considering that I—along with Kage —was the damned face of the franchise and our entire team had *put in work* in order to get us to a post-season that should have been impossible? The ask wasn't that big when you compared it to the potential that we had to do some really amazing things with this team. The money was there, that much I knew from listening to the conjecture on ESPN daily. I don't know why the Lloyds were dragging their feet with extending the official offer, but I wasn't going to stress myself out about it. The fact of the matter was that what number they came to me with would be one that I accepted regardless. I was *that* dedicated to this team and seeing it through for us to bring another championship back to Nashville under my leadership. I did, however, know my worth and hoped that they knew it too.

Moms finished up the pancakes and I hopped up to bring all of the serving platters of food she'd had warming in the oven over to the table. Scrambled egg whites with cheese and spinach, turkey sausage, and real bacon rounded out the meal. We said a quick grace and commenced to grubbing. Ma fussed over my leaving so soon after breakfast and I assured her that I'd either fly them down or make another trip back up here before the season began.

I got to the airport and checked my phone noticing that I still hadn't gotten a reply from Jayde. I didn't want to be that dude, super pressed about it all, so I didn't send another text. If she wanted to play me off now, I guess that was how we were going to roll. I couldn't front like I didn't *feel a way*...because I did. And that way was... confused as all hell. Did I foresee us crossing that line? Honestly, at some point because it was evident that there was a certain something brewing between us and unlike her, I was not bound and determined to fight it. I was a man who believed in taking complete advantage of the pleasures of life...all within moderation of course. It made zero sense to me for either of us to deny ourselves of the magic that our connection wrought. But over the past few weeks I'd learned more about Jayde than she probably realized. One of those things was her sense of pragmatism. So, she had probably awakened with all sorts of questions about us and what sleeping together meant for how we'd progress going forward. But instead of bringing any of that to me, she'd internalize it to the point of driving herself crazy. I'd seen her do it with others, regarding silly interpersonal issues with her bandmates or friction she'd encountered when she went on songwriting dates with good ol Nashville boys who played her to the left. So, I'd give her that space to work through whatever she needed...for now, anyway. Fact of the matter was being inside of her felt entirely too good for it to be a one-time thing...and if she needed some convincing from me to prove it to her, I had no problem doing that at all.

"SOMETHING TOLD me you would be the first one out here," I heard as I strolled up to the front of the massive house that I would be calling home for the next five days.

I smiled, extending a hand to shake the hand of the man who I'd spoken to more often than anyone else at the label—Ro Ashe.

"Always a pleasure, brotha," I replied in greeting, "You know I had to make sure I got in here before everyone else...just in case."

Roosevelt chuckled, "Still about the big reveal huh? You know at some point we will have to let the people know who you are exactly, right?"

I nodded, "Yep. But for now, the mystery is kinda comforting, you know? I'm able to really step out and take risks, without being put into a box or risking pre-judgement."

"I feel you, man. So, you ready for this though?"

"As ready as I'll ever be. So what's the set up here? I know you sent over the floor plan and I kinda already staked out where I wanna crash, but are we...on a schedule, expected to interface with the other finalists regularly, there gonna be challenges? What's to it?"

Ro just chuckled and shook his head, "No inside information, pimp. You'll get the parameters when everyone arrives. Gon head inside though...you'll see a familiar face in there."

The smirk that crossed his face with that last remark had my interest piqued. I wondered who in the world could be familiar to me in this house as I walked in. The only folks that I knew were Ro and Rucker, my fellow contestants and I hadn't really interfaced like that. Melina had tried sliding into my DMs on some "let's collaborate virtually" type math, but after hearing about Jayde's past with her I was cool on anything that would link she and I together. The last thing I needed was anyone getting any wrong ideas about anything happening between Melina and me. My question about familiarity was quickly answered as I walked into the living room to see Jayde sitting at the piano, singing and playing while some cat grinned a little too hard in her face.

I recognized the song she was playing instantly and couldn't help myself from joining in when she got to the chorus.

'Cause I've never felt this way about lovin'
Never felt so good
Never felt this way about lovin'
It feels so good

Jayde abruptly stopped playing and turned toward me, "Nikolas...hey."

"Hey yourself," I replied easily, moving closer to lean down and wrap her in a quick hug, "This is a...unexpected surprise."

I felt her stiffen briefly in my embrace before softening and returning it. I pulled back with a question in my eyes that she shut down with a quickness as she shook her head almost imperceptibly.

"You know Rich?" Jayde said, sliding out of my embrace and turning back toward dude who was now mugging me.

I extended a hand, completely ignoring whatever he thought he was about to be on with me, "Pleasure to meet you, man. Nikolas."

He ignored my extended hand, instead nodding at me, "Yeah, I know who you are."

"Okay then...well, I guess I'll let y'all get back to it. I need to settle in, but Jay...I'll catch you later?" I said, looking her directly in the eye, hoping that my gaze conveyed that wasn't a suggestion, but a command.

She made a noncommittal sound in the back of her throat instead of actually responding verbally which almost made me press her a little, but I knew that this wasn't the time. Especially in front of this clown who was skinning and grinning in her face once again after her perceived dismissal of me. I didn't know what the deal was between those two, but I knew for damn sure she wasn't about to play me off in front of some dude whose lining looked like my eighty-seven-year-old grandmother had done it. I went to the room I'd initially staked out over the garage to see that it was already taken with a duffle bag strewn across the bed and a rolling suitcase near the door, so I went back into the main lodging area to find the room that was my second choice free and clear. This one wasn't as secluded as the garage room, but it would definitely do for when I needed my space. I settled in, unpacking my shit, and then taking a quick shower before changing out of the clothes I'd driven down here in. I'd just re-dressed when I heard a light knock on my door. I crossed the room to open it fully expecting to see Jayde, but instead another...semi-familiar face peered up at me.

"Holy shit," she breathed in a sultry low timbre, "See, I just knew your ass would be fine and I was right. *Whew, I just didn't know how right until this very moment though.* Whassup, baby, I'm Melina."

She pressed her body into mine, causing me to take a big step backwards and stretch a hand in her direction. She ignored the proffered hand, gushing, "No need to be all formal, babe. We're about to be all up in each other's space for the next ten days. Might as well make the best of it, right?"

"Uh..." I replied, scratching my head, "I guess."

She giggled, pulling her lower lip between her teeth, "Ain't nothing wrong with mixing a lil pleasure with business, you know?"

"I wouldn't know anything about that. I've got more of a single-minded focus," I replied.

"Mmmm, I do have something you can focus on..." Melina trailed off as another knock sounded on my door.

What the fuck was this the local watering hole? I thought as Ro peeked his head in the doorway.

"I see someone got sidetracked, Melina was supposed to come up here and let you know that everyone was here, and we were ready to meet, Nik. You good to go?"

"No doubt," I replied, "Let's ride."

Both Ro and I stepped aside to let Melina precede us out of the room and she definitely spared no step, twisting her ass and hips so hard I thought she might pull something. It took everything in me not to laugh out loud at her ass as Roosevelt and I met each other gazes with raised brows and twin smirks.

"All I gotta say is, beware bro," Ro laughed.

"Man, I can spot a barracuda a mile away. The basketball groupie life prepared me for the likes of Miss Melina," I replied with a chuckle of my own, "She ain't getting far with me at all."

As we came down the stairs and walked into the living room, I saw that we had been joined by a handful of unfamiliar faces to me. Of course, I recognized Jayde, Rich and *Double R Records* CEO Ryan Rucker, but there were more people in the room that I'd never seen before in my life in addition to the other finalist. My entrance into the room garnered a few curious stares, but no one said anything outright.

"Aight, now that everyone is here, we can go around the room with introductions. I'll go first though I'm sure everyone in this room should be more than familiar with me. I'm Ryan—President and CEO of *Double R Records*."

The woman next to him spoke up next, "Hey everyone, I'm Rita. An engineer who'll be working with you all to get those vocals recorded and mixed."

Next up was Jayde. "Hey y'all. I'm Jayde—I think *Double R* brought me in to be a songwriter, bass player, background vocalist, basically a Jayde of all trades," she giggled, those dimples in her cheeks seeming to wink at me as they deepened with her prolonged laughter, "But for real—I'm looking forward to collaborating with you all and seeing what magic we can make."

Melina muttered something under her breath after Jayde finished speaking.

"What was that, Melina?" Ryan asked, "Speak up."

"I...didn't say anything," she stammered, attempting to distract him with a smile, but Ryan didn't seem too fazed by her.

"Oh...okay, seemed like you had something to say. I guess not...aight Rich you up next."

"I think you already introed me big homie," the Rich cat laughed sounding like a damn dweeb, "But yeah, like Double R said, I'm Rich. I'll mostly be working on music and vocal production. Maybe Jay Jay here will let me sit in on some writing sessions or something, too."

Jay Jay? This cornball... I thought, halfway paying attention to Melina's introduction.

After Melina were another two producers named Didi and Jean, another two songwriters named Carl and Abani, the other finalist besides me and Melina, Vanilla Ice aka John C.—a name that Ryan cracked dude would have to change so he wouldn't get mixed up with his forefather Jon B. After John, it was my turn.

"Whassup y'all, I'm Niko aka Okin," I started before Carl cut in.

"Aye man, we know who the hell you are! I'm a huge fan, bro. Those calls against y'all in that Boston series were bunk as hell. Y'all got robbed."

I shoot him an appreciative grin, "Thanks, man. Appreciate it."

"And I'm Ro...the reason why y'all are all here in this crazy ass arrangement," he said, garnering a few laughs from the group at large, "Actually, you can blame my soon to be wife for the reason why y'all are out here. She was the one who brought the idea up and Ryan's ass ate it up like it was a piece of chocolate cake. Matter of fact, let me get y'all her email address so you can air out your grievances there."

The room erupted in laughter once again.

"But for real, I'm glad y'all were game to give this a try. It's going to be really reality TV adjacent, unfortunately. We're going to have live streams in all of the common areas starting tomorrow. Please try not to play too much to the camera, just behave like you normally would. The whole purpose of the livestream thing is so folks can get a feel for who you are beyond those couple minute clips you all have been uploading to your Instagram accounts. Nik, I know your anonymity is a big thing, so there will be a semi-tape delay just in case the team we have monitoring the streams see that—"

I cut him off, "Actually...I've been thinking about that since agreeing to this whole being taped thing. Might be time for the man behind the mask to be unveiled."

Jayde's eyes met mine in surprise. She was the only

other person besides Roosevelt who was aware of how intent I was about keeping the Okin secret.

"We...can talk about that later," Ryan said, immediately and it was like I could see the wheels in his head turning on how he could flip my reveal into something that would catapult the coverage of this contest to his advantage.

"Yeah, definitely," Ro said redirecting attention onto himself, "Why don't me, you and Ruck meet after this, actually?"

I nodded.

"Where was I?" Ro asked.

"You were talking about the tape delay before you were rudely interrupted," Rich piped up.

"Thanks, man," Ro said, narrowing his eyes briefly at the unnecessary additional commentary before continuing to lay out how we would be given a schedule of time that we'd be expected to be in the studio with either producer/songwriter pair working on material for the four song EP each of the finalists would release. The sales and streams of those projects would help determine the winner of the overall contest. Seemed simple enough, so when Ro asked if anyone had any additional questions no one piped up. I figured any questions I'd have would be answered along the way, so once we were dismissed, I made no time making my way over to Jayde.

"Sup coach?' I said with a grin.

She grinned right back, blushing a little as she asked, "You got a minute?"

"For you...as many as you need," I shot back

smoothly, which just made her giggle again and roll her eyes a little, "C'mon."

She took off walking and I followed behind without a second thought.

"Before y'all get too far," Ryan called out to everyone as the crowd dispersed, "Family dinner is a prerequisite of this arrangement. So I'll expect to see all of your faces around the dinner table at six thirty sharp, nightly."

"You got it, boss man," John C. responded with a mock salute.

I halfway expected him to give a wink and the gun along with it. But he just turned on a heel and strode from the room. I looked over at Jayde and she looked like she was holding back another laugh, lips twitching in barely concealed amusement.

"C'mon," she urged again, taking off down the hall that led to the garage apartment.

"Oh, it was you! I should have known by the obnoxious pink suitcase left in the room," I joked, "You stole my spot."

"I did no such thing, sir. I merely took one of the many rooms that was available to me when I arrived this morning," she grinned again, tongue peeking between her teeth, "Shut the door behind you."

She walked into the room and perched herself upon the surface of the desk that was set up in a corner of the room in front of a large picture window. I stayed close to the door, leaning against its closed surface.

"So whassup?" I asked after we stood there in silence looking at each other stupidly.

"I...I wanted to...apologize to you," Jayde started,

looking away from me as she continued, "I, um...you know I had that early flight to catch on my way back from visiting Nyema and then you know life...so I...er...didn't have a chance to..."

Instead of letting her continue to stammer through paper thin excuses I crossed the room to stand directly in front of her, cupping her chin gently to bring her gaze back to mine.

"This...doesn't have to be awkward, Jay. I'm following your lead here. If...that was just a one and done, then we're good. You don't have to worry about me going off the wall on you."

"And if I don't want it to be one and done?" she asked, so softly I barely heard it.

"Then all you gotta say is the word, sweetheart," I replied, gently caressing her lower lip with my thumb.

A small shiver ran through her body before she whispered, "the word."

I peered down into her eyes and saw nothing but pure lust shining back at me, so I lowered my mouth to hers capturing her lips in a sweet kiss. Jayde wasn't with the soft and sweet though, immediately threading her hands together behind my neck and crushing our lips together in a torrid mashup of lips, tongues and teeth. My hands slid from cupping her face directly down to her ass, palming both cheeks easily. The feel of my hands on her ass drew a ragged groan from Jayde as I settled my hands on her in a firm grip, turning my palms into a seat for her ass to rest upon as I lifted her to a comfortable height for me to take over the kiss effortlessly. Wrapping her legs around my torso, Jayde ground into me insistently—her intentions and expectations made instantly clear as she moaned, "I need to feel you again, Nikolas."

Within seconds of that utterance we were completely disrobed, nothing between us but the latex of the condom I'd retrieved from my wallet and used to sheath myself in record time before plunging deeply into Jayde's wet folds. She bit down on my shoulder to muffle her sharp cry of pleasure as I used my hands on ass to bring her onto me over and over again, each stroke taking me deeper than the previous until I was drowning in her.

"Shit, Nikolas," Jayde breathed, the words coming out in more of a hiss than anything else, "You feel s-sooooo good."

"That's all you, sweetheart," I grunted out as I slowed the pace of my strokes.

I needed a chance to regain my bearings, before I ended up busting way before Jayde had been thoroughly satisfied. I moved my hands from her ass to her hips, directing her frantic up and down into blissfully slow circular movements of her hips, bringing her clit in direct contact with the base of my shaft on every rotation. The change in tempo made Jayde burrow her nails into my skin as she panted in harsh breaths for me to bring it back up. I was enjoying this slow grind, though, in no rush to bring out connection back up to the pounding breakneck speed with which we'd started. I dipped my thumb into her pussy, coating it with her juices before using it to rotate against her clit in the opposite direction of the circles of her hips.

Within seconds, I felt her thighs quickening as she panted, "Niko, I'm about to..."

Once again, I took her mouth with mine as she was about to scream her release, muffling the sound in another urgent kiss. I picked up the pace of my strokes as Jayde shuddered though her orgasm, determined to keep her aftershocks going as I reached my own release.

A few moments of silence passed as our breaths returned to normal. I stroked a hand gently up and down Jayde's back and she burrowed deeper into my chest, inhaling deeply.

"You always smell so damned good," she murmured into my neck as she took another deep inhale.

"Okay...that's not creepy at all," I laughed, causing her to sit up and smack me across the chest.

"Hey!" she exclaimed.

I just kept laughing, shrugging my shoulders, "So you gon act like if I snorted your skin like a line of coke you wouldn't be in ya lil group chat app with your girls talking mess about whether or not I was gonna skin you and wear it as a jacket? Oh...okay..."

That caused Jayde to let out a loud cackle, "Something is *wrong* with you. And no I wouldn't. I'd be...flattered."

I smirked at her, "Yeah okay."

"Hey?"

"Whassup?"

"You...didn't accept my apology?" Jayde said, worrying her lower lip with her teeth. Her eyes held a bit of uncertainty, almost as if she hesitated to bring it up, but now that she broached it we could rewind.

"This," I said, gesturing to our completely naked and satiated bodies, "wasn't acceptance?"

Jayde rolled her eyes, "I'm being serious. Are we good?"

"We are more than good, Jay. So long as you don't play me off in front of that nigga with the etch-a-sketch lining again like you did earlier."

"Etch-a-sk...oh my God," Jayde giggled, "Rich? Ain't nobody checking for that dude at all. Trust me. He is *nothing* but a friend."

"He knows that?" I asked, an eyebrow raised, "Because the energy I got when I walked in earlier...I wasn't so sure."

"He should *absolutely* know that. I've *never* seen him in that way. Won't ever see him in that way," Jayde shuddered, "I'm low key insulted that you think *Rich* was my type."

"Man, I ain't know what to think when you hit me with the church hug and then played me off in favor of continuing whatever y'all were doing before I'd arrived."

"We...weren't doing anything. I was messing around on the piano and he hadn't walked up much sooner than you had actually. And I did not give you a church hug earlier! I returned your hug."

"Man, I know that, 'let me give this fool a lil attention so he'll move on hug'," I said, "I got more than enough of them growing up when I went through my awkward phase—from chicks who were playing me off."

"Oh, I do not believe you *ever* had an awkward phase," Jayde said.

"I most definitely did before I got braces, grew eight inches in four months and finally added some weight to my string bean frame. Hell, my ma would gladly show you pictures from the era she calls 'if nobody else loved you then, I loved you'," I laughed.

Jayde giggled too, "Oh, you fought the braces battle too? Man...those were the worst two years of my teenaged life."

"Yeah, my teeth looked like they were throwing up gang signs," I chuckled.

"Wouldn't be able to tell now," Jayde mumbled as I flashed her a grin.

"Dr. Bradley earned his paycheck for sure by wrangling these joints," I cracked, referencing my childhood orthodontist, "and I definitely still make use of my retainer every now and again."

"All these years later?" Jayde asked.

"Well it ain't the OG one, but I definitely keep my dentist appointments and ask for aligners every one to two years. Gotta keep this Colgate smile together."

Jayde shook her head at me, sitting up completely and moving from where she'd previously straddled me.

"So...how are you feeling about all of this?" she asked, gesturing around the room, "I know how you feel about your privacy...autonomy...all of that is gonna be nonexistent in this place."

"All a part of the game, right? And I'm playing to win so I can make the necessary adjustments. Nah, scratch that, I *will* make the necessary adjustments."

"Ahhhh, that's why you're willing to do the big unveil on *Okin4thegram*, huh?"

I nodded, "I figured with this Real World shit they were tryna pull the likelihood that it would stay quiet for long was slim to none, but I'd rather have it come out on my own terms and not someone else's you know? And I'm sure that *Double R* can make that happen without it turning into some other shit, you know? Speaking of... shit, I was supposed to be talking to them after out little introductory thang downstairs, but somebody lured me into her sex den..."

Jayde's mouth dropped dramatically as she clutched her invisible pearls, "Me? I invited you up here to have a conversation, Nikolas. You, on the other hand..."

"I like to think that my mouth served a better purpose this time though."

"I mean, that I can't refute," Jayde grinned, leaning down to capture my lips with hers, "Can't refute that *at all.*"

I indulged her a bit, making out like teenagers before we disengaged to get ourselves together before we had to sit around the dinner table with everyone else. After a few moments more I crept out of her room to take my second shower of the evening and headed down to dinner. *Double R* spared no expense with this trip I soon came to see as we were served a steak dinner with all the trimmings. I would definitely have to make sure I got my ass up early to go for a run or something to work off all of this decadent food. Since I wouldn't have access to my normal facility I used to get my daily workouts in, my running would have to be ratcheted up to even the score. The road that I drove down to get to this little tucked off ranch seemed to be about a mile and a half, so a couple times down to the main road and back should get me right where I needed to be.

Conversation flowed around the dinner table as we

all settled into getting one another. I'd only had to field a couple of crazy ass questions about my place in the league, otherwise the night went off without a hitch. I made a plan to talk to Ryan and Roosevelt in the morning about the veil on my anonymity being lifted. They wanted to do it incrementally, with the big reveal coming right before the winner of the entire shebang was announced. I was cool with them letting it roll out their way, knowing that it didn't matter when the connection was revealed, it would end up being news for a brief moment in time before the next pop culture moment took over in the gossip blogs.

TEN

MY ALARM WENT OFF SO EARLY that it was still damn near pitch black when I hopped outta bed to begin my day. I was so grateful that I'd packed my headlamp. We were in the middle of nowhere, so I didn't expect there to be anyone else on the path I'd be running, but I just wanted to be safe. I'd shower after my return, so I slipped out of bed, donned my running gear, and headed downstairs. I'd just stopped right outside the front door to stretch and select one of four carefully curated playlists when movement in the corner of my eye caught my attention. I turned my head to see Nikolas, similarly attired—a look of pleased surprise settled upon his face.

"Good morning," he rumbled in a low baritone that traveled through my body, settling in a tingle between my legs.

There was just something about a deep voiced man I thought, a quick shudder running through my body.

"Morning," I whispered, "I...didn't think anyone else would be up this early."

"Well you know what they say about the early bird... but hey, how did you being a runner sneak past me as a fact about Jayde I should know?"

I shrugged, "Dunno, guess it...never came up."

"Well, you mind company on your run or..."

"I don't mind a little company at all. C'mon," I said, heading in the direction to round the back of the house where I'd scoped a little path around the man-made pond that decorated the back yard.

When we came upon the path, Nikolas breathed out, "Man, how'd I miss this? I was about to run my fool ass up and down that road that led to the house until my watch told me I'd run three miles."

I giggled, "The email they sent us about the house mentioned the running/walking path around the lake. I checked it out yesterday when I arrived to make sure it was paved because I hate running on gravel and couldn't bear to not get my morning miles in. Something about pounding the pavement always gets my creativity brewing."

Nikolas nodded, "Shall we?"

"You said you do three miles?" I asked.

Nikolas nodded.

"Okay, the loop is a little less than a mile total, so... ready when you are," I replied, bending over to stretch out my hamstrings one last time before taking off.

As I straightened, I felt Nikolas' gaze pinned to my ass and I bit back a grin, "You runnin' or you creepin'?"

"That depends, you runnin' or you servin'?" Nikolas replied in that deep grumble of his.

I giggled, before taking off in a light jog, "Runnin'."

Nikolas easily caught up to and kept pace with me, keeping up a steady stream of conversation as we ran the loop around the pond. I normally couldn't stand to talk as I ran, preferring to use the time to work out complicated melodies or incomplete lyrics that'd stymied me when I was working, but chatting with Nikolas as we jogged was very...*pleasant.* It was weird, this budding dynamic between us—one that I, admittedly, thought would turn awkward after I pulled my smash and dash move. A move which hadn't deterred Nikolas in the least...which honestly made him even more appealing. By the time we finished our run, which ended up being closer to five miles than three, it appeared the rest of the house had awakened and were getting ready for breakfast.

"Y'all got some early morning strategy sessions popping off?" John C. cracked as Nikolas and I reentered the house, "You know you here for all of us right, Miss Jayde?"

I rolled my eyes. Not even a full twenty-four hours in this house and I wasn't looking forward to working with neither him nor Melina. I couldn't get with the "down ass white boy" vibe that I got from John. He had to let the fake ass Timberlake persona go because he actually had a really good voice. I didn't need all of the extra and neither did his target audience.

"I'm here to work with all of you, Jonathan. How I choose to spend my spare time is completely my own. You'd do well to remember that, love," I said with the most artificial saccharine I could churn up.

The last thing I needed being said was that I was being preferential towards one person in this house over another. A major stipulation of my entering this mentorship adjacent situation hinged on me being able to maintain a lack of bias as I worked with my assigned daily producer and artist. The idea was for us to all sit with the finalists in one on one time, getting to know them and the rest of the mentors brought in for this final phase of the contest, in order to create a product that would hopefully catapult whomever won to musical stardom. This portion of the contest reminded me of *The Voice* on steroids, but I was low key into it. Well...I should say I was looking forward to working with everyone but Melina. And as the fates would have it, as I gazed upon my morning schedule, my first session was with Melina and Didi. *Fantastic,* I thought with a groan. I had no doubt in my mind that this little collaboration was set up in order to help them get some livestream drama popping off for their first day of the general public being able to view the process of the *#forthegram* finalists recording their LPs. I sighed, skipping breakfast in lieu of getting up to my little cove of seclusion and taking some time out to meditate after my shower. I needed to steel my brain so that I didn't fall for whatever tricks Melina would pull out of her bag to make me pop out of character. I didn't trust her ass no further than I could throw her and my arm was wild trash.

As I was leaving my room to head to the makeshift studio space that we were meeting in, my phone chimed with an incoming text.

Etch-a-sketch lining better tread lightly with me in this session. - NV

I giggled before typing out a reply.

Your little girlfriend needs to behave, too.

Nikolas' response made me laugh even louder as I headed down the hallway. He'd sent a gif of Snoop Dogg saying "Who?!"

Haven't you heard, sweetheart. I'm a free agent in more ways than one this summer. – NV

You better make sure your girl is aware with way she was grinning in your face at breakfast this morning…

Didn't you abandon me? - NV

I did, but the live streams didn't.

Oh, they were for real with that starting early this morning, huh? Well hopefully I looked good since you had me out there becoming a hot sweaty mess this morning. – NV

Oh…and I see you couldn't get enough of the kid. But you didn't have to check me out online when you could have me in person? – NV

I giggled again, shaking my head. While it was true that I could definitely have him in person, watching the live stream wasn't something I'd planned, but when it came down my timeline while scrolling social media, I'd indulged a bit. I wouldn't front like I wasn't annoyed to see Melina in Nikolas' face the entire time that he was in the kitchen eating. It did, however, make me extremely happy to see that he was barely paying her dust. I couldn't hear what they were talking about fully, but from his body language, Nikolas was just being polite and not entertaining her blatant attempt at flirting. I didn't know why I was so territorial...after all he and I had barely established what we were exactly doing here. Screwing someone a few times didn't give me the license to act like he couldn't talk to another woman. I knew that talking was all that it would be, since he didn't strike me as a dirty dicked type to be sleeping with multiple woman concurrently.

& on that note...enjoy your session, Nikolas.

And, you'll have me later? — NV

I grinned in spite of myself.

We'll see.

Sounds like a yes to me. Until then... - NV

My session with Didi and Melina went off without a hitch, surprisingly. I'd worked with Didi before, writing to some beats she'd given *Double R*, but we never were in the same space physically. Getting to share the room with her today was everything because the energy that she brought to the space was just...*ethereal.* Before we even began working, she grabbed both Melina and I by the hands, saying she needed to release the negative energy that was swarming the room before we could actually get going.

I'd hoped that she wasn't trying to turn this into some woo woo, let's get our feelings out on the table kind of session, but instead she spoke in a stern, firm voice to the both of us, impressing the fact that despite how we felt about each other that there were bigger things at stake here. She refused to move forward until the both of us accepted the tentative truce terms she'd laid forth between us. I readily accepted, as I was not interested in going the distance with Melina. I refused to give her more space in my head than she deserved, which was none. I was brought in to do a job and I'd planned on doing it to the highest level of my ability, personal feelings be damned. It'd taken Mel a bit longer to acquiesce, hell bent on the idea that I would be a saboteur in her attempts to win this contest. After we sat there in silence for fifteen minutes because Didi wouldn't even play a hint of a beat until Melina agreed to squash the beef on her end and we proceeded forth.

Surprisingly the song we'd managed to put together in the few hours that we were in the session turned out really well. Despite not being the biggest fan of Melina, I was acutely aware of her range, vibe, and what it would take to make her successful. Didi played us four records, but it was the one with the bass heavy, summer sway to it that ended up being the best fit for Melina's style. The end result was a cocky girl power anthem with a chorus centered on being *that bitch*. It was swaggy without being denigrating, boastful without being haughty. I could definitely see it turning into a summer anthem to accompany the hot girls as they continued to act up this season. Didi's production went a long way in helping highlight the scant range Melina possessed and I had to admit it to myself that she didn't sound half bad. Nikolas and John C. mighta wanted to make sure that they were coming correct with their contributions.

I left the session feeling good and literally ran into Nikolas as I moved down the hall. His hands steadied me at the waist as I bounced backward from his body and damn near fell right back onto my ass.

"Whoa there!" he chuckled, "Where's the fire?"

I laughed right along with him, "In the kitchen, I am *starving*."

"You...didn't get my text?" he asked, eyebrows arching, "I'd wondered if you wanted to get lunch...off campus. Did a lil yelping and found a bomb ass BBQ situation not far..."

"Oh! I must've forgotten to take my phone off airplane mode. Usually when I'm in the studio, I do that to kill my distractions," I said, reaching into my back pocket to switch my phone back in to cellular mode. About twenty different notifications went off as I joked to Nikolas, "Just how many texts did you send?"

Eyebrows raised with a little smirk playing about his lips Nikolas answered, "Just one little miss popularity."

I looked down at the notifications seeing that most of them were coming from my social media accounts which was strange because I hadn't posted anything new on Instagram or Twitter in days. I opened up Instagram to see what the hullabaloo was about and saw a shit ton of new followers and hella comments on a post on the *Spilling That Hot Tea* Instagram account. Curious I navigated over to the post where I was tagged in the comments and damn near dropped my phone.

"You...might want to look at this," I said to Nikolas, handing him my phone.

Nikolas grabbed the phone I held in his direction with a puzzled look on his face before immediately breathing out a low curse once he realized what I was showing him. It was a short video of us on our run earlier this morning. Right before we'd gone into the house to rejoin everyone else, we'd shared a quiet...*sweet* moment. I was about to head into the house when he grabbed me by the wrist and pulled me into him. We stayed in that embrace for no more than fifteen seconds, a quick moment of solace as he pressed a kiss to my forehead when we parted and walked into the house. That little bit of time was enough for someone to not only see it, but film it and send it off to *STHT*. And of course, their shady little caption about me looking to do more than mentor in the *#forthegram* competition did nothing but fan the flames of speculation as the caption also hinted at who the mystery man was behind Okin. Something that I knew that *Double R* was still trying to keep under wraps for a little bit longer.

"Jayde," Nikolas started, and I cut him off with a shake of my head.

"Nope, we're going to talk to the boss. He'll figure out who was behind this little leak and get ahead of all of the speculation in the comments," I said.

We quickly found both Roosevelt and Ryan who were both well aware of the *STHT* post and neither were too pleased. The caption clearly outed Nikolas for anyone who was even the tiniest bit of aware of anything to do with basketball. Nikolas had been all over the sports news as the negotiations for his free agency contract were being settled—a thing I knew had to be unnerving because of how much he valued his privacy. To be put out here on terms that were not his own was probably driving him up the wall, despite the ultra-cool demeanor he displayed right now.

"Nik, Jayde, I want to apologize for the awkward ass position this put y'all in," Roosevelt said, contrition lacing his tone, "And I also want y'all to know that whoever was tryna make a quick buck and put your business on front street will be dealt with. That ain't some shit that *I'm* gonna let fly. Not to mention we're caught with our pants around our ankles because *Double R* was working on our own gradual reveal of *Okin4thegram*. So not only has whoever sent this over to the folks at *...Hot Tea* violated your privacy, but they've also pissed me off because they're fucking with my project. I've got my assistant communicating with *...Hot Tea* now to figure out what's the price for them to reveal their source because clearly it was someone who we loaned a bit too much trust to. And I can't bang with that, at all."

Roosevelt's face was pulled into a scowl that spoke volumes to the degree at which he was pissed off. Ryan was a bit more diplomatic, giving us some party line about being sorry that our privacy was violated in this way, but also saying that we could flip it to our advantage. He wanted to divert from the whole mentor/mentee storyline to us having some sort of sit down interview and talking about how this contest not only led us to fulfilling musical goals but finding love along the way and the look on my face must've said it all as Nikolas interrupted

Ryan's spiel with a gentle redirect—a plea to just be able to take over the live stream and come out on his own, leaving our connection or anything to do with me out of it. I appreciated his discretion but was still thirty-eight hot at whoever in the house wanted a little bit of extra coin and was willing to sell us out. I had my ideas on who it could be, but I was treading lightly. I didn't want to jump to conclusions and accuse anyone, but this had Melina written all over it honestly.

Of course, I wouldn't be able to prove it without confrontation and quite frankly that was the last thing I needed at this point. I didn't need her to take me out of character and possibly tarnish my reputation with *Double R* like she had done to countless other folks in the past. I wouldn't become her latest victim. We ended our meeting with Ryan and Roosevelt with their promises to find out who was behind this or at the very least regaining control of the narrative and allowing us to be back in the drivers' seat with how much we wanted to reveal or not reveal with regard to mine and Nikolas...relationship. I wasn't quite sure that was the proper designation for whatever it was we were doing currently, and I certainly was not in the mood to try and decipher that right now. I was cool with us playing it by ear, but this social media shit might have forced my hand

"...So, lunch?" Nikolas asked with raised brows and a smile.

I sighed, then nodded. I needed the distraction and we had a couple hours of free time before we'd be going back into our sessions for the evening. Nikolas took his hand in mine and led me thought the house and out to his car, opening the door for me to get in, then rounding the car to slide into the driver seat.

"I hope you like BBQ," he said, as I gave a noncommittal sound of assent.

My mind was still on the social media shit. I wasn't really for putting too much of my business in the streets nor had I ever been linked to anyone who had a slither of the notoriety that Nikolas has due to his basketball career, so I was on edge. I was trying not to let that completely shine through, playing the cool girl role but Nikolas saw right through that. We hadn't been driving for more than three minutes before he spoke up again.

"So...how are you feeling? You know...about all of this?"

"I'm...processing," I answered, truthfully.

Because I was. I didn't know what to think. There were too many conflicting factors and just the thought of having to parse them all and figure them out? Ugh, my head hurt already at the fact. Soon, however, Nikolas was pulling up to the restaurant that he'd promised would blow my mind according to the Yelp reviews. I thought it was cute, his blind trust in internet strangers to determine whether or not he'd really enjoy a place. I wasn't a person who operated in that way, much preferring to stumble upon gems without meticulous research. Nikolas waited until we were seated and had placed our orders before asking me, "Still processing?"

I grinned, pulling my lip between my teeth, "I...don't know what you want from me, Nikolas."

"Who said I wanted anything at all?" he replied, and I felt my hackles instantly raise, "Wait...that came out wrong. I mean...I don't want any more than you're willing to give, sweetheart. No pressure, no stress. I just...I don't want this little hiccup to disturb our groove we got going here."

I laughed at his music reference and shook my head, "I have to be completely honest with you, Nikolas. I'm a little out of my wheelhouse here."

He lifted a brow in askance, a silent plea for me to continue. I swallowed the lump that had suddenly formed in my throat and shifted in my seat a bit. It shouldn't be this hard to express my feelings, but I wasn't wholly comfortable with being put on the spot either.

"Why do I feel like I'm in the hot seat here?" I asked, trying to deflect.

Nikolas held up his hands, palms out facing in my direction, "Hold up...I don't want you thinking I'm trying to force your hand here, Jayde. I'm just...hoping that you're open to the possibility of exploring. I mean, shit... you can't deny this thing between us." As if to prove his point Nikolas laced our fingers together and that slight shift sent a shiver through me.

"I'm not trying to deny anything. I just...I'll need your patience. And actually, if we're being honest, I'll probably try your patience a bit too," I laughed, "But...I'm open...to exploring...with you. I like you...I like this."

Nikolas nodded once in my direction, a slow grin creeping on his face, "That's good enough for me...for now."

I matched his grin with an equally giddy one of my own, squeezing his fingers as the waiter brought out our food and conversation came to a temporary lull as we both dug into the plates laden with barbecue. I hadn't indulged in some good ol' barbecue in a while, even choosing to skip most of the grilled foods at Nyema's parents' cookout that I attended. Nikolas had made a very good choice with this place because the brisket that I ordered was tender as hell and the barbecue sauce was both sweet and tangy, a delight for my taste buds. I swallowed my first bite and looked up self-consciously because I definitely dove straight into that food, my starving sensation from earlier returned in full force. Luckily Nikolas was just as enthralled with his selection, so I had nothing to be ashamed of. I reached for my glass of water and took a long sip before restarting our conversation.

"Well now that that's settled. Who do you think is behind that leak to *Spilling That Hot Tea*?"

"I low key think it's Ryan..." Nikolas said.

"What? Ryan?!" I screeched, causing the few diners who were in the restaurant to turn in our direction, "Why do you think that?"

"I don't know. He seemed a little too...go with the flow about it for me. Who do you think it is?"

"Melina. Violating someone's privacy is her m.o. And I wouldn't put much past her conniving ass to ensure that she came out on top in this competition." I gritted out.

"How was she in your session today? Still on her regular bull?" Nikolas queried.

I shook my head, "She was actually super pleasant, and we got along for the most part. The song we actually got brewing with me, her and Di...I hope you put in work this morning because that shit is a *guaranteed* banger. Might put her ahead in the game once it's out there."

"And you think she'd really risk her place in this contest to...hell, I don't even know what whoever leaked that was seeking to do. The angle they had barely showed my face, but uh...it definitely showed one of *your* best assets," Nikolas grinned sheepishly.

"Oh my god," I groaned, disengaging our hands to cover my face with mine, "can you not?"

"I could, but where's the fun in that, sweetheart?" Nikolas teased before flicking up his wrist and glancing at what looked to be a very expensive timepiece, "We should probably be heading back soon for the afternoon sessions. Especially since I now know that I gotta pay nice with etch-a-sketch lining to ensure that we create something that's half as dope as whatever you and Didi have come up with for Melina."

"I'm just saying...you might wanna get your basketball fan base in there to skew the voting if this hit we created this morning is any indication of just how real this competition can be.

Fleetingly, a looked passed over Nikolas' features before he schooled his face back into a more normal expression.

"Hey, I didn't mean that in...a bad way," I stammered, "Just shit talking."

"Yeah," Nikolas nodded, "I know...but you know I wondered about that with this big reveal thing, right? If I'd really be winning on my own merit or would letting folks know who I was for real would skew this whole thing?"

"Can I tell you a secret?" I asked, leaning in, "And if you tell anyone I told you this, I will deny until the end of time."

Nikolas leaned in a little closer himself, "Ok, I'll bite. What's up?"

"*Double R* is going to be the final say in who wins. Not the public vote," I whispered, as if anyone in that place cared about our conversation.

It was a little factoid that was spilled to me from a chatty receptionist at *Double R* when I was sending back my paperwork. I couldn't exactly remember how we even got down that road of talking about the competition that deeply, but I did remember the receptionist immediately clamming up after she'd spilled the beans. She clearly had gotten too comfortable and forgot she wasn't talking to someone who was completely in the know. And quite frankly, I was a bit relieved to know that it would ultimately be the decision of the label and not the general public because I was still salty that America made Taylor Hicks our American Idol in season five over Katharine McPhee. And that orange asshole who currently occupied sixteen hundred Pennsylvania clearly showed that the American public should not be left to their own devices to make decisions of grave importance. Not that a singing competition on a social media platform held the same gravity of being the leader of the free world, but... Americans en masse had yet to prove they're to be trusted consistently.

"Wait what?" Nikolas asked, "Says who?"

"Says a Chatty Cathy *Double R* employee I had a convo with," I replied, "This boot camp is to see how you work well with multiple people in the industry as well as a way for them to observe you all's work ethic in person to see if whoever wins would have the endurance to go the distance when it comes to recording a full project, doing promo, all of that."

"Hm," Nikolas mused, "Interesting."

"So yeah...you definitely better play nice with...what do you call him, etch-a-sketch?" I laughed, "The streets is watching."

"So, the cameras are for more than the lil livestream or whatever, huh?"

"Mmmmhmmmm," I nodded.

"Noted."

When we got back to the house, we barely had time to spare before it was time to go into our afternoon sessions. And the energy in the space when I reunited with Melina and Didi was decidedly different than our morning session. Whatever bug that resided in her ass when Melina had to interface with me had lodged itself there once again, unmoving and trying every inch of my patience. If I said go, she said stop. If I said zig, she said zag. I was at the point of just leaving her and Di to it....and even normally super Zen Didi was at the end of her rope. When she snapped at Melina after she'd disrespected me for the third time in as many minutes, I finally spoke up.

"Ok, you know what? Let's just get this shit completely into the atmosphere, Melina because I'm not doing this hot and cold shit with you. I thought whatever stress was between us previously we'd both agreed to look past and put behind us for the sake of ensuring your success in this competition, but apparently sometime between the morning session and lunch you decided that didn't work for you. So please, enlighten me, what is exactly your problem with me?" I asked, hands on my hips, head tilted in exasperation.

"My problem is that you don't know how to work with a man without throwing your pussy at him. Have some self-respect, Jayde, honestly," Melina tutted.

"Bi—" I started before taking a second to collect myself and taking a deep inhale, "First of all, you'd do well to mind your own pussy, Melina. My home girl Juju has a whole series of videos about it that I can refer you to on YouTube if you need some pointers. Secondly—and I cannot stress this enough—what I do with my body is none of your business. And not that it bears any weight on what we are doing right now, but baby girl I don't have to open my legs or mouth to get ahead. My vocal abilities and writing skills do more than their fair share in helping me succeed. You might wanna work on both for your career ascend to the heights that you believe I fucked my way to."

"Oh please," Melina sighed, "Don't try to act all high and mighty. Everyone knows you fucked *Double R* and that's the only reason why you were invited here as a mentor or whatever. And now you're trying to fuck Niko to hitch your wagon to his star light too. You ain't low, Jayde."

I moved closer to her to make sure that I was right in her face so that nothing I was about to say would be misconstrued. We were damn near nose to nose when I whispered, "Let me be clear about one thing. You open your mouth to speak about me, my pussy, or any of my relationships ever again? I will dog walk your ass. I'm done playing nice. And don't think this won't get back to Ryan or Roosevelt because that's my first stop on my way out of this door."

And with that I took off out of our little makeshift studio and headed downstairs in search of one of these niggas whose first name began with an R so that I could speak my piece. I didn't have to put up with this kind of treatment, unprovoked from *anyone*, let alone Melina's wack ass. And of course, she was hot on my heels, damn near knocking me over when we came upon Ryan and Roosevelt lounging in a common area.

"Hey guys, can I get a moment of your—" I started before Melina rudely cut me off.

"I want her gone, Ryan. She has it out for me and is trying to sabotage my chances in this contest," she pouted.

I took a deep breath before speaking again, "Nobody 'has it in' for this dingbat, but my foot is gonna be *in her ass* if she doesn't keep my name out of her mouth. I know that much."

The sound of our raised voices drew everyone else for their sessions as the room soon was filled with everyone converging trying to figure out what was going on. Ryan and Roosevelt split the different, each of them taking time to speak with Melina and I respectively while ushering everyone else who wasn't directly involved back into their sessions.

Nikolas hung back a little, catching my eye and mouthing, "You good?"

I nodded once before mouthing back, "We'll talk."

Then I followed Roosevelt out onto the screened in porch so that he could get my side of what exactly happened between Melina and I. Didi also came out to where we were to co-sign my side of things, so that my word against hers shit was dead, since I had at least one witness that realized her ridiculousness ass flip-flopping and helped me maintain my sanity. I had no idea what even set Melina off but I didn't care. I was not going to be disrespected by someone who probably sucked all of the necessary dicks she needed to get ahead. And that wasn't even on some slut shaming steez, the girl was known for the behavior in the past—a tried and true pattern. I mean, I'd heeded Tricks' wise words in *Players Club* too, to a certain extent, definitely using what I had to get what I wanted, but I never stooped to the lowest common denominator of making my vagina community property. Like I'd said to Melina earlier, my talent superseded the necessity for me to do such. And honestly, if I were being objective, she had a passable enough voice that she could make things shake without shaking her ass on every available lap. But hey, to each her own, I guess.

I couldn't be bothered to keep up with her PussFax when my career, reputation, and good name were on the line with her foolishness getting started in the house. The last thing I needed was anything shifting my focus or putting me in a bad light. I'd planned on not only showing *Double R* that I could be the epitome of professionalism, but that my voice was an important one to be amplified within our community. Roosevelt heard all of my concerns and after listening to Didi's unbiased version of the events that transpired, definitely seemed to be on my side with everything. Something that delighted me, and I'd only hoped his boss/homeboy would feel the same way after hearing from the both of us.

However, when I had my one-on-one time with Ryan, he seemed less convinced of my innocence and stopped just short of reprimanding me for his perception of my alleged behavior. Instead of arguing with him, I ate it. Swallowed all of my rebuttals in favor of my belief that he just wasn't thinking clearly because of his clear affection for Melina. I wasn't sure of the origin nor depths of their connection, but one thing I knew for sure was that whenever it came to her being at the center of some mess, Ryan tended to side with her over anyone else involved. I knew it was kind of fruitless for me to argue back and forth with him and had hoped that the levelheaded, fact-based thinking that Roosevelt tended to employ would hold some weight with regard to both mine and Melina's presence in this space going forward.

By the time all of the drama of the afternoon concluded I was wiped, heading straight to my bed to lay down and decompress. I didn't even want to show my face at our little mandated dinner time, honestly. Because I didn't know what I would do or how I would react to Melina intentionally needling me further. And knowing her? She would definitely push her luck, to further her agenda of me being some sort of loose cannon with an ax to grind when it came to her. As if I'd ever let someone like her hold an iota of space in my brain that could be better served by damn near anything else. In order to maintain my Zen, I pulled out my cellphone, intent on opening up my favorite meditation app, *What's Going Om?* When I went to navigate toward the app, I remembered that my phone was on airplane mode when I was in that session earlier and I toggled my cellular service back on. Just like earlier, before I went to lunch with Nikolas, my phone chimed with a cacophony of sounds, notifications going off back to back. I groaned aloud, thinking that maybe something else may have been leaked to *Spilling That Hot Tea*, but these notifications were all texts. I also had ten missed calls. Navigating to the iMessage app, I wondered who had been trying to get a hold of me and I had messages from both of my brothers and sister in law in a group text thread. Reading the first of those messages made my heart drop into my stomach and I felt ill. Without thinking I jumped up and ran from my room, intent on hopping into the Fiat and taking off.

ELEVEN

"WHOA, WHERE'S THE FIRE?" I asked Jayde as she flew past me.

I'd been on my way to her room to get the real information on whatever had happened between her and Melina earlier that afternoon. She gave no answer, seemingly moving in a daze, her eyes unfocused and wild as she breezed past me and down the stairs. I gave chase, trying to catch her and figure out what was going on. By the time I caught up with her, she was sitting in the driver seat of her little toy car, hyperventilating.

"Jayde," I said, touching her shoulder, trying to get her attention, "Baby...what's going on?"

"My...my...moth—oh God, oh God oh God," she said before collapsing onto the steering wheel and breaking out into soul wrenching sobs.

Hearing her cry like this, in obvious pain was tearing me apart as I tried to get some answers out of her. She just kept screaming half words and sobbing as I pulled her out of the car and into my arms, rubbing her back in soothing circles. From what I could make of her frenzied speech, something had happened with her mother. I knew we weren't that far from her hometown—a fact she'd mentioned on our drive back from lunch, so I immediately jumped into action. Transporting her from her car to mine, I pointed my GPS in the direction of Belt Buckle, TN, the small town she'd name dropped in our conversation earlier.

Eventually Jayde's chest heaving sobs devolved into a more contained cry, but she still struggled to fully articulate what was going on with her. She calmed enough to unlock and hand me her phone. There, I saw texts from who I assumed were family members saying that her mother had been rushed to a local hospital after her blood sugar had spikes to incredibly high levels. I updated the GPS to reflect the hospital in Manchester that had been mentioned and moved Jayde across the bench seat of my ride, deep into the crook of one of my arms as I drove us with the other one. I kept a steady pattern with my hand rubbing circles on her back as she burrowed into my chest and cried. After about ten minutes of driving, she'd gotten a bit of her composure back.

"You must think I'm a mess," she said, hastily wiping her face with her hands.

"There's napkins in the glovebox, babe. And no, I don't think you're a mess. We're at that age where getting a message like the one you got about our parents is more than enough to send us into a tailspin. You're good, sweetheart, trust me."

Jayde sniffled, "It's just...when I got the news about my daddy? It came in this same kind of way...they texted me that he'd been admitted to the hospital and in the ninety minutes it took me to get home from Nashville? I wasn't quick enough. I should have drove faster. Because by the time I got there..."

She trailed off, looking out of the window before shaking her head and redirecting her attention back to me.

"I just...I know Jonah said Momma was okay, but I just..." she broke down in tears again.

I maneuvered to the shoulder, unable to take hearing the pain lacing her sobs and not doing anything about it. After I'd safely pulled off and shut the car off, I pulled her in close, enveloping her in a bear hug, and whispering words of comfort into her ear as she let it all out. Her phone had been pinging as we had this moment, but I couldn't be bothered to untangle from her to see what had come through. It was more important to me, to give Jayde this time to get all of her emotions out. The last messages sent from her family that I'd seen in the thread said that the doctors at the hospital were working to bring her mother's levels down. That had been sent a couple of hours ago, so hopefully things were in a much better place or at least would be once we finally got to the hospital. After a few minutes, Jayde's sobbing quieted and she leaned into me even further with a heavy sigh. I pulled back to look into her eyes to try to gauge what she was feeling. If you let her tell it, she had a poker face, but Jayde's countenance was actually hella expressive, most often telling her true emotions.

"I'm okay..." Jayde said, after a few seconds of my

perusal, "Come on, let's get to on down to Manchester and see about my momma."

I stared at her a few moments more, before pressing a quick kiss to her forehead. Jayde shrugged out of my embrace, instead choosing to keep our hands intertwined as she used her untethered hand to text her family for updates on her mother's prognosis. I turned my attention to starting the car navigating us toward the hospital quickly, but more importantly safely.

"She's okay," Jayde breathed out after we'd been back on the road a couple minutes, "Sid says her levels are still entirely too high, but the doctors are confident that they'll get them back on track. She's gonna have to stay in for a few days though."

"Good," I said, bringing our laced hands up to my mouth to place a kiss on hers, "I know you won't be settled until you lay eyes on her yourself and see that she's all right. GPS says we'll be there in twenty."

"Nikolas, thank you," Jayde breathed.

"It's nothing, sweetheart," I replied back, breezily.

"No. It's everything," Jayde insisted.

When we pulled up to the hospital, I let Jayde out at the Emergency entrance, telling her I'd catch up to her once I'd parked the car. She looked shocked momentarily before nodding and hopping out of the car. I know she didn't think I was just gonna drop her off, absolutely not. I parked the car, shot off a couple texts to Roosevelt informing him of what had happened and where we were now so that our absence from dinner wasn't the fodder of more rumor mill talk. When I walked into the hospital, the stares were almost instantaneous. I ignored them in favor of heading to the triage desk and asking for directions to where the Turner family was. The nurse informed me that only close family was allowed back in the room where Mrs. Turner was resting comfortably until they moved her upstairs into a regular room.

"I'm sorry, I probably should have led with the fact that she's my mother in law. My wife...her daughter just came in."

"Oh...of course Mr. Verette..." the nurse chirped with a decidedly friendlier tone than the gruff, no nonsense one that she'd employed this far throughout the conversation, "right this way."

I followed her back down a couple of hallways to a decently sized room where Jayde was next to the bed, fussing at her mother while two men and a woman looked on. The men I assumed were her brothers as they carried the same complexion and dimpled faces as Jayde, but I had no idea who the woman was.

"Mama, what the hell is Niko Verette doing in your hospital room?" the shorter of the two men crowed, before coming over and dapping me up, "You got something to tell us? Is he our long-lost brother? Nice to meet you, bruh. I'ma big fan. Longtime fan. I'm Jonah."

I returned his handshake, laughing, "I'm actually a friend of Jayde's. Nice to meet y'all."

"Jaybird, this man is your *friend*?" Mrs. Turner asked, making Jayde blush at her emphasis on the word friend.

"Momma, don't be embarrassing. *Please*. Yes, Nikolas is a friend. And he was the one to make sure I got here in one piece so you should be thanking him that your knuckleheaded sons frantic blowing up of my phone didn't cause me to get into an accident."

"Man, my first text said don't freak out," the other brother said.

"Sid! You know the number one rule of telling someone potentially bad news is not to tell them not to freak out because what do they invariably do? Freak the hell out!" Jayde groused, sneering in her brother's direction.

"Say bruh, I coulda just not told you shit," Sid reasoned.

"And you coulda got your ass kicked by your baby sister," Jayde shot back.

"Jaybird! Language!" Mrs. Turner said.

"Really mama? Sidney said s-h-i-t, but you're policing my language?"

"Still a narc," Jonah muttered, shaking his head.

"And y'all still get away with everything!" Jayde whined, crossing her arms over her chest.

"Y'all too grown for this mess!" Mrs. Turner laughed.

"Jay started it," Jonah said, sounding like an overgrown child, causing all of us to burst out into laughter.

"Nikolas...is that what my Jaybird said your name is baby? C'mon over here so I can get a better look at you since I don't have on my glasses," Mrs. Turner said, beckoning me with a wave of her hand.

"Mama, you don't even wear glasses," Sidney cracked, making all of us laugh again.

As I drew closer to the bed in which she laid I could hear her trying to whisper to Jayde, "Oh baby girl, he's simply too handsome to keep as just a friend."

Jayde mumbled a response I couldn't quite catch as I approached the bedside with a hand out for a shake, "It's nice to meet you too, Mrs. Turner. I hope you're feeling a lot better than earlier."

She waved off my hand, stretching her arms in my direction and I fully acquiesced, leaning down to give her a hug.

"Oh, and he's *strongbackeded*, too, Jaybird!" she crowed when we separated.

"Momma, please," Jayde groaned, embarrassment reddening her face.

"I'm just saying, this handsome, *strong* young man is right here, and you aren't getting any younger. Since those two," she said, throwing a hand in the general direction that Jayde's brothers stood in, "refuse to give me any grandbabies, you're my last hope, Jaybird."

"Hey! Sid's married, why don't you get on him and Faye about babies," Jayde argued.

"I said what I said," her mother shot back, "So Nikolas, do you want children?"

"I..." I attempted to reply but was cut off by Jayde.

"Oh my God, momma, can you not? Since when are you okay with out of wedlock, babies anyway?" Jayde laughed.

"Hey! I'm ready to have me a little bundle of joy that I can snuggle and spoil, by any means necessary, little girl. So, Nikolas?"

I was saved from having to answer when the nurse who'd led me back to the room came in to check Mrs. Turner's vitals and update the family on the status of getting her moved upstairs to a different room. Before she left the room, she looked around at everyone and remarked, "You're so lucky to have such a loving and involved family here with you. I see so many folks come in here alone or bickering so much that you almost want to send them home to give the sick one some sort of respite."

Mrs. Turner smiled, "I am blessed to have children who love me so."

"And your in-laws too," the nurse replied as she walked out of the room, throwing a hand up indicating me and the woman I now knew was named Faye, "Both of them were so worried about you when I brought them back."

Jayde craned her head in my direction, brows up to her forehead when the nurse lumped me in with her sister in law.

"Babe, she was only letting family back here so I mighta had to stretch the truth a little to get back here to make sure you all were good," I quickly replied, soon as the nurse was out of earshot, "I guess celebrity only goes so far."

"Babe?" the younger of Jayde's two brothers asked, "Aye fam, I thought you said you and this man was only friends, Jaybird. Don't none of my friends call me babe."

"Because you ain't got no friends, JoJo" Jayde gritted out.

Mrs. Turner hummed in question but didn't say anything further as an awkward silence took over the room.

"So...Nikolas, you stayin' with the *Trojans*, right?" Sidney suddenly piped up, "I've been getting all my

Bleacher Report alerts about free agency, but I hadn't heard anything about you yet."

And our conversation devolved into discussing all of the summer trade shakeups in the league that had been making headlines over the past few weeks. While I was choppin' it up with Sidney and Jonah about sports, Jayde and her mother carried on a very hushed toned conversation as Faye looked on. Jayde's brothers were cool as hell, super down to earth brothas, folks I knew I wouldn't mind being around for any extended amount of time if this thing with Jayde and I actually flourished into...something more than having mutual physical needs sated. I mean, I'd already gotten her to admit that she was feeling me, which took a load off of the stress of trying to figure this all out in my mind. Hell, I wasn't in the market for a relationship, none of that, but being with her and round her quickly changed my mind. We could move at her pace for now, as long as it kept us moving.

About thirty minutes after the nurse had left, the porters came to move Mrs. Turner to her room upstairs. Jayde and I sort of hung back from the rest of the group as we all made our way up to the new room.

"Hey," I said, nudging her shoulder, "You good?"

She swallowed, "Yeah, I just...needed to see for myself that she was good, you know?"

I nodded, "Look I'm sorry about..."

Jayde cut me off, with a teasing grin, "Nothing to apologize for...*hubby*."

"That wasn't too...much?"

I'd wholly expected her to tear me a new one when we were on our own.

She shook her head, "Quick thinking. But hey...you don't have to stick around. I can have JoJo or Sid drive me back to Shelbyville. I know you hadn't planned on having your day usurped by sitting around in a hospital with my family."

"Have I complained?" I asked.

Jayde shook her head again.

"All right then. I'm good, sweetheart. I'm not staying anywhere I don't want to be, okay? Besides, ain't shit in Shelbyville but a house full of annoying folks, and Ro."

Jayde giggled, "Well damn, tell me how you really feel, then!"

I bit down on my lip, shaking my head, "Nah...you ain't ready for all of that yet."

We ended up chillin' up at the hospital for another few hours before her mother put us all out because the ones who came from her womb were working her nerves. *Her words, not mine.* Jayde insisted that she would be back bright and early in the morning as soon as visitor's hours allowed, and her mother pleaded with me to distract her daughter enough that waking up to get on her nerves would be the least of her thoughts in the morning. I wisely kept my mouth shut instead of answering verbally, sending a wink Mrs. Turner's way that made her blush.

On the drive back to the Real World: *#forthegram* house, my phone rang with a call from my agent, Al.

"Nik the sneak, what's goody?" he crowed as soon as I pressed the button on my dash to connect the call.

"What up, Al?"

"It's about that time, G. The Lloyds have finally met

our number in the middle and they want you to come on down to the house to make it official. Is your little pop star camp over yet?" he laughed.

I shook my head, smirking, "Nah, man. I'll be back home at the end of this week."

"That doesn't work for me, Nik. Phil wants you in ASAP to sign."

"Phil, yeah okay call Mr. Lloyd anything but his proper name to his face if you wanna play, Albert."

"Nigga...can you come home to out your John Hancock on these papers in person or nah? I told the Lloyds I'd be getting you in the office soon."

"Shouldn'ta made a promise you can't keep, fam. Let me figure out when's the earliest I can get back to Nash and I'll call Mr. Lloyd's receptionist myself on get on his calendar."

"You tryna freeze me out, Nik?"

I laughed, "Naw, man. Never that. Ten toes down forever, Al. But you tryna hoe me right now and I ain't goin'. I told you I was busy, and you refuse to respect that. I caught that "little pop star" jab earlier. Not gonna be playing ball forever, man. Gotta diversify my interests. I'll get back at you when I'm in Nashville though."

"Nik..." Al was trailing off when I pressed the red button to disconnect the call.

I let out a harsh breath, gripping the steering wheel a little tighter. After a couple seconds I felt Jayde's soft hand massaging the tension from my neck and shoulder.

"You know, when you get upset, it's like all of your anger just bunches right here," she said softly, still massaging the part she'd indicated, "You wanna talk about it?"

"No one understands why I'm doing this...you know? Why I even entered the contest to begin with? Why I'm dead set on putting so much into it. According to them I should be putting the energy I'm giving this toward recovering from last season and rebuilding for the next season. But maybe...I just wanted a break. Basketball has been my everything for more than half of my life at this point. And I pour so much of myself into it, only to barely see the rewards of it. And I don't want to go all "poor little rich boy" right now because my life is excellent. I am paid extremely well to play a sport I love and get to travel the world and connect with folks from all over while doing that. And I'd never take anything away from that, but maybe I want to be more than number eighteen on the *Trojans*."

"I get that," Jayde agreed, softly, "Honestly, no one understands being put into a box or pigeonholed more than I do. It's a big part of why I am where I am in the industry currently. Because I refuse to be neatly packaged into folks' preconceived notion of who I need to be. I think it's admirable, that you're doing something different, Nikolas."

"Thank you?" I replied, laughing.

Jayde joined me in the laughter and then sobered, "But seriously, when you win this contest and the world falls in love with your voice...everybody who had something to say about your "little singing thing" is gonna be on ya dick once again."

"I appreciate your confidence in my success," I replied, and Jayde groaned.

"Really, Nikolas? You don't think you have this in the bag?" she asked, genuine curiosity lacing her tone.

I shook my head once quickly, "Thought I had going to the league straight out of college in the bag. That didn't happen. Thought I had upsetting the entire Eastern Conference in the bag this season. And you were there to see how that turned out. I don't take anything for granted sweetheart, even when I have the clear edge or advantage."

"Hm. Interesting," Jayde replied as we were pulling onto the road that would lead us back to the house.

"Interesting how?" I asked.

"You move through this world with such surety, that I wouldn't have taken you for a guy who weighs and calculates your risk to such a high degree is all," Jayde replied.

"Why does that sound like you're trying to goad me into a reaction?"

"I'm not," she replied, shrugging, "Honestly, it was just something new I learned about you today."

"Learned a few new things about you too, Jaybird," I shot back, grinning as she blushed.

"Oh my goodness, *please* forget that little nickname. Momma refuses to let it go."

"Not a chance in hell, sweetheart. Don't worry though, I'll keep it just between us, JB."

Jayde rolled her eyes, but a smile spread across her face, belying whatever annoyance she was feigning. We pulled up to the house to see Melina departing the house with her luggage. As we got out of the car, Jayde and I looked at each other wondering what exactly had happened in the few hours that we hadn't been in the house. We barely got in the door good before Roosevelt was summoning everyone to the media room for an impromptu house meeting.

"Aye Ro, what is going on, bruh?" Rich asked as he walked into the room.

Roosevelt ignored his question, instead waiting until everyone was in and seated before he began speaking.

"Aight y'all, I'm just gonna keep it a buck because there's already been too much garbage floating around since we've been in this house. Melina is no longer in this competition. For reasons I won't go too deeply into with the group at large because not everyone was involved in the shit she was stirring up. Ryan also has decided to head back to LA for the remainder of the week, leaving me the man the ship here. I've rearranged the recording schedules, so check the bulletin board for those updates. I want to wrap things up here by Friday at the latest because I know y'all have lives you need to get back to and quite frankly, I'm ready to be somewhere where the humidity isn't working actively to kill me by suffocation."

At that everyone in the room burst out into laughter.

"Aight, y'all. That's all I got," Roosevelt said once we'd sobered, dismissing us, "Nik...lemme holler at you for a sec?"

"You got it," I said, following Ro out of the media room and settling into the room he'd turned into his makeshift office this week, "What's going on?"

He blew out a breath, running his hands over his head before speaking, "This Melina shit, man...you ain't gonna believe this. I need to bring you up to speed just in case your team needs to get out ahead of any shit she tries to conjure up since being dismissed from the contest."

From there he told me the most unbelievable story about how the videos got on *Spilling That Hot Tea* as well as the aftermath of finding out all of that information and how it led to Melina being disqualified and escorted from the house.

"Wait bruh, escorted?"

"Fam, you ain't notice that big nigga walking along-side side her when y'all came in?"

I shook my head.

"You did seem...*otherwise occupied.* For the record... there isn't a no fraternizing rule, I'm just sayin'..." Roosevelt tossed out.

"So, what does that mean for the competition going forward? It's just down to me and John?"

"Well, about that..."

"YOU WILL NOT BELIEVE this crazy shit I just heard," I said, walking into Jayde's room to share with her all of the knowledge that Ro had dropped on me in our damn near thirty-minute chat.

"Damn, niggas don't knock no more? You mighty comfortable up in here, hoop dreams," Rich said.

"Aight, Rich...we can catch up later. Thanks for coming to check in on me," Jayde said, ushering him out of her door.

"I don't like that nigga, JB. He got one more time," I said, kicking my shoes off and settling onto Jayde's bed.

"Make yourself comfortable," she mumbled as she sat down on the other side, sitting cross-legged facing me.

"Don't mind if I do," I replied.

"Niko, focus...what crazy shit did you just hear?"

"Wait. Did you just call me Niko?"

"That's...your name, right?" Jayde asked puzzled.

"Yeah, but *you* don't call me that. *You* call me Nikolas. Let's go back to that."

Something about that made her blush before she asked again, "So what did you just hear?"

"Well for starters, you were right. It was Melina that leaked that video to *STHT*."

"I knew that trash ass..." Jayde cut me off, but I held up a hand.

"It gets better."

"Go on," Jayde prodded.

"Remember how you said she got all of those folks fired at *Double R*? Turns out Melina is Ryan's sister... half-sister or some shit. I can't remember which Ro said exactly, but the term outside child was thrown around in there. But that's the reason why she kept getting off the hook with all of her antics in the past with the label. I guess it's bankrolled by their pops and he threatened to cut the cash flow if Ryan didn't find a place for Melina somehow. Which is how she even ended up a finalist in the *#forthegram* contest. Apparently, the majority of the buzz around her entries was paid propaganda by the Rucker family."

"Wait, so why didn't he just give her a vanity contract

and just leave the rest of us out of their narrative?" I asked.

"From what Ro says, she came to Ryan with some sob story about how she had grown from her manipulation in the past and wanted to earn something on her own merits. Clearly some bullshit, since she had daddy buying her likes."

Jayde shook her head, mouth agape, "This is...unbelievable. So, wait...what was the final straw?"

"Apparently, she had planned on leaking my identity before *Double R* could do it. Since her little trick to slander you didn't exactly go off as planned," I replied, almost laughing at the satisfied grin that settled upon Jayde's face, "What she didn't know was that Ro had paid a few of the blogs in advance to do the reveal once we were out of the house *and* to let him and his people know if someone tried bringing the info to them. Guess he smelled a rat after that first leak. So yeah, Melina apparently reached out to *The Tea Report* and their folks contacted Ro's assistant almost immediately. Once Ro got confirmation and copies of the correspondence from Melina, he brought the information to Ryan. Which is how he learned that they were related and all of the rest of that shit. From there, Melina got the boot and now you're just as caught up as I am."

Jayde's mouth stull hung open in surprise, "You're... right. That is some crazy...no, beyond crazy mess."

"Yeah, so Ryan headed back early to basically narc on Melina to their pops and hopefully get folks to do some PR work to spin why she would no longer be continuing in the competition."

"So, then it's just down to you and John? Nikolas, you know this means you basically won, right?"

"Not so fa—"

"Man, enough of your humble superstar persona, you can let that go with me. You know hand-me-down Timberlake can't fade you. Melina was your only true competition here and now that we know that all of that was basically fake...*Nikolas, you've got it*! Period. Save that fake humility for the basketball court."

"Speaking of the basketball court..." I said, gesturing toward the oversized shirt Jayde wore, a player exclusive *Trojans* shirt that I hadn't even realized I was missing, "Nice shirt."

"Right?" she smirked, "A perfect fit."

"So...do you make it a habit to steal shirts from men regularly or am I just lucky?"

"*Steal*? Me?" she was going for an innocent tone, but immediately broke out into giggles.

"Cute. Real cute. You weren't the one who had to leave their friend's girl's place looking like a thot on a walk of shame without a shirt. Your girl and Langston clowned me mercilessly."

"I have no recollection of the crime in question, sir!"

I chuckled, "So you gon deny it 'til the end, huh?"

"Deny what?" Jayde asked, moving closer to me on the bed, "That I'm a really big fan of the *Trojans*? I could never do that. Hometown team and all...and I'm the loyal type."

"Yeah yeah," I said, grabbing her by the leg and bringing her to straddle me, while pressing a series of kisses on her neck, "So what I gotta do to get my shirt back?"

"This is a good start," she said, angling her head to give me better access as I ran my tongue along the side of her neck before kissing my way up to her ear, "An even better one would be you stripping me out of this shirt and making good on the promises that your dick is currently making."

"Say less, sweetheart. I'm way ahead of you."

TWELVE

"NIKOLAS," I whispered on a harsh breath, "You have to get up. *Now.*"

It was like I hadn't said a word as he didn't budge an inch, still completely in a deep sleep if his even breathing was any indication. And even though my room was mostly secluded from the rest of the house, I didn't want anyone to catch him creeping out of my room. Especially with the way that Rich liked popping up to my room unannounced. Despite that video showing up on Spilling That Hot Tea, Nikolas and I still played it cool around everyone else in the house. I was sure there were murmurings—though decreased a bit more since Melina's dog ass was gone—and I didn't want to give them fuel to their fire. Which is why...instead of getting up to get ready for my run, I was trying desperately to get this man to wake up and get out of my bed. My run was completely out of the question at this point, my legs still feeling like jelly after Nikolas did his best to get his shirt back from me.

No way in hell was I giving it back. It still managed to smell like him—a clean woodsy fragrance that delighted my senses which was why I'd stolen it from him in the first place. Well technically, I didn't really steal it as much as I was in a hurry to get out of dodge after that first night we'd spent together at Nyema's place and just threw everything that remotely resembled my stuff into my bag before I hightailed myself out of there without a backwards glance. I wasn't even that type of girl, on some Destiny's Child when you're not here I sleep in your t-shirt type of math, but when I found Nikolas's shirt in my things when I got home and emptied my bag, readying it for the laundry? I definitely slipped it on quickly and it had become my newest nightgown since. I didn't even give it a second thought when I threw it in my bag while packing to come out here in this house. Probably because I hadn't anticipated that Nikolas would end up in my space like that, but you know what they say about the best laid plans.

Since he refused to awaken even after I pinched him a couple times, I sat back...taking him in like a creep. His physical presence all but usurped this full-sized bed that could not have been a comfortable fit for him in any way. But all six foot seven inches and two hundred seventy-six pounds of him were in here resting peacefully. I'd obsessively Googled him after our first real encounter and could probably spit his stats—*physical and game related*—verbatim by this point. I'd read his Wikipedia so many times that if he found out he might be a little less enamored with me. But...it was a way to sate all of my curiosity about the man who I was supposed to be avoiding instead of...laying up with.

Apparently, all it took was my laser-like focused glare on him to finally rouse Nikolas from his sleep. His half-lidded eyes gaze landed on me and a slow grin crept across his face as he began to fully awake, sitting up to try and stretch a little.

"Good morning," he rumbled, his low baritone making me shiver, "How in the hell do you get comfortable on this hard ass mattress?"

"Judging from the way you were sawing logs when I tried waking you up, you found a way," I joked, "Morning."

"Did I keep you up?" he asked, contritely.

"Nah...I'm a pretty light sleeper...and early riser."

"Hey! It's still plenty early," Nikolas replied, looking over my shoulder at the digital clock that was on the nightstand, "You tryna get a run in today?"

"That was the plan," I responded, biting my lip to stop myself from grinning like an idiot.

"Was? What changed it?"

I tapped a finger to my chin, pretending to think, "Hm, I dunno...maybe it was somebody being intent on—how'd you put it? Fucking all of the feeling out of my legs. I'd say you definitely accomplished that mission. When I got up to go to the bathroom this morning, I busted my ass hopping out of bed."

Nikolas chuckled, "Gas me up, sweetheart."

"Oh, you think I'm playing? I'm serious," I whined, rubbing my hip, "My ass still hurts a little."

"You want me to kiss it and make it better?" Nikolas crooned, moving to make good on that promise.

"No sir! That's how we got here in the first place," I said, letting that grin I'd been biting back go.

"Is it? Because I thought recovering my shirt from a little thief was how I got here. A shirt that is noticeably missing," he said, looking around the room.

I shrugged, laughing, "I have no idea what shirt you're talking about."

"Yeah, okay..." he said, getting up from the bed and stretching fully, "Well...I'm gonna go get my day started, get a couple miles in by myself since someone isn't up to it. See you at breakfast?"

"Okay," I replied, tilting my head up to meet him halfway as his face descended toward mine for a quick, closed mouth kiss, which quickly devolved into a tongue lashing, torrid kiss that had him pressing me back into the mattress.

I freely welcomed the weight of his body pressing into mine, surrounding me and consuming me fully. My hands moved from being clasped behind his neck, down the glorious trail of his pecs and abs and into the shorts he'd thrown back on at some point during the night. At the feel of my hands on his dick, Nikolas pulled back, looking me in the face.

"I'm not going running, am I?"

I slowly shook my head no, pulling him back into a kiss while helping him get rid of those shorts. He stripped me out of the tank and shorts I'd thrown on after my middle of the night shower, donned a condom and slid into me quickly.

The connection of our bodies drawing ragged moans from the both of us as the delicious friction of Nikolas stretching me to capacity drove me out of my mind. I'd had my fair share of men inside of me, but none of them had managed to consume me fully like Nikolas did every time we were together. Having sex with him felt like a wholly new experience with someone who was more in tune with me than I seemed to be with myself. He adjusted to my needs intuitively, slowing his strokes to dole out unending pleasure with each breach and retreat, the maddeningly slow pace driving me out of my head with need.

"Nikolas, please," I moaned, not giving a damn how helpless or...powerless I sounded.

When he had me at his mercy in this way, I had zero second thoughts about letting myself completely succumb to his whims. I rocked my hips to the agonizing slow pace he set, expressing exactly how good he felt inside of me with moans and a keening cry when he finally picked up the pace and pounded into me mercilessly with powerful, purpose-filled strokes. His sole purpose was to drive me out of my mind with ecstasy, as he refused to let up even when I let him know it was too much...he was too deep...I was too...*far gone.*

"Nikolas, *please,*" I whined, not even sure what I was pleading with him to do because he was hitting every one of my spots with his dick deeply embedded in my walls and his mouth licking, sucking, nibbling, and biting on every piece of available flesh that he could reach.

"Goddamn," he grunted, as a gush of my wetness caused him to slip even deeper within me, drawing a gasp from me.

"Ni-ni-nik-*Shiiiiit*," I screeched, unable to hold it back and not giving a damn who heard me.

I lost all sense of decorum or the necessity to keep anything that Nikolas was doing to me or my body under wraps. He deserved to have the adulations I praised him with shouted to the rooftops. And Nikolas wasn't far behind me, cumming with a loud roar that I was certain not only everyone in the house heard, but anyone within a mile radius probably heard it as well. Collapsing alongside me, Nikolas turned my face in his direction, plying me with soft, soul-stirring kisses that prolonged the aftershocks of my orgasm, my pussy contracting around his still hard dick that was still deeply embedded within me. I felt my eyelids growing heavy and instead of resisting, I gave myself over to it, knocking out almost instantly.

When I awakened again, it was just after eight am and Nikolas was nowhere to be found. The soreness between my legs was the only remnant of the fact that he'd been sexing me out of my mind all through the night and through the wee hours of the morning. I groaned in delight as I pulled myself from the bed to shower—*again*—then headed downstairs and to grab some breakfast. On my way down, I glanced at the schedule for today, the second to last day we'd be here and saw that I was going to be working with Rich and John C. today. *Oh boy* I thought *this should be good.* I wasn't too much of a fan of John C. because he reminded me of the white boy who grew up in the hood and thought that meant he was also one of us. No one had thought to tell him he was not. And when I found out that he'd actually grown up nowhere near the hood and had assumed this...*persona* during his undergraduate years when he discovered that some Black folks just couldn't resist a white boy with a passable falsetto? Yeah, I was definitely cool on buddy. Because he could easily slide into a space that we'd gladly welcome him into, but just the *thought of me* singing country was too much for his people to wrap around their brains? I got riled up just thinking about it, might need a brief interlude with *What's Going Om?* before I had to interface with this poseur.

I stepped into the kitchen and it was—*thankfully*—empty. I didn't know if I was too early or too later for everyone else, but I delighted in the silence as I pulled out the ingredients to make myself an omelet. I'd just poured my eggs into the hot skillet when I felt a hand at the small of my back as someone leaned in to speak into my ear. The voice, however, was the one I was expecting with that familiar of a touch, so I quickly turned around, shoving Rich's hands off of me.

"Rich...dude...*what is this*?"

"This ain't how you greet your friends? That's what you said you and *Like Mike* were, right?"

I turned to the stove to turn off the eye and back around to face him, "What is this energy, Rich?"

"I don't even know what you mean, Jay."

"Nah...we ain't doing that. We're clearing this up right now, right now. I'm not heading into another session to be ambushed by someone. So, I'ma ask you again. What is going on with you, Rich?"

"Let me ask you something, what's going on with you and Jackie Moon?"

"Who?" I asked, genuinely confused.

"Don't play dumb, Jayde. We've all noticed that you two can't stay away from each other. Hell, was your mom even sick or did y'all just leave the house so you could make all of those sounds you were making last night at an even higher pitch?"

"First of all, you've lost your goddamned mind, Richard and I'd suggest you find that shit real quick. What kind of creep shit were you on to even know about me and any sounds I was making last night?"

I knew good and well that Jesus the Christ probably heard how loud I got last night, but I couldn't grasp what would ever make Rich think that he could call himself confronting me about what I was doing with whom and when. We...didn't even get down like that. Had *never* gotten down like that. And I'd never given him any impressions that the possibly for us to get down like that was ever a real one, so I was completely blown away by all of this, seemingly, coming out of left field.

"I'm just saying, we're here to work, not so you can be a groupie hoe for a nig..." he barely got his last word out before I smacked the shit out of him.

Rich glared at me in stunned silence for a second, I think partially shocked that I'd fired off on him, before turning to walk away. I scraped my half-cooked eggs into the garbage can and didn't even have an appetite to start another batch, so I put everything else I'd taken out for my omelet back into the fridge and headed back up to my room.

"We can't keep running into each other like this," Nikolas crooned as he was walking down the stairs that I was ascending, "Hey, you good?"

I made a non-committal sound, which wasn't good enough for him as he reversed field, dragging me into his room since it was closest.

"What's going on? Everything okay with your mom?" he asked, his face frowned with concern.

"Yeah...yeah, she's good. I talked to her briefly after I showered. She told me not to bring my narrow ass down to that hospital today because she was on her way home," I laughed, shaking my head, "But...okay, before I tell you this, you have to promise me you're not going to get upset."

Nikolas shook his head, "Nah, I'm not gonna be lying to you like that. What happened?"

"Can you at least promise me that you won't have a big reaction when I tell you this?"

"Please stop stalling and just tell me what happened, Jayde," Nikolas said, voice kind of stern in a way that almost made me forget what I was even supposed to telling him.

I quickly regained control of my senses and held my hand out, threading my fingers with his when he grabbed mine before I began to speak. I could feel his body tensing as I recounted everything that had occurred between Rich and me in the kitchen. When I finished speaking, Nikolas said nothing, urging me to my feet.

"Wait...where are we going?" I asked.

"To find Ro so you can tell him exactly what you just told me and get this nigga outta this house before I fuck him up," Nikolas replied calmly.

"Nikolas!"

"Oh, would you rather the other option of me fucking

him up? Because we can definitely make that happen, too sweetheart. Just let me know which way we're going."

"Neither way! I handled it. It's fine!" I said, pulling my hand out of his and pacing back and forth, mumbling under my breath, "No need to make another big deal where I'm at the center of some drama once again."

Nikolas caught me by the hand again, bringing me in for a hug. I sank into him, sighing heavily as he wrapped me up tightly, pressing a light kiss at the top of my head.

"None of this is your fault, JB," Nikolas said firmly, pulling back from our embrace and tipping my head up so our eyes met, "You hear me? There was nothing you did to make neither Melina nor Rich behave in the ways that they did. But...hey if it's good for the gander, it's good for the goose, baby. And that nigga being able to stay in this house after disrespecting you? It's not flying with me. So, like I said...which way are we handling this? *We* going to talk to Ro or am *I* going to knock a proper lining in buddy's head?"

I rolled my eyes, "I'm supposed to be working with him and John today. This whole thing is just so unnecessarily awkward. I just don't get it. Rich is my boy....*was* my boy? Hell, I dunno. None of this makes any sense. And like, I don't wanna be responsible for him being put out and this possibly reverberating through the industry and having some sort of impact on him. Though... honestly, whenever some shit like this happens the woman ends up getting dragged more than the man, so I'd be the one bearing the brunt of whatever fall out."

"All right, so that settles it. I'll be talking to ol' etch a sketch since you're so conflicted. He might be a lil fucked up in the head to build a beat, but I will have definitely beat some sense into him when it comes to having respect for a woman. That's for damn sure."

"Nikolas!"

"Don't Nikolas me! It's a simply resolved issue. Couple different approaches, but we can definitely get the shit handled in no time."

"I...appreciate your energy right now. I *really* do."

"That feels like a but is coming and quite frankly, I'm not tryna hear it, JB. It's bigger than this competition. I don't care about whatever you think is at stake because what it sounds like to me is that you're saying that I should be cool with letting some cat disrespect my girl for the sake of saving face."

"Okay." I said, trying to hide the grin that was fighting to spread across my face at hearing him call me *his*.

And seeing the sheer amount of anger on his face as he talked, let me know that if I let him loose on Rich, he'd do some serious damage. Something that we needed to avoid at all costs considering that he was about sign a new, *huge* contract for the upcoming few seasons and didn't need any outside drama doing anything to detract from that. The fact that none of this was a thought in his mind as he sought to protect me was...*beyond appealing*. I'd interrogate what all of that meant for us going forward later, but for now, we had some business to attend to.

"Okay what?" Nikolas asked.

"We can go talk to Roosevelt about what happened. Let him sort it out,' I said, "You've got too much at risk to go about it your *preferred* way."

Nikolas kissed his teeth, "It would nip that shit right in the bud though."

"Alright killa, c'mon, let's go find Roosevelt."

We found him pretty quickly in his makeshift office and I recounted my run-in with Rich once again to an astonished Roosevelt.

"Aye, what the fuck is in the water in Tennessee?" Roosevelt blurted after I finished, "Excuse my complete lack of professionalism, but why is everybody wildin' out here?"

I laughed, completely at a loss for words as Nikolas shrugged.

"Thank you for bringing this to my attention, Jayde. I'll definitely address it with Rich ASAP. Before that, I need to round everyone up once again to give the latest updates on the state of *#forthegram*. Y'all can meet me in the common room in about twenty minutes. I'm about to go round everyone else up," Roosevelt said, leaving me and Nikolas in his office.

He walked out mumbling something about this real world bullshit being the worst idea anyone could have ever thought of.

"I thought he said this was his girl's idea?" I giggled.

"Man, she bout to get an earful when he gets back to LA, I know that much..." Nikolas agreed, laughing.

I shook my head, thinking, *that poor, poor woman.* When we got to the common room everyone, but John C., was there. He bopped in about a minute after Nikolas and I had, holding a conversation on FaceTime.

"Aight bae, I gotta let you go. Yeah...we bouta get it crackin' in here," he said.

Couldn't hear the woman's reply because he had in AirPods, but whatever she said drew a low chuckle and, "You know how I do, baby boo" from him. It took everything in me to not have a verbal reaction, but my face must've said it all as Nikolas nudged me, laughing. I rolled my eyes mouthing John's words, which made Nikolas laugh even harder. Justin Timberlake and Robin Thicke had walked so he could run and here he was with this blaccent put on and horribly out of touch AAVE. Once John had ended his phone call, Roosevelt began speaking.

"Aight y'all...I'ma just keep it a buck with, y'all. The contest has been put on ice...indefinitely. Due to the mess with Melina, a few things happening behind the scenes, and some very recent situations," he said with a pointed look at Rich, who had the nerve to look like he was confused about the reference, "things...are not going as planned at all. So, y'all are free to hang out in this house for the length of time that we were scheduled to be here or if you'd like to get back to your normal life, come see me and I'll get my assistant on booking alternative travel plans for you. Producers and songwriters, you guys will be compensated the rate quoted in your contracts for the length of the entirety of this debacle."

Didi raised her hand, "What about any other... portions of our contracts? Will that be fulfilled as well?"

A question I'd also had because of the carrot they'd dangled in front of me about possibly bankrolling my country album. Hell, I'd forego that little payment they were giving us for this week if it meant that possibility would be turned into a reality.

"Those we can discuss on a case by case basis," Roosevelt said, "But I know litigation is not a favorite thing of anyone at *Double R*, so all things outlined in your contract will definitely be fulfilled. Any verbal agreements or promises? I can't speak to any of that right now. Any other questions?"

Though the room hummed with folks having sideline conversations, no one else directed anything else to Ro.

"Aight," he said, clapping his hands, "If you need to find me, you know where I'll be."

With those words of dismissal, I got up, intent on heading to my room and packing my things. I could use these extra free days to go bug my mama up in Belt Buckle.

"Jay...can I talk to you for a minute?" Rich called out.

"Nah," I said, not breaking my stride.

I had to pass him on my way out of the room and he grabbed my arm, which was the most wrong thing he could have ever done. Nikolas was on my heels, throwing his arm off of me almost instantaneously.

"She said nah, fam," he barked, "Go find something else to do."

"Oh, I was unaware that the motherfucking leader of the Monstars was your spokesperson now, Jay. It's cool though..."

Nikolas was in Rich's face before I could even draw in a breath to say don't. Immediately I hopped into action, trying to get between them.

"Nikolas...please. I already told you he isn't worth it."

"Oh wow, Jay. That's how you feel, huh? Coach

Carter's protégé got you that sprung that you'd turn on your friends. Damn, you hate to see it."

"Say bruh, I thought I told you she was good on you talking to her," Nikolas said, evenly. The calm in his tone making me a little scared because I could feel the intensity of his tightly wound body as my hands rested on his abs, using all of my strength to keep him from going after Rich.

"*Nikolas*," I said, coating my tone with all of the honey I could muster, "Baby. Please."

He exhaled, slowly and I could almost see him doing a mental countdown to re-center himself.

"Come help me pack," I said, which earned me a grin.

"Aye man, she just saved your life. But please don't let me happen to run into you when I'm in your city. She won't be there to save your ass then."

Rich jawed back saying something that didn't even register to me as I tugged Nikolas out of the common room and up to my space. I sat down on the bed and Nikolas sat in the desk chair facing me.

"You know you shoulda just let me beat his ass right then and there, right?"

"While that would have been satisfying in *so many ways*...I couldn't let you do that. Oh my goodness, could you imagine if tape of you two piecing Rich got out?" I collapsed back onto the bed in giggles.

"Nigga need to know these hands do more than dribble," Nikolas grumbled.

"Oh, I'm well aware of that..." I said, sitting back up to make eye contact with Nikolas.

He grinned, biting down on his lip as he rolled closer to me in the chair.

"Mmmmhmmm, I *know* you know," he said, running his hands up my calves, settling upon my knees so that he could spread my legs apart as he stood from the chair, settling between them.

He was leaning down to connect his mouth with mine when his phone chimed with an incoming message. I groaned as our mouths were centimeters apart and he said, "Hold that thought", backing up to read the message, and then shoot a quick reply back.

"Two questions—first, what are your plans? You staying here for the next few days or are you heading back up to Nashville?"

"I'd actually planned on driving over to BB and bugging my mom for a couple of days, why?"

"Well, that leads me to my second question—any interest in going to a *Nymphs* game with me in a few days? That text was from my agent. I texted him while Ro was making the announcement about the contest changing it up so I could get my meeting set up with the *Trojans* front office so I could sign my contract and all of that. While Al was getting things settled, apparently they mentioned that I'd yet to show my face at any of the W games this season and since one of my teammates has been Mr. Perfect Attendance at *Nymphs* games as he thirstily chases after Selena Samuels, I figure I need to make my way there to show my support sooner rather than later."

"Ooh, actually...yes I'd love to go to a game. I've been

tryna get in there to see my girl *The Sharpshooter* in real life action, but the timing hasn't worked out."

"What you know about Selena Samuels?" Nikolas asked, a bit of shock in his tone.

"Besides being my home girl and neighbor? She's easily the best pure shooter out there—NBA or the W," I said, confidently, "Who's touching her?"

"Ouch," Nikolas breathed, "Present company excluded?"

I shook my head, laughing, "Nah, boo. You're great... but Selena is always a sure bet. *Always*."

"Tough crowd," Nikolas fake pouted before chuckling, "So it's a date?"

I grinned, "It's a date."

THIRTEEN

IT FELT INCREDIBLY good to be sleeping in my bed after my cramped quarters out in Shelbyville. I'd been back home for nearly a week and in that time, I'd thanked God for my bed no less than five hundred times. What I hadn't thanked God for, however, was the fact that for the entire time I'd been home, Jayde had been in Bumblefuck, Tennessee with her family. Her mother had been released from the hospital and Jayde had taken it upon herself to be the nursemaid, helping her mother get her eating habits on track. We'd been in constant contact, pretty much every day checking in multiple times a day via various modes of communication, but it was nothing like the energy that flowed between us when we were in the same room. It wasn't even on some purely sexual shit, I just liked having Jayde around and that time in Shelbyville, spoiled me with her everyday presence. I couldn't remember the last time I'd willingly wanted to surround myself with one person for more than a few hours at a time, if ever. That damn Jayde though...there was something about her. And today...finally, blessedly, we'd be in the same place at the same time.

The *Nymphs* had a home game, and we'd agreed upon going together before I left Shelbyville, so like a teenage girl counting down to the prom—I'd been eagerly awaiting this day. I was more than ready to take in some good ass ball, with my best girl by my side. I'd been up early, spending a few hours in the gym getting back into shape and a couple more after that in my little makeshift home studio that I'd set up. With my free time I bought some equipment, kind of mimicking the setup we'd had out in Shelbyville, trying my hand at song composition and writing. It was...an *interesting* experience by myself to say the least. I'd learned to pluck out a few chords on the keyboard back in the day when I was in the church choir, but having not really put any of that training into practice in almost fifteen years? It was rough the first couple of days, but at some point, muscle memory kicked in and I'd been able to cobble together a track or two that didn't sound *too* terrible. Nothing too refined, but definitely enough to bring to a collaborator to flesh out.

I'd been in my little makeshift studio when the downstairs concierge let me know that Jayde had arrived. I eagerly abandoned my little music set up to go let her into my condo. When ten or so minutes had passed with no sign of her, I called back down to the concierge desk to see what the holdup was. Peter, who was working the desk today, informed me that he'd let her up on the elevator and that they appeared to be working properly, which confused the hell out of me. I opened the door intent on trying to figure out where

Jayde was and she was standing right in front of me—in the tiniest pair of white shorts and a bedazzled, red Selena Samuels jersey that she'd clearly customized on her own as it was cropped and clung to her body like a second skin.

Before I could open my mouth to say something about her outfit, Jayde groaned, "Oh God. Are we gonna be one of *those couples*? Really with the matchy matchy, Nikolas?"

I looked down at what I was wearing and laughed because we were both decked out in red and white—though mine was in the converse of hers. I wore a fresh white tee, paired with red shorts that had the *Trojans* name logo on the front, and my retro 4s in white with red accents.

"And you're really going outside with the word Trojan on your dick, huh? Wow, bold choice, Nikolas."

I laughed, shaking my head, and pulling her into my arms. I'd really missed her smart-ass mouth and leaned down to show her just exactly how much. She greedily accepted the kiss I laid upon her lips, opening to receive my tongue less than a nanosecond after I snaked it out seeking entrance. Placing my hands squarely upon her ass, I hoisted her into the air so that we were level and I didn't have to bend down damn near a foot to keep our mouths connected. Not breaking our kiss, I backed us into my place, kicked the door shut and navigated over to the couch, landing with Jayde straddling my lap. When the necessity of breathing pulled us apart, Jayde grinned, "Hi."

"Hey."

She placed a light kiss on my lips, "Missed you. Missed *that*."

"You sure took your sweet time coming to get it," I said, referring to the lull between her trip from the lobby to making it to my apartment.

"Oh! I ran into Eddie on the elevator. And I was telling him my good news and got carried away. But...hey, guess what?"

"What?" I asked.

"You will never believe this," Jayde gushed, "Because hell, I didn't believe it until I showed up to the place and everything was legit. So, a few days ago I got an email from an exec over at Wagon Wheel Records, said that someone had hipped them to me and they liked my sound, wanted to have a meeting with me and talk about some things. Me, not thinking much of it, agreed to the meeting even though it felt like I would be yet disappointed by another record company promising me one thing and delivering another. But nope! I get to the meeting with them, at the *Pancake Pantry* of all places, and Nikolas, guess what? You are now hugged up with the newest contemporary country artist on Wagon Wheel Records!"

"Say word?"

Jayde nodded, grinning broadly, "They are...a dream come true honestly. You know I was wary after all of the false starts I've had in this town, but Sid looked over my contract and everything that they said would be in there was in there, with a few more perks. I just...I can't believe this, and I have you to thank, kinda..."

"Me?" I asked, "I didn't do nothing..."

"Oh yeah you did, remember that video you posted of me from the Sham? That was how I'd gotten back on their radar."

"Wait, *back* on their radar?"

"Yeah, way way back in the day I interned for Wagon Wheel when I'd first come to Nashville. All of the work I did then was purely administrative though I was not shy about letting them know I had musical aspirations as well. The president of the label at that point, however, wasn't feeling ya girl. But...fast forward to damn near ten years later and the new label head was actually my old boss, Jamie, from when I was interning, small world right? And *her intern* was the one who showed her that video."

"Sort of like a full circle moment, huh? We gotta do something...go out and celebrate!" I said.

"Honestly? I'd rather stay in and celebrate," Jayde replied, leaning down to connect our lips once more.

"Now that's something I can certainly accommodate," I murmured when we parted.

"*After* the game, though. I look too cute for nobody but you to see this look, let's go lover boy," she laughed, hopping up off my lap and going over to the small mirror on the wall in my living room to make sure she looked presentable before we headed out

Walking to our seats in the arena had all of the bittersweet feelings running through me. The last time I was on this court, it was after a heartbreaking loss culminating a season that might have been one of the best that I'd had in my professional career. I was, however, looking forward to getting back in here in September and getting that work though. We'd made some acquisitions in free agency that would round our team out a little bit more and give us even better chances of repeating our post-season run from this year once again.

"Aw shit, the prodigal son finally found his way home huh?" a familiar voice called out behind me.

I turned around, unsurprised to see Kage's ass decked out in a Selena Samuels jersey. I chuckled a bit to myself, thinking of all his antics on social media trying to get her attention. The rookie had heart...and a never-ending will when it came to trying to win over Selena. I wasn't too familiar with her personally, so I didn't know if he had a snowball's chance in hell, but I did know that it was entertaining to say the least.

"What up, K?" I said, turning in his direction to dap him up as he approached, "This is my girl, Jayde. Jayde, Kage Steele."

"What up, shorty?" Kage said not really looking in Jayde's direction, "Man you see who they let back in here from the gutter? Nigga shouldn't even be allowed to step foot in this arena."

I turned to look in the direction that he was glaring in to see Dre Leonard. Damn, I hadn't seen that man in a while. I'd heard rumblings that he was on the *Nymphs* staff, but I wasn't sure of the truth of it. From the looks of it, he seemed to be doing well.

"What beef you got with Dre?" I asked Kage.

He didn't give me a direct answer, mumbling under his breath.

"Oh, Nikolas. Selena's over there...I'm gonna go say hi."

"I'll come with you, babe, hold up. Aight K, I'll catch up with you later," I said, following Jayde who'd not listened to a single word I was saying and was already over hugging it up with Selena.

Selena must've asked who she was here with because Jayde pointed at me. I waved in their direction before heading over to where Dre was standing on the sideline.

"Niko Verette," he said as I approached, "What up, boy?"

"Shit, I can't call it," I said, slapping the hand he held out for a shake and pulling him in for a hug, "You looking good, bro. Just couldn't stay out that Cardinal Red, huh?"

"You know I make this shit look good, so..." Dre smirked, laughing, "Nah for real...when the Lloyds make you an offer though..."

"You definitely don't refuse," I replied, laughing myself, "We need to catch up though, man. Go shoot around or something. Put me up on life coaching in the W now."

"Now...you really don't want me to bust your ass like I used to do back in the day, do you Nik?" Dre joked.

"Man, *here you go*," I replied back, "I can keep up with your ass now. This ain't undergrad."

"Coach Leonard, can I speak with you for a second?" someone called out before Dre could make another smart comment back.

"Duty calls...but we'll get up, Nik," Dre said, with another quick handshake before jogging over in the direction of the voice that had called out for him.

Jayde was walking back in the direction of our seats and as soon as she fell into stride with me, I looped an arm over her shoulders, "You want something to eat or drink before tip-off?"

She shook her head, "I'm good. Thanks though."

Within minutes the festivities of the game were starting and at the singing of the national anthem, I fought back laughter as Jayde cringed through the singer's choice of...*unique* notes to hit during her rendition.

"Hell, even Melina could have done a better job than this," Jayde whispered to me as the singer wrapped up.

"Tough room," I cracked.

"I'm just saying...if you're gonna be charged with singing that song, at the very least you should sing it in one key—preferably on the musical scale—and stay there. Home girl sang that shit in z flat and q sharp," Jayde quipped.

I shook my head at her before focusing on the game in front of us. The *Nymphs* were comprised of an excellent young core and played with a skill that was beyond admirable. Hell, I wish we had Selena in the back court with Kage on the *Trojans* because shorty was bad as hell. There wasn't a spot on the floor that she couldn't sink a shot from. And Jayde...you would have thought she was Selena's mother with the way she hopped up and cheered any time Selena made a shot. Watching how much she got into cheering from courtside amused me. She was beyond appealing in those little ass shorts, but her laser focused intensity on the game as it progressed just made her even more attractive to me. At halftime I was ready to take her ass out of the arena and back to my place where I'd strip her of those tiny shorts and let her know exactly how much I'd missed her in the past couple of weeks that it had been since we'd seen one another. But I had priorities, namely supporting my sister squad as they balled their asses off, so my horniness would have to take a backseat...for now.

The game ended in a victory for the home team and after a quick stop to congratulate the ladies on a hard-fought win, Jayde and I left the arena in search of dinner. We ended up at Tànsuǒ, a Chinese restaurant co-owned by some Food Network chef that Jayde seemed super excited for us to be eating at. We were seated fairly quickly, and the waiter had taken our drink orders. As we sat awaiting our wine, Jayde looked at me grinning.

"What's that grin about?" I asked.

"So...is this like...our first official date?" she asked, the grin still stretched wide across her face.

"Oh...so does that mean you don't have enough for your half of the bill?" I cracked, laughing.

Jayde rolled her eyes, "I really can't stand you, sometimes. I'm just saying, you keep introducing me as your girl to folks, but ain't never took me out on a proper date. Might have to rethink coming back to your place after this, Nikolas. Can't keep giving you the milk for free."

The smirk on her face let me know that she was still playing.

"I mean...we're *friends*, right?"

Jayde nodded slowly, "Big facts."

"Sharing is caring. So your...*milk* is just another form of sharing," I laughed, as the waiter approached with our drinks, then took the food order which put a pause on the conversation that we were having.

"So...Nikolas...I...I wanna ask you something, but I don't want to come off as like...a stereotypical insecure type."

"I'm an open book, baby. Ask away."

Jayde sighed deeply and ran her fingers through her hair, threading a bit at the nape around a finger as she chewed on her lower lip. I'd never seen her nervous before, so now I was getting a little on edge because I wondered what, *exactly*, she wanted to ask me. I reached a hand across the table, intertwining our fingers and tugging on hers a little so she'd look up at me.

"Tell me what's going on in that head of yours?"

"I just...what are we doing here, Nikolas?"

"I thought we were grabbing a bite to eat," I joked, which just earned an eye roll from Jayde.

"Can you be serious? Please..."

"JB. I thought it was clear, but I guess not so I'll spell it out for you completely," I said, grabbing her other hand so both of hers were enveloped in mine, "We're *dating*... working towards commitment. Or at least that's what I'm doing. Am I out here by myself?"

She shook her head, lowering her eyes.

"Naw naw, don't get all embarrassed now, babe," I said, letting go of one of her hands, to cup her chin and make her resume eye contact with me.

"I'm...I'm not embarrassed. Just...Nikolas, I'm a little shook," she whispered.

"Shook, why?" I asked.

This wasn't a conversation that we should be having in the middle of an upscale contemporary Chinese restaurant, but since she'd brought it up, I certainly wasn't going to sidestep it. I wanted my intentions toward her to be clear and for us to be on the same page going forward. I certainly hadn't planned on entering into anything resembling a relationship this summer, but I couldn't deny this thing with Jayde and me. I genuinely liked her company, wanted her around for as long as she wanted to be around. What I didn't want was some one-sided thing popping off. I'd done the whole, being more into a woman than she was into me—sniffing up behind her like a little puppy—begging for a whiff of her attention.

"I...don't do this. Like relationships and all of that. I... am a girl who is more into moments and brief connections, but there's just...you bring something out in me that makes me want to throw away all my former conventions and try something new. I just...like being around you, a lot. And I guess I wanted to just be sure that this wasn't a one way street," Jayde shrugged, now looking off into the distance at the people around us instead of at me right across from her.

"Aight, well let me be extremely clear then, Jayde," I started, calling her attention back to me, "I...Nikolas Verette...am wholly and fully into you...Jayde Turner... and I am looking forward to exploring this thing between us and seeing where it leads. Now, you turn..."

"Well, I mean, I guess I can't let you stay out here being on your Lewis & Clark expedition steez by yourself, huh?" she replied, biting back a grin, "Just promise me one thing."

"I'm listening."

"Don't have me out here looking stupid. If at some

point you decide I'm not worth the trouble or this isn't what you want, I need you to be straight up with me."

"When have I ever had a problem telling you exactly what I think about you, Jayde?"

"Touché," she replied, taking a sip of her drink as the waiter approached with our meals.

The conversation was briefly tabled as we tucked into eating. We ordered a variety of dishes because Jayde was indecisive and basically wanted to try everything on the damned menu. We compromised by ordering three appetizers and three entrees to share between the two of us. Whatever we didn't finish could be bagged up for us to bring back to my places and dig into a little later if our activities later in the evening left us a bit more peckish. I guess my answers to her questions were sufficient as Jayde completely switched the dinner conversation to speculation about the culmination of the *#forthegram* contest. I still hadn't heard anything further from anyone at *Double R*, but I wasn't tripping too hard on it.

"I just don't understand why they would have you all go through doing all of that stuff to get the contest off the ground and get people's interest ratcheted up about it only to never give us any resolution," Jayde grumbled.

"Yeah, I guess," I shrugged, "I don't look at it that way though. This whole thing was me doing something that was completely out of my comfort zone and taking a risk on something I'd been dragging me feet about putting any real concerted effort into anyway."

"But don't you also risk never seeing anything come to fruition? I mean...I may sound a bit hypocritical here, given my circumstances in this industry. But is the taking that leap to no reward worth it?" Jayde asked.

"If there isn't a risk, is it worth wanting at all? Think about it...everything you do, that's not a given, there's some sort of risk associated with it in some way. So, I can either go through life only participating in sure things—being completely risk avoidant or I can apply the philosophy that one of my coaches in AAU ball told me that's been the driving force of my entire basketball career. Hell...my life's driving philosophy, honestly."

"And what's that?" Jayde queried.

"You miss one hundred percent of the shots you don't take," I replied, simply.

"Profound," Jayde giggled.

"I know, I know...it's hella cliché. But think about this...how many times have you had an inkling to do something, but you eschewed it because you were scared? Either of the outcome not being what you wanted it to be or afraid that whatever effort or energy you put toward a thing wouldn't be enough to ensure your success. Then you see someone else out there doing the thing you wish you had the courage to do, while you're sitting back worried about the shots not taken over the course of your life. Shooters shoot, babe. So as far as *#forthegram*, if it ends up being a dud? Ain't no skin off my nose because I proved everything, I needed to myself already. And, if I should decide, I know that I could go forth and create music and folks would embrace it, wholeheartedly. Unless most of the appeal of *Okin* was the anonymity."

Jayde shook her head laughing, "Nah, it was actually the abs. Like eighty percent of it was for sure. The price of your bag went way up when you let me and Phar convince you to do that D'Angelo cover."

I shook my head laughing, "Yeah, okay. But seriously...reward always outweighs the risk for me. *In all things.*"

"Message received," Jayde responded before she went back to nibbling on the spread of food on our table.

We ended up doggie bagging more than half of what we ordered and headed back to my place. With a quick stop to Jayde's car to pick up her overnight bag, we got back to my place and neither of us were in much of a condition to do anything more than shower and climb into my bed and watch some TV since we were so stuffed from dinner. I'd showered in the master bath and Jayde in the guest bathroom. I was finished up before her and was laid in bed, mindlessly scrolling through my phone when she reappeared, wearing another one of my shirts.

"When in the hell did you steal this?" I asked, tugging at the hem as she launched herself into the bed and snuggled into my side.

"I have no idea what you're talking about, sir," Jayde replied with a straight face.

"Yeah okay," I laughed, pulling her deeper into my embrace, "What you tryna watch?"

She shrugged, "I don't really care, honestly. I'll probably be knocked out in about five minutes flat."

Knowing I'd likely be in the same boat as her in an even smaller time frame, I just picked some random show that was in the new releases section and pressed play. I couldn't tell you what the show was about or who was in it because I was deep off into nod land very quickly after the credits had begun to roll.

The next morning, I woke up in bed alone, but with my house smelling like a goddamned bakery. I quickly washed my face and brushed my teeth before heading out to the kitchen to see what Jayde had whipped up and saw her and Pharris yakking it up as they sat in front of a plate of what looked to be homemade cinnamon rolls. I glanced over to the clock to see exactly how late I'd managed to sleep in and was shocked to see that it was barely ten am. Since Jayde's back was to me, Pharris was the first one to notice my presence in the room with a quick, "What up, Nik?"

I was about to ask him why the hell was he in my house so early skinning and grinning in my girl's face, but Jayde got up from the table and made her way over to me, tilted her face toward mine and pursed her lips. I took the hint and leaned down to capture her mouth in a kiss that went on a little too long if Pharris' groans about us needing to get a room were any indication. I pulled back from Jayde, dropping another quick kiss on her lips and murmuring good morning before going in on Pharris.

"Man, you the one in *my* house this morning and not with one of your fifty girlfriends. What the hell you doing over here anyway?"

"Left my wallet over here, g. Been out here riding dirty and ain't even know it 'til I tried to stop at Krystal and grab me a lil something on the ride home this morning."

I shook my head laughing, "I can't believe you eat that mess, man."

"Hey! It's the closest thing to the Castle and you already know how I feel about the Castle after a night of...activities," Pharris replied, slyly.

"Oh, you were out with your girl Cyn last night?" I asked.

"Who?" Pharris asked.

"Shorty from the fourth of July? Invited you out to the family thang?"

"Oh," Pharris said, shaking his head, "That didn't work out. Nah I was out with Jos last night. She might be the one, Nik."

"I'll believe that when I see it...anyway, what's smelling so good in here?"

"My famous caramel pecan sticky buns," Jayde piped up, grinning, "You want a taste?"

"You know good and well I always want a taste of whatever you're serving, sweetheart," I growled, burying my face in Jayde's neck as she giggled.

"And on that note," Pharris said, grabbing another bun from the plate, "I'll leave you good people to it."

"Thanks for the ride to the store again, Pharris," Jayde called to his retreating back.

He threw a hand up in acknowledgement of her statement but didn't break his stride or verbally reply as he left.

"Now where are these sticky buns?" I asked

FOURTEEN

"OH, you *do* still live here, huh?" a voice called out from across the street as I got out of my car.

I looked over to see Selena grabbing mail from her mailbox at the end of her driveway and jogged over.

"What up, All-Star?" I called out, crossing the street to chat with her briefly, "Yes, I do still live here."

"Hm, I couldn't tell from the Barbiemobile's lack of presence in your driveway lately. I guess that confusion you were dealing with at the game a few weeks back has... passed?" Selena asked, a sly grin on her face.

"Somethin like that," I said, returning the grin.

"Well, must be some other girl named Jayde that I've seen all hugged up with Niko Verette on *Spilling That Hot Tea*, huh?"

"You sure you wanna go there because I mean...I've seen a certain fine ass visitor rolling through the cul de sac on occasion when I was home over the past few weeks."

"You know what? I'ma change the subject, what's new, girl?" Selena replied, laughing.

"Everything...how much time you go?" I asked, jokingly.

There had been so many changes in my life over the past month that I honestly felt like my head was swimming with all of the new parts of my life. The biggest change, though, was the one that initiated this conversation. Selena wasn't far off-base with her assertion that I'd worked through my initial trepidation with fully leaning into the feelings that I had for Nikolas. When we went to the *Nymphs* game that day, I'd tried playing it off when she asked what was up between the two of us, and she'd actually given me some pretty good advice. And the courage to woman up and ask Nikolas about his feelings about me. Hell, we probably still would have been dancing around the whole "what are we" portion of courting that we were now, thankfully, past and firmly implanted in a full-blown relationship.

Selena flicked her wrist up, "Not much, actually. I have to be at the arena in less than an hour."

"Well hell," I breathed out, "How about we try to get together soon? Share some wine and I can update you on all the goings on in my life?"

"Now that sounds like a plan, sis. I'll text you to see what your schedule is looking like this week."

"Alright, girl," I said, and headed back to my original destination—my place for a few hours of respite.

I was supposed to be recording a track for my album, but when I showed up to the studio the power was out on the entire block and there was no known time of when it would be back on. Someone had run a truck into a pole that held up power lines and whatever damage they did was pretty intense. Since none of us involved in this process were too keen on working by candlelight—there were a few lyrics we weren't still completely satisfied with—we'd decided to reconvene the next day. Nikolas was busy helping out at a camp that one of his teammates put together for disadvantaged youths in the summer, so I decided I'd come home and get some much-needed rest. I'd been burning the candle at both ends, but it was completely worth it. I was fully living the life I'd envisioned for myself when I left Belt Buckle for The Big City.

No sooner than I'd stepped over the threshold of my townhome, my phone sounded off. Looking down at the display I grinned, seeing a new text from Nikolas.

Dinner at my place, tonight? – Nikolas Verette

Works for me :).

Any requests? – Nikolas Verette

Whatever chef's feeling.

Copy that. Save some vocals for me when you leave the studio. – Nikolas Verette

You tryna make me sing some high notes? ;)

Always. Until later, sweetheart. – Nikolas Verette

Until then...

Knowing dinner time for Nikolas meant eating

between seven and eight in the evening, I stripped down and slid into bed, setting an alarm to get me back up at around five so I could shower, dress, and make my way back downtown to Nikolas' condo. Just when I felt myself sliding into sleep my phone rang. Groaning I reached over to retrieve it, perking up once I saw who was calling.

"Hey Momma!"

"Jaybird, when you bringing that strongback young man back down here to see me?" my mother crowed, greeting be damned.

"Oh, I'm doing well, mama. Thanks for asking," I grumbled.

"Don't get smart with me, little girl. Now answer my question."

"I feel like this is a set up...when do you want Nikolas and I to come visit you?"

"Well actually...I was thinking I may have Sidney bring me up there to come visit with you for a few days."

"Okay, mama, we can arrange that. Just let me know when you are thinking about coming and I'll make sure my schedule is..." she interrupted me, "Well Sid's driving up to Bowling Green tomorrow and was gonna drop me off along the way, so does that work for you?"

"I...guess it will?" I replied, shaking my head.

"All right, baby. I'll let you know when we get on the road tomorrow. I'll just be staying a couple days, Sid'll pick me up when he's done with his business in Bowling Green. Talk to you later, love you...bye."

"Bye, Momma," I replied to dead air because she'd already hung up.

Great I thought. Knowing my brother, he'd be dropping my mom off hella early on his way to Kentucky for whatever business he had to handle up there, which meant that I probably should reschedule dinner with Nikolas tonight. I needed to make sure that I was home because if I wasn't when my family pulled up, I'd never hear the end of it. Instead of texting, I called Nikolas via FaceTime.

"Hey, baby, what's up?" Nikolas answered.

"So...you haven't had Chef start preparing anything yet have you?" I asked.

"Nah, not yet...why?"

"Change of plans. Come over here and I'll whip something up for us," I said.

My irritation at the change in plans must've shown on my face because Nikolas asked, "What's wrong?"

"Nothing's...*wrong* per se, but my mother just called. Said my brother's driving her up for a few days for a visit. Which...fine...but I'd like a little bit more advanced notice than twelve hours you know? And...I'm busy—I've got sessions scheduled tomorrow and Saturday. I already know she's going to want to tag along, but then I know she'll complain about being stuck in the studio all day."

"How long will she be here?"

"She said a couple days, but in my mother's language that could be anywhere from a literal two days to an entire week."

"Ah," Nikolas breathed.

"Yeah..."

"Well, if you need someone to entertain her for a few hours, you know I have no problem with that, right?"

I couldn't help the smile that spread across my face at his words, "I know. I should be fine, for the most part."

"And if you're not, you'll tell me?"

"Sure," I replied, breezily.

"That sounds like a half truth. I'm serious, JB. I don't mind hanging out with your mom for a bit. She likes me... and you know the feeling's mutual."

"Aye, don't tell me I'm in danger of my mother stealing my man," I joked, making Nikolas break out into a low chuckle.

"I mean...she is the original recipe version of you, babe. I'm just sayin'..." Nikolas laughed, quickly sobering when he saw the look on my face, "Too far?"

"Just...gross. Anyway, hey, when you come over can you bring a bottle of that white wine you always have that I like."

"Which one, baby?" Nikolas asked, face scrunched in fake confusion.

"You know damn well which one, Nikolas."

It was a sweet German white whose name I'd always had problems pronouncing. All I knew was that it started with a z, had way too many vowels, but was hella refreshing. I should have just stuck to Riesling, but the other wine was too delicious to deny. Even if I couldn't properly pronounce it.

"C'mon try to say the name of it just once more," he cajoled.

"Man, just bring the wine," I laughed.

"Anything else, your highness?"

"Yeah, make sure you're ready to get your dick rode

off into the sunset since I don't know how long Momma will be here so that means no sleepovers."

"Wait, what?"

"Don't hate the player, hate the game. See you later," I grinned.

"Later, baby."

I adjusted my alarm since I'd have to get up to throw something together before Nikolas arrived, so now my nap would be more like a cat nap since I had just over an hour to rest.

THE TWO OF them were getting on my nerves. Between my momma going through her mental rolodex to come up with every single embarrassing story from my adolescence that she could drudge up and Nikolas greedily lapping up her tales, I was over them both. Sid was, thankfully, coming back to get Momma today and though I loved my mother dearly I was ready for her to go. She'd had something to say about every aspect of my life, unbidden. Not everything was negative, because she definitely heaped loads of effusive praise on me for following and conquering my dreams, but she also tempered that with consistent references to me not getting any younger. The phrase geriatric pregnancy had been thrown around more than once in the nearly three days that she'd been here.

Currently, we three were enjoying a very nice picnic spread in Centennial Park. It was Nikolas' idea and Momma hopped onboard immediately when he showed up at my door with a picnic basket and that damned panty wetting smile of his that he knew was impossible for me to resist. We were outside enjoying the nice day, spread out on a blanket in a corner of the park. A few *Trojans* fans had noticed Nikolas but were super respectful and did not approach him for autographs or pictures as we sat talking. Hell, even if they had approached, he and my mother were too wrapped up in each other to notice anyone else was there anyway. My phone dinged and I prayed it was Sidney telling me when he was coming to get Momma, but it wasn't. It was my friend Eddie.

Bluebird. Tonight. 8pm round…you want in? – Eddie Kane

Oh my God. Was he serious?! I'd been playing in piece of shit bars and writing with everyone and their mother for the past decade, hoping for an invite to a songwriter round at the *Bluebird Café* one day. The *Bluebird —along with the Opry and the Ryman*—was on my bucket list of venues I'd like to perform in one day. Some other places that rounded out that list were *The Gorge* in Seattle, *Red Rocks* in Colorado, *The Kennedy Center* in DC, and *The Hollywood Bowl*. I had a list of over thirty venues in the states alone with stages I'd longed to rock, and so saying yes to this invite to the *Bluebird* was a no brainer. I excitedly responded with an all caps hell yes. Eddie called shortly thereafter with the details of the night. Apparently, someone who was supposed to be in the round had gotten sick at the last minute and the person at the *Bluebird* reached out to Eddie to have him join, but he was currently out of town. I was the first person he thought of as replacement and he wanted to make sure I was cool with him passing my contact information along.

I was glad that he let me know before just passing it along because I would have certainly thought it was someone trying to prank me and would not have taken it seriously. After confirming with him that he could absolutely pass my info along, he and I rung off. I jumped up from where I was seated, not giving a damn about who saw me looking like a fool as I danced around, too excited to stay still. My sudden movement captured the attention of my mother and Nikolas who both looked at me like I'd grown a second head.

"Uh...you okay, Jaybird?" my mom asked, skeptically.

"I'm *more* than okay, Momma. I am freakin' fantastic!" I crowed, alternately dusting off my shoulders while singing, "I'm playing the *Bluebird*. I'm playing the *Bluebird*."

"The Bluebird *Bluebird*?" my mother screeched while getting to her feet as well.

"The actual *Bluebird*!" I replied, flinging myself into her for a hug.

She gladly accepted it, drawing her arms tightly around me and whispering into my ear, "You're doing it, baby! Everything you said you would...you're doing it."

And I don't know what it was about those whispered words, but they broke me down for a second and my happiness dissolved into tears, not of sadness but of euphoria. Momma was exactly right. Signing with *Wagon Wheel* was just the first in many steps of creating a life that I was thrilled to wake up to each morning. I felt utterly blessed to be in this position and knew that without her endless support, I might not have ended up here. I pulled back from my mom and she wiped my face with the pads of her thumbs.

"Oh Bird! When are you performing?" Momma asked.

"Tonight," I replied.

"Tonight?!" she screeched, "Oh, c'mon we've got to get out of here and find you something to wear and do your hair and..."

Her laundry list of commands was cut short by her phone ringing. From the ringtone I knew it Sidney and he sounded irritated when she answered. While Momma was talking to Sid, my phone began to ring. I walked away a little to answer the call and it was Eddie's friend John who was organizing the round this evening, giving me all of the details. He informed me that I could bring up to three people with me to see the show tonight and that I needed to arrive about forty-five minutes before the round was to begin. I thanked him for the opportunity and ensured him that I would definitely be there on time. He said the pleasure was all his after my glowing recommendation from Eddie. He also informed me that I needed to have at least four songs ready for the round-robin style format that the show would follow. We'd be tasked with not only talking about the process of writing the song, but also performing a little snippet of the song. As I was wrapping up my call with John, I noticed that Momma and Nikolas were packing up our leftovers from the picnic.

"Sidney'll be here in about half an hour, Jaybird. So,

we're gonna head back to your place so I'll be ready when he arrives," Momma said.

"But...I wanted you to come to the show at the *Bluebird* tonight. Call Sid and tell him I'll bring you home tomorrow."

"Now, baby girl didn't you tell me that you had that meeting at your label tomorrow? It's fine. You can get Nikolas here to record it all for me and you all can show it to me when you come down for Labor Day."

Come down for Labor Day? I thought. Damn, they'd really made whole plans without consulting me at all.

"No," I whined, "I want you to be there in person, though. I can call Jamie to see if I can push our meeting out a couple days."

"It's fine, baby. You don't have to go through all of that trouble for me," Momma replied, shaking her head, "You doing all this fussing when we could be getting a move on and heading back to your place so you can get ready to play and I can get ready to get on the road."

"I can take you back tomorrow, Mrs. Turner," Nikolas piped up, "I don't mind, and I don't have anything going on that would need to be moved. That is... if Jayde doesn't mind..."

"I absolutely do not mind in the least. See, Momma. I'll call Sid back and tell him to just head straight on home. He'll probably be thrilled that he doesn't have to make the extra stop, so everyone wins!"

"Swear I don't know who raised you to think you are always supposed to get your way," Momma groused as I pulled out my phone to call my brother.

As I suspected he was super happy to not have to

come pick up Ma and told me to pass along his thanks to Nikolas for coming through in the clutch. Nikolas dropped Momma and me off, with a promise to return in a few hours ready to drive us all over to the *Bluebird Café*. After getting back home to get ready, time seemed to pass in a blur because I swear it felt like no more than ten minutes had passed when Nikolas was back ringing my doorbell. The *Bluebird* was a very short drive from my house and by the time we reached our destination I was on the verge of a full-on panic attack. I didn't know what the hell brought this on, as I'd performed hundreds upon hundreds of times before, but something about tonight felt different. I tamped my feelings down, appearing outwardly calm, but inside all of my organs felt like a swirling mass of confusion. Once we were inside and John showed me to the area that they had for the artists to chill in before we went on, I walked back out to make sure that my momma and Nikolas were settled in at a table. I'd barely made it three steps when I literally ran into Nikolas.

"Hey...I was just coming out to make sure you and Momma were good," I breathed.

"And I'm coming to make sure you are good. I know you're trying to hold it all together, but I just...don't make fun of me for this one...but your energy felt off. So, I wanted to make sure you were really doing all right."

"I'm..." I hesitated, contemplating lying, but it was no use, "I'm freaking the fuck out, Nikolas. Why did I say yes to this?"

"Because we take all of the shots when the ball is in our hands, remember? This is your moment, baby. You gotta gon head and heave that half-court shot up and trust it'll go in—all net."

"Easy for you to say," I giggled, "You don't have to get up in front of all these folks and bare your soul. My songs...the ones I write for myself and others are a glance into the deepest parts of me. Shining a light on those places, and really digging into the genesis of some of these records could possibly get..."

"Emotional? I know you don't like showing that you have them, but you honestly couldn't write the beautiful songs you do without having some pretty damn deep emotions. You don't have to always tuck them away, babe. Holding onto all of that emotional baggage eventually becomes too heavy to bear, you know? Sometimes baring your heart is good for release."

"Ok Dr. Phil," I joked.

"I'm serious. If there's any place you can lay your burdens down and not be faced with judgement, it seems like this would be the one. Now...scale of one to ten, where's your anxiety?"

"The limit does not exist," I deadpanned.

Nikolas burst into laughter, pulling me into his body and pressing a kiss into my forehead. We stayed like that, pressed together in an embrace until I felt the storm swirling inside of my body calming back into the normal, relaxed state I was usually in. The longer we stayed close like this, our heart rates synched, my breathing evened out and my anxiety dissipated. As if he sensed the exact moment that the calm took hold of my spirit, Nikolas held me for a couple more beats before releasing me and bending down to place a quick kiss on my lips.

"I'm gonna go back out there with your mom. Looking forward to seeing you kill it, babe."

He'd gotten a couple steps away when I called out his name. Nikolas turned back, a quizzical look on his face.

"Thank you," I grinned.

"Anytime," he replied with a grin that matched mine, and then turned back toward the center of the *Bluebird*.

Soon it was time for me and the other three songwriters to take the stage for our session. I'd never met any of the other guys on the panel tonight but was intimately familiar with a lot of the songs they'd written that were all over country radio. I was up here with some heavy hitters as a relative newcomer to this specific scene, but I held my own. We ended up only getting through a couple songs each and by the time the night had ended I felt fantastic. All of those earlier nerves were nowhere to be found as Momma, Nikolas, and I drove back to my house and I couldn't stop grinning. I was completely over the moon about having checked off one of my life's bucket list items.

I was beyond content, I was downright elated. And rode the high of the night right on into the next day when I had a meeting with Jamie about starting to shape my debut album. Turned out, it wasn't just Jamie in this meeting, but the A&R, a couple of producers, stylists, and additional songwriters were in the room too. I thought that this gathering of folks was kind of foreboding and would possibly lead to me being told how I was going to be presented, what I should be representing and the type of music that would be included on the album, but it was quite the opposite. The meeting was easily one of the most collaborative situations in which I'd been included as Jamie gave me the space to really spell out what I wanted my album to sound like, what I expected from the label and all of that.

Later that evening, as Nikolas and I laid on his couch not watching Netflix I felt like a broken record as I recounted the meeting and my immense happiness at landing there.

"I swear, it's like God handpicked *Wagon Wheel* for me and said, 'ok girl, you claim this is what you want? Prove it!' I just cannot get over how dope my team is, how dope this experience is, it's just..." I sighed.

"Everything's coming up Jaybird, huh?" Nikolas smiled.

I bit down on my lower lip, "Something like that."

"You deserve it all, Jayde. You've paid your dues, time to reap the benefits," he said warmly, "It's your time, girl."

I blushed before thanking him in a low voice. It was amazing how supportive he was of me, constantly reminding me that my time in the sun was more than overdue. The man gassed me daily and I couldn't get enough of it. I felt kind of guilty about it though, knowing that a major part of the reason that we'd even gotten a chance to get together was still hanging in the balance. He hadn't heard anything further from *Double R Records* and even though he hadn't talked about it, I knew that had him feeling a way. One thing I'd learned about Nikolas was that he was a sucker for a full circle moment and having things left unresolved or with the loop hanging wasn't something he enjoyed in any fashion.

"You know...I've been thinking," Nikolas said suddenly.

"About?" I prodded.

"Maybe I don't wait on *Double R*. Maybe I just do this shit myself. I've got the money, means, and access," he grinned, "I could put together a lil LP or something and release it myself."

"I think you absolutely can. Now the question is would you release it as Okin or as yourself?"

"As me...that Okin ruse was a test really, to see if my voice was really something worth sharing with the world without being burdened by people just telling me I was good because of my already established celebrity. And now that I know I got the juice..." he shrugged with a grin.

"You tryna let it loose. I feel you," I giggled, "I think that's a great idea, baby."

"Yeah, I've been messing around a lil bit in my music room, trying my hand a songwriting and everything."

"Wait...and you're just now telling me?"

"Get outta here with your fake offense," Nikolas chuckled, "I wasn't keeping anything from you intentionally, JB. I just...needed to get comfortable with the idea myself before sharing it, you know?"

I nodded, "I get it. So, what are you thinking about the theme for the LP? Any ideas on producers you want to work with? If it's someone I know I can put a bug in their ear. And I'm pretty sure that Jamie will let you record at *Wagon Wheel's* studio for a modest fee...not that you need a hook up but I'm just saying and..."

"Whoa, slow down, lil mama," Nikolas laughed, "I

was thinking about baby stepping it since the pre-season is rapidly approaching, which means free time is gonna be scarce as I get back into go mode. But...I did have an idea I wanted to run by you though."

"I'm listening..."

About thirty minutes later, after a quick call to Ro Ashe, we were down in his media room the both of us sitting in front of his keyboard with his phone live on *Instagram* in front facing camera mode. He'd just gotten through explaining to the thousands of folks who'd joined the live within seconds of the notification going out that he had been a part of the now defunct *#forthegram* contest and the story of music being his constant companion along with basketball from his youth through his adolescence and into adulthood. The reason I was here was because he wanted to sing a little bit, unmasked and asked me if I'd be into doing a duet because the song, he had in mind that he wanted to sing had a male and female vocal lead. It was a no brainer for me to say yes because I absolutely adored his voice and knew ours together would sound like lemonade on a hot summer day—crisp, refreshing, and soothing to an agitated spirit.

We bantered back and forth a bit before Nikolas situated his hands on the keyboard, "You ready, baby? I'll do my best to keep up...don't show off too much, okay?"

I giggled, playfully shoving away from him as I responded, "Just make sure to keep up, mister basketball crooner."

As he played the introductory chords, I snapped my fingers in time, grinning at the choice of song he'd made for our duet. It was the perfect summation of my feelings...our feelings that night at Tànsuŏ before we'd laid all of our feelings bare. And when we got to the first chorus, I couldn't help the broad grin on my face as I turned to face Nikolas as we sang in unison.

So if you love me, just say so

'Cause I can't play these games with you no more

We hadn't said those three words to one another yet, but it was clearly evident. In the ways that we cared for one another. In the ways that we supported one another. In our everyday actions. But sitting here singing this song with him, really absorbing the words and not wanting there to be any doubt in his mind about how I feel about him, I knew I needed to say those words to him. The song wound down and Nikolas played the last notes of it before ending the live stream and turning to me.

"Thank you," he said, "for being willing to do that for and with me."

"I love you," I blurted out instead of the you're welcome that had been building on the tip of my tongue.

If he was surprised, Nikolas didn't let it show as he leaned down to capture my mouth with his, drawing me into a sweet, delicate kiss, then pulling back to say, "I love you, too."

FIFTEEN

"AYE, you ready to hand these niggas their first L of the season or nah?" Kage said, coming up to me as I headed from the locker room to the gym for pre-game shoot around. We were up in Milwaukee for our first game of the season and their home opener.

"G, you stay on one, huh?" I laughed.

"I'm just sayin', we handed them their last L of last season in this place, only right that we keep that same energy upon our return," Kage shrugged, jogging down the tunnel ahead of me.

All I could do was shake my head. Dude was bound and determined to be a damn mess. Then I remembered how young and cocky I was at his age and had to just chalk it up to youthful arrogance. He'd learn one day. I was less concerned with that and more concerned with the arrival of my special guests when I saw Ricky coming toward me with the two people I was looking for in tow. Both decked out in *Trojans* gear from head to toe, I couldn't help but laugh when the little George let go of his father's hand to run straight toward me, holding out his hand for dap.

"Whassup Niko!" he exclaimed.

"What's good, lil man? You excited for the game tonight?"

Lil George nodded as Rick and his dad finally reached us.

"Thanks, man. Again...for all of this. I appreciate it," the elder George said.

I'd arranged for them for them to have dinner at a nearby restaurant, get a private tour of the Fiserv Forum and now they were able to hang out in here while we got some shots up pre-game. I'd also sent them most of the gear that they were rocking tonight. My offer was extended to their entire family, but George said his wife had zero interest in attending a basketball game, no matter how swank the accommodations would be, and their other son was barely a year old so the experience would be lost on him. I was just glad it all worked out for me to uphold my end of the bargain. My fans—especially ones as loyal as these guys—were important to me and I loved being able to show my appreciation on a micro level as often as I could.

"No doubt, man,' I said, replying to him then turning to his son, "Aye lil man, you wanna help me warm up?"

His eyes damn near popped outta his head before he turned to his dad, as if he were seeking permission. Big George grinned, nodding and Lil George followed me onto the court, staring up at all of the empty seats in awe.

"You hoop lil man?" I asked, dribbling the ball before passing it in his direction.

He caught it quickly, dribbling a bit before crossing it between his legs and nodding, "I play with an AAU team. Daddy coaches us."

He kept on dribbling as we talked and moved closer to the hoop to get a few shots up. Shorty had handles, I was impressed with his ball handling skills and he had a lil shot on 'im, too. We ran through a few shooting drills, getting up shots from the baseline beyond the arc, a few scattered spots on the court for mid-range, and from the free throw stripe. Lil George's father was definitely putting in work with the kid because his skills were well beyond his seven years of age. Kage eventually came over and the four of us—Big George came out to join us on the court—played a game of two on two. It was me and Big George against the little and the rookie. We only played to ten, and their asses almost took us out, but Big George hit a big last shot for us when we were tied up at nine. Soon it was time for Kage and me to head back to the locker room, but I thanked the Georges once again and told them to enjoy their night.

I was excited...more than ready for the game to begin. Despite my outward reply to Kage, I was ready to hand the Bucks an ass whooping in their house, too. We needed to start this season off with the kind of energy that showed the league who we were and what we were capable of doing this year. Even though no one really took games before the All-Star break seriously when it came to determining the front runners in the league, I wasn't playing into any of that. All eighty-two of the games we would play this year in the regular season were just as important as the ones we'd eventually play in the postseason. I needed folks to be on notice to know what we'd done in the postseason last year wasn't a fluke or dumb luck. It was the concerted effort of a team that was hell-bent on making their way to the finals and eventually a championship.

Before Coach came in here with his pregame pep talk, I pulled out my phone to call Jayde. Last month she'd released her album to much anticipation and it was blowing up on the country charts. She was currently on tour and with my season starting up, our time face to face lately had been hit or miss. I couldn't complain as we were both making major moves in our respective careers, but I'd be goddamned if I didn't miss my girl. The phone rang and rang and rang, with no answer which was strange. Usually, even if she didn't answer, her assistant would and have her call me back within minutes. I didn't bother leaving a message because Jayde believed that leaving voicemail should be a federal offense. Instead I shot off a text, letting her know that I missed her and was looking forward to seeing her in a few days. She'd be home for a few dates before heading up to the east coast to do some shows out there.

Turning my attention back to the locker room, I tuned in just as Coach was urging us to go out there and do what we'd come to do. Whole room was hype, everyone clapping it up as Kage hopped in after Coach, talking his shit and gassing the entire squad up. And all of that energy worked as we moved into the half with a commanding twenty-point lead. Everybody was playing out of their minds in this first half on both ends of the ball. All of our starters were in double digits and we'd had some of our key bench playmakers coming in to grab some buckets too. I sat on the sidelines as the second half started, turning around and making eye contact with the Georges who were seated a few rows behind our bench. George the younger greeted me with an exuberant grin while his father gave me the homeboy head nod.

Our commanding lead was short lived after our opponents came into the second half, beasting. I don't know if they had their Wheaties during halftime or something, but by the time the fourth quarter rolled around our twenty-point lead had dwindled to three. And now, with five minutes left in the quarter we were all tied up, trading bucket for bucket as the game progressed. After the Bucks hit a go ahead three, Coach called a timeout. The look on his face let me know he was getting ready to cuss us out for the next minute and fifteen seconds. Instead I was shocked as he calmly asked what had happened. And when no one could provide an answer, that's when the clipboard went flying and he cussed us out about being cocky and lazy in this second half. After having our asses handed to us, we went back into the game with a different sort of fervor. Coach was right, we were coasting after the first half, but now wasn't the time to take our feet off our opponent's necks. First game of the season or not, we still had something to prove. And we did just that, turning things around and ending the game with a ten-point lead to give us our first victory of the 2019-2020 season.

Post-postgame presser, my teammates once again were trying to get me to go out and enjoy the Milwaukee nightlife, but I passed, eager to get back to my hotel, ice down and lay down. Tonight had been brutal on my body, I'd played almost all of the second half and I was worn the hell out. I guess the adrenaline of the younger ones had them ready to keep it going, but I was good with going back to the hotel and vegging out in front of the TV with some late-night room service action. In the lobby of our hotel, Zeb tried convincing me once again to hit the streets with them.

"Y'all got it, man. Ain't nothing out there for me," I begged off.

"Damn, Nik, used to be a time you'd be the first one out here," he replied, shaking his head.

"All good times must come to an end, my guy," I laughed, extending my hand for a dap, "Looking forward to hearing about what y'all got into on the flight home tomorrow though."

Zeb shook his head, with a solemn look on his face, "Nah, man. What happens in the Kee, stays in the Kee."

We looked at one another for a few moments before both breaking down into laughter.

"Man, you dumb as hell. Enjoy yourself out there... and y'all be safe."

"Enjoy...your marathon of *Lemme Upgrade You with Will & Way*, dawg," Zeb jeered.

Jayde had gotten me on the wave of watching channels I never even knew existed and the home improvement show starring two brother who were brothas had made its way into my repertoire of in-flight entertainment this season.

"You watch one episode of a show on a flight and the clowning won't stop," I griped, laughter in my voice.

I got off the elevator on my floor, grateful that my room was only a few steps from it. I was over ready to lay it down. Approaching my door, I could see a sliver of light underneath the door, which had me on edge. I knew I'd left all of the lights off when we left because it was the middle of the day and I'd had no need to turn any of them on. Pressing my keycard to the sensor on the door, I opened the door cautiously—desperately hoping that some helpless groupie hadn't convinced anyone in the hotel to risk their job by letting her into my room. Maybe I'd accidentally left a light on. However, when I walked past the bathroom and reached the area of the room containing my bed, I was greeted with a sight that made me utter, "*Goddamn.*"

"Surprise, baby," Jayde said, with a sultry grin settled upon her face.

She was splayed against the all-white linen of the king-sized bed clad entirely in red lace looking like the sweetest vision out of my dreams. I had so many questions about how and when she'd gotten here, but all of them were cast aside as I grabbed her by an ankle, pulling her down to the foot of the bed so I could take her mouth with mine, kissing her with all of the pent up and repressed desire I'd been carrying with me for weeks. We'd FaceTime after every show of hers...even taking advantage of the video technology to find other ways to sate our sexual desires for one another, but having her here in living color? Oh, I was definitely energized and ready to tear that ass up.

And Jayde was equally ready, pulling me into the bed with her and attacking my mouth with vigor. I took my time stripping her of the lingerie and showing her exactly how much I'd missed her with my mouth all over her satiny smooth skin, teasing and tasting. Soon we were both completely undressed, and I was slowly sliding into her, letting out a groan as I was fully seated. I took a moment before I began to move in deliciously slow strokes that had Jayde panting, begging me to pick up the pace. Unable to help myself against her pleas and cries, I eventually picked up the pace, slamming into her with quick hits, my hips pistoning in rapid movements that sent her over the edge. I wasn't far behind her, growling my way through completion.

I collapsed onto her and she welcomed the weight of my body with a smile. After a couple moments, I slid out of her, collapsing alongside Jayde and lifting her chin for a kiss.

"Hi," she smiled when we pulled back.

"What are you doing here?" I asked, matching her smile with a grin of my own.

"Couldn't wait 'til we got home. I was trying to make it for the game, but a jackknifed semi on the highway put a kink in that plan. I missed you, baby."

"Missed you, too. I was about to come in here and blow up your phone since I hadn't heard from you."

She grinned, pulling her lower lip between her teeth, "Had to not answer otherwise I woulda given away this surprise. You know I can't keep my mouth shut when it comes to you."

"Well aware. I've reaped the benefits of that open mouth more than often enough," I teased, making her blush.

Couldn't have asked to a better end to my day, honestly. Everything that I'd ever wanted in life and some things I'd hadn't even realized that I wanted was right in my grasp—literally and figuratively.

Jayde rolled her eyes before slapping me across the chest and leaning into me, "So, this was a good surprise?"

"The best," I replied, kissing her on the nose and pulling her tighter against my body.

-the end-

EPILOGUE

...SIX MONTHS LATER

"WHERE THE HELL IS HE? I am going to kill him," I groused, pacing backstage at the *Ryman Auditorium.*

"Calm down, Bird, you know that man is gonna be here," Momma said, rubbing my back soothingly, "There's no way he'd miss tonight."

Tonight...was one of the biggest of my fledgling country music career so far. I was headlining a showcase put together by my record label of all of their acts. When Jamie approached me about it initially, I was super excited because I knew it would be a good time, then she mentioned it would be in the *Ryman* and I damn near lost my mind. When I played my hometown shows on my tour a few months ago, I'd hoped that they would be in the Ryman, but there was a scheduling conflict that did not permit it. When this opportunity arose, however, I was over the moon thrilled with it. And everything about the scheduling worked out so that all of the most important people in my life would be in town to attend the show. My mother, brothers and sister in law had driven up. Nyema and Langston came to town. Hell, I was even able to get my girl Selena and her guy on the yeehaw agenda. Even Nikolas' parents had traveled down for the show. I'd officially been introduced to them over the holidays when we traveled back to his hometown for Thanksgiving since the *Trojans* were playing the Bulls. All of these people...some of the most important in my life were all here backstage...except for my *soon to be ex-boyfriend* who was nowhere to be seen.

I'd been with him all morning before the show, actually, until he said he had an errand to run and would meet me at the venue. But that was almost two hours ago, and I hadn't heard a peep from him. Not a text, not a phone call, not a tag, not a tweet and I was beyond annoyed. I was just getting ready to grab my phone and tell him to not bother showing up when his big, fine ass loped into the backstage area. Ignoring everyone else, he came directly over to me.

"I know. *I know*. I'm sorry," he started, with that damn grin he knew made me weak in the knees spread across his face. Leaning down he spoke directly into my ear, "I'll do whatever you want me to do to make it up to you."

The low growl of his voice making an involuntary shiver pass through my body. I stepped back, trying to give myself a little space to recover my annoyance with him, but Nikolas stayed right up in my space, wrapping his arms around my waist and pulling me into his body, "I'm here now. The show hasn't started. You're about to go out there and kill it. We cool?"

I sighed and rolled my eyes, pulling back to look up at

him. I'd opened my mouth to say something smart but was bereft of speech when I saw the clear love and adoration that he had for me shining in his eyes. How in the hell could I even pretend to still be mad when I wasn't at all? So, I wisely said nothing, as Nikolas lowered his head and finally greeted me properly with a public appropriate kiss. When he pulled back, the fire in his gaze let me know that he'd make good on the promise of making up his tardiness to me once we were alone together.

"I got you something," Nikolas crooned, before calling over his shoulder to Pharris.

I hadn't even noticed Phar with Nikolas since I was too focused on being fake mad at him for running a little behind.

"Hey Phar, which of your sixty girlfriends did you bring with you tonight?" I teased, as he handed Nikolas a long rectangle shaped box.

"I'm ridin' solo tonight, Jay. Tryna see if your fine ass boss will give me some play, where she at?" he asked, looking around the room.

"Oh Lord, can you not...please?" I giggled.

"Baby," Nikolas said, "Focus. So tonight, is a pretty big deal. The first of many, many times you'll play on this storied stage. I had to get something special made to commemorate it. Here."

I took the proffered box that he held in my direction, ripping off the pretty wrapping paper that he'd probably paid someone to do for him. Once I got all of the paper off and opened the box to see what was inside, I gasped loudly before turning to him with eyes full of tears.

"Oh hell, you better not cry!" my makeup artist

Janielle called out from across the room, "I don't have time to reapply!"

I tried blinking back the cresting tears to no avail as I lifted the frame from the box.

"I can't believe you got this made. How?" I screeched.

"That's why I was late," Nikolas grinned sheepishly, "I was over there at the Hatch Show Print shop waiting for them to get this together. We had a couple of trial and error runs, which put me a little behind schedule. Do you like it?"

"Are you serious? I love it!" I squealed, launching myself at him to press kisses all over his face.

When I moved to Nashville over ten years ago, I became obsessed with finding cool and unique Hatch Show prints for concerts that artists have performed in Nashville and worldwide. My front room and media room in my house were decorated with almost all of the ones I'd owned, and I'd wanted to have exclusive ones made for this performance at the Ryman, but we'd had the idea too late and Jamie was unable to get us on the Hatch Show Print schedule. I don't what Nikolas did or how he was able to get this made for me, but it meant the world to me. I looked down at the print, on cream paper, it had been stylized to look like the pink bass guitar that I played in my act with my name in huge letters at the top and the details of the show's location, date, and time in progressively smaller fonts. It was legit one of the coolest gifts I'd ever received in my life.

"Thank you, baby...I love it and I love you," I whispered before capturing Nikolas' lower lip between my teeth and drawing him into a kiss.

"All right, all right...y'all got plenty of time for the lovey dovey later," Jamie called out, entering the room with a grin, "You ready to play the roof off this place, Jayde?"

"Let's do this," I said, striding out of the green room backstage toward where my band was waiting for our normal ritual of a quick prayer and then the individual handshakes that we'd crafted between me and each member. It had been a long few months on the road when we were out, so we did a little bit of everything to pass the time including creating intricate secret handshakes.

The moment I got on stage, I felt electrified. The crowd was on their feet, hands clapping, feet stomping, and voices raised high to sing along with the words I'd written. The feeling of being on that stage and playing the music I wanted to, in the manner that I loved never got old. I switched up the set list a bit tonight and right before I closed the show with the title track on my album "My Greatest Mistake"—a tune I'd written about Nikolas before we'd actually gotten together, I talked to the crowd a little bit.

"I want to thank all of y'all for being here tonight," I said, stepping back and taking in the massive applause that followed that statement, "Now before we get on out of here, I got a couple more songs I'm gonna do for y'all if that's all right?"

The enthusiastic yes that roared from the crowd made me grin broadly before I continued speaking, "We got any *Trojans* fans in the house? Well...I happen to be a bigger fan of the *Nymphs*, but...one of my favorite

Trojans is in the house tonight and I'd like to invite him up here to say hello to y'all."

The crowd cheered once again as Nikolas strode on stage, coming right over to me and pressing a sweet kiss on my upturned lips. We made our way over to the keyboard and bench that the roadies had set up, with a microphone for Nikolas.

"So," I started, with a giggle, "You may have seen us do this before a time or two. But you guys seem to really like it, so it only made sense to make him come up here and out sing me once again, y'all give it up for Niko Verette."

He spoke into the mic, "How's everybody doing out there tonight?", and of course the crowd went up once again as he asked me, "You ready, babe?"

I nodded and he began playing "Say So" by PJ Morton and JoJo. I closed my eyes, getting lost in the song, the energy of the crowd, the beautiful melding of our voices as we sang to one another. After the last chorus that was supposed to be the end of the song, Nikolas kept playing and sang, "*So if you'll marry me, just say so...coz I ain't tryna play these games no more.*"

I turned to him wide eyed as he held up a beautiful, rose gold diamond ring with a glimmer of mischief in his eye.

"Quit playing with me," I breathed out, all as one word as the crowd laughed at my response.

Nikolas got up from the keyboard, grabbing his microphone and coming to get down on one knee in front of where I still sat in shock on the bench.

"Ain't nobody playing with you, girl. Jayde Elaine

Turner, I never would have predicted that I would be here, with you on a stage in front of two thousand of our closest friends," he turned to smile at the crowd like the true ham he was, "asking you to be my wife, but here we are. I love everything about you, and I cannot imagine my life without you in it for as long as I am on this earth. So, will you do me the honor of becoming my wife?"

Speechless, I could do nothing but nod emphatically, as I held out my trembling hand for him to put on the ring. He slid on the ring and placed a sweet, chaste kiss on my lips as I looked at him crazily. He chuckled and lowered to speak directly into my ear, "This was the real reason I was late. Stuck in traffic on my way back from the jeweler. Gon head and finish the rest of your show, we can properly celebrate later."

Hearing the word show brought me back to the present, reminding me that we were onstage with a crowd waiting for me to wrap up this show. I quickly gathered myself and shouted out to the crowd, while holding up my hand, "I's gettin' married, y'all."

As expected, they erupted with applause and laughter and I settled into my last song of the night. Singing this after having the man who inspired it propose to me on stage at the *Ryman* felt so surreal. Tonight, I felt like the luckiest girl in the world who couldn't ask for anything more.

AFTERWORD

If you enjoyed this book, please consider leaving a review on Amazon and/or Goodreads.

Keep up with my podcast #FallsonLove at:

www.nicolefalls.com

Follow me on Twitter:

www.twitter.com/_nicolefalls

Follow me on Instagram:

http://www.instagram.com/_nicolefalls

Like me on Facebook:

https://www.facebook.com/AuthorNicoleFalls

Join my Facebook Group:

https://www.facebook.com/groups/NicsNook/

ABOUT THE AUTHOR

Nicole Falls is a contemporary Black romance writer who firmly believes in the power of Black love stories being told. She's also a ceramic mug and lapel pin enthusiast who cannot function without her wireless Beats constantly blaring music. When Nicole isn't writing, she spends her time singing off key to her Tidal and/or Spotify playlists while drinking coffee and/or cocktails! She currently resides in the suburbs of Chicago.

ALSO BY NICOLE FALLS

Accidentally in Love Series:

Adore You

Smitten

Then Came You

Holliday Sisters Series:

Noelle the First

Brave Hearts

Started From A Selfie

The Illumination of Ginger

Standalone Titles

Sparks Fly

Road to Love

Last First Kiss

sugar butter flour love

All I Want for Christmas

A Natural Transition

Distinguished Gentleman Series

Switched at Bid

Made in the USA
Middletown, DE
14 June 2020